Meant for You

ALSO BY MICHELLE MAJOR

Meant for You

MICHELLE MAJOR

Montlake
Romance

Text copyright © 2017 Michelle Major

Published by Montlake Romance, Seattle

www.apub.com

Amazon, the Amazon logo, and Montlake Romance are trademarks of Amazon.com, Inc., or its affiliates.

ISBN-13: 9781503943667
ISBN-10: 1503943666

Cover design by Damonza

Printed in the United States of America

To Dr. Kircher—down the block or several states away, I'm grateful for our friendship. Thanks for keeping me sane, making me laugh, and mixing the best beergaritas ever.

CHAPTER ONE

Jenny Castelli was late, as usual, but it wasn't her fault. There were simply too damn many people living in Denver, most of whom had descended on the swanky Cherry Creek North neighborhood for lunch this beautiful June afternoon.

If life were fair, Colorado natives like Jenny would be awarded some sort of special parking pass for the crowded streets. Unfortunately, the parking gods didn't seem to give a flying fig about her place of birth. During her laps around the block, she'd passed the cars of the friends she was meeting. All three were Colorado transplants, but none had her issues with getting to places on time. They'd order for her, but Jenny rarely ate much during their monthly lunch dates, thanks to the familiar nervous flutter in her stomach. Jenny liked having girlfriends, but she wasn't exactly a pro at the whole "sisters from another mister" vibe.

Up until her best guy friend, Ty Bishop, had met local reporter Kendall Clark two years ago, he was pretty much her only friend other than her mother. Everyone knew moms didn't count.

Kendall had looked past Jenny's rough edges—and there were plenty—to make her part of a tight-knit group of women that had quickly become Jenny's lifeline. Not that she'd ever admit how much their friendship meant to her, or that she still sometimes expected Kendall, Chloe Haddox, and Sam Carlton to realize that she didn't belong as part of their group. She couldn't help running her mouth, and she didn't get the subtle nuances of female friendship that other women seemed to have been born knowing.

She swore under her breath as she rounded a corner to another street lined with cars. Almost immediately, she mentally committed a dollar to her son's swear jar. At twelve, Cooper was determined to cure her potty mouth, and while she tried her best not to curse in front of innocent ears, all bets were off in traffic.

A parking space finally opened only a miraculous half block from the restaurant, and she maneuvered the behemoth of a truck she was driving into it. Part of the reason she was running late was an issue at a job site, so she'd driven one of the hulking Rocky Mountain Landscapes vehicles instead of her own cutie-patootie Mini Cooper.

She shoved quarters in the meter, flicking a bit of dirt from her jeans with her free hand. She'd also planned to change from her work uniform of faded denim and a company T-shirt before lunch, but she took a bit of comfort in knowing that even if she got sidelong glances from the upscale customers in the cafe, her friends wouldn't care.

"Jenny Castelli, is that you?"

The bright Colorado sun couldn't prevent the chill that thrummed down her spine at the sound of a voice she hadn't heard in a decade.

She tried to ignore the woman speaking, until another voice piped in. "Of course it's her. Look at that crazy red hair. It's as wild as it was in high school."

Blowing out a breath, she turned to see Dina Sullivan and Brenna Holt, two of the posse of mean girls that had ruled her private and exclusive high school.

"Hard to believe I've avoided you ladies for so many years," she muttered. "I guess my luck's run out."

"Seems about the same as it ever was," Dina said in her tinkly voice. She'd always sounded to Jenny as if she'd just huffed a helium balloon. But the voice fit with her blond hair and brightly patterned Lilly Pulitzer dress. The woman was more Barbie doll than human. She pointed a pink-polished finger at Jenny's truck. "Still a gardener?"

"I actually opened my own nursery on a property northwest of downtown." When the women just stared, Jenny added, "I'm also a senior consultant to the design team at Rocky Mountain Landscapes." She couldn't help the note of pride in her voice, even though it was a job she was desperate to quit. Women like them never failed to put her on the defensive.

"But it's Ty Bishop's company," Brenna said smoothly. "The Bishops have always taken such good care of those less fortunate than them." She smiled like a cartoon cat trying to hide the canary in its mouth. "Especially you and your poor mother."

"My mother was the one who took care of Ty and his brother and sister when we were growing up. Any of them would tell you the same thing."

Ty's father, Eric Bishop, had insisted on paying Jenny's tuition to the prep school where his children attended high school, to thank Jenny's mother for her years of service as the Bishops' housekeeper. Although Jenny would have been a better fit at the local public high school, her mom had wanted Jenny to have an education that would pave the way to new opportunities.

But all the Summit School had offered was a lesson in heartbreak and humiliation. And these women knew it.

"You know our ten-year reunion is just around the corner. Brenna and I are, of course, on the committee," Dina explained in her chirping voice.

"You haven't RSVP'd yet," Brenna said, her tone faintly disapproving. "Our numbers aren't where we want them to be, so Dina and I are personally following up with people. You might be interested to know we've gotten confirmation that Trent is playing in the golf tournament that day." Her glossy mouth pulled down at the corners. "That rascal had better make an appearance at the reunion as well. Maybe he'll bring his wife. I heard she's lovely." She plastered on a phony smile. "Do you two still keep in touch?"

Jenny felt her throat go dry as anger swept through her like a desert sandstorm. "No."

Her lack of an RSVP had nothing to do with her ex-boyfriend, Trent Decker. She'd hated most of her classmates from high school when she was a teenager. Why would seeing them as adults be any different? But the thought that Trent would be there . . .

Brenna leaned slightly closer. "I understand why it would be difficult for you to attend. I mean, you live with your mistake every day."

"If you're referring to my son, you'd better shut up before I fu— mess you up." Cooper would hate her outburst, but at least she'd managed not to swear.

Both Dina and Brenna gasped, and Jenny took a step closer to them. "Cooper is the best thing that ever happened to me, and Trent is an idiot and a jackass for walking away from him." She felt her hands fist at the thought that anyone would reject her beautiful, smart, talented son. "We don't need or want Trent in our lives."

Brenna tsked softly. "You have to admit there are studies that prove that it's important for a boy to have a strong male role model in his life."

Jenny narrowed her eyes. "We don't need Trent," she repeated, "because Cooper has . . ." She paused, then said, "Someone who is proud to be a father to him. And he's a million times the man Trent could ever be."

A thrill of satisfaction flashed through her as both women's jaws dropped. Jenny didn't give a rat's ass what the people she'd grown up with thought of her, but she'd be damned if anyone would diss her son. Of course, what she'd told them was a lie, but Jenny wasn't known for her good judgment, and the feeling of being trapped by these women only obscured her internal compass even more.

"A father?" Brenna asked after another moment of gaping. "Does that mean . . ." Her gaze dropped to Jenny's unadorned left hand.

Jenny drew in a breath. In for a penny, she supposed. "Of course I don't wear my engagement ring when I'm working. It's quite valuable." When Dina's eyes widened, she added, "And large. Yep, it's a rock all right."

As soon as the words were out, she bit down on her lip. She'd always had an issue with running her mouth, especially when her temper got the best of her. She was laying it on too thick. These two queen bees would call her out on her obvious lie, and then she'd look like the foolish social misfit most of the people she'd grown up with thought her to be.

Dina shifted closer, her voice dropping to a conspiratorial whisper. "I always thought Trent was a bit of a prig for dumping you the way he did. But my mom still keeps in touch with the Bishops, and I haven't heard about you and a man since . . ."

"You certainly aren't privy to everything—or anything—about my life, and neither is Libby Bishop. But . . . he's someone I've known for a while." A tiny part of her had imagined Owen Dalton's gentle brown eyes when she'd been crafting her lie. They may have only dated for a nanosecond almost two years ago, but he'd been the nicest person she'd ever met. True to form, she'd screwed up the relationship before it even had a chance to blossom.

Brenna sucked in a breath. "You don't mean—"

"Yes, I do," Jenny answered automatically, still lost in a mix of daydreams and regret.

Both women whipped out their cell phones and began furiously thumbing.

Jenny blinked. "Wait. *What* do I mean?"

5

"Owen Dalton," Brenna answered. "I remember when the *Denver Post* ran a story on him a couple of years ago and mentioned you were his girlfriend. I heard you'd broken up, but no one in their right mind would let a catch like him go." Her thumbs tapped at an almost inhuman speed. "I'm posting to the event page on Facebook, right now."

"Posting what?" Jenny's voice came out sounding like she was Dina's twin. She felt her own version of a helium rush pound through her head.

Neither woman seemed to notice. "This should get our numbers up," Dina said. "We'll call the DJ next. We thought we weren't going to be able to afford him, but—"

"Stop." Jenny tried to snatch the phone, but Brenna managed a shockingly quick shoulder block. "What did you do?"

Brenna grinned triumphantly. "I posted your engagement."

Jenny felt her lungs seize as if someone had just dropped a two-ton boulder on her chest. "You're joking, right?"

"Don't worry." Brenna patted Jenny's arm like she was soothing a toddler having a meltdown. "I didn't say his name. I hinted you'd be bringing a surprise guest and that no one who had used a device from Dalton Enterprises would want to miss it."

Jenny clutched her stomach. She was definitely going to puke all over Brenna's expensive-looking wedge sandals.

"We should tweet it, too," Dina said, nudging Brenna.

"Can I get a photo of you wearing the ring?" Brenna asked. "I can Instagram the big rock."

"Right after I insta-punch you in the throat," Jenny growled, her heart hammering in her chest.

"You really haven't changed," Dina murmured.

Jenny stared at the ground in front of her, trying hard to convince herself that her entire world wasn't spinning out of control.

"You have to come to the reunion," Brenna said quietly. "It's on social media. Everyone will expect it."

Jenny wanted to say that she didn't give a damn about anyone's expectations. But as much as she liked to pretend not to care, she couldn't stop herself.

"You weren't making it all up?" Dina asked after another moment of awkward silence. "The father for your kid and the big engagement ring?"

Tell them, a little voice inside Jenny's head whispered. A voice that sounded a lot like her mother.

You are enough for Cooper. You are enough.

She gulped in air and raised her head, pasting a smile across her face. "Owen's protective of his private life, but I'm sure I can convince him." Her heart was pounding double-time as the lies continued to spill out of her mouth. "To tell you the truth, he has trouble denying me anything. He's super romantic that way."

"Lucky," Brenna said. "Mark and I have been married almost five years and already we're just a boring couple who fights over the remote."

Oh, how Jenny wished for boring right then.

"I'm late to meet some friends for lunch," she said, her voice sounding far away in her own ears. She stood like a statue as each woman gave her a short, awkward hug. They'd been ready to tear her apart five minutes earlier, and now they were hugging? Behold the power of her fake fiancé.

She let it happen, too stunned to do anything else. Like explaining that she'd just had a mental breakdown and could she get a do-over on the conversation? On most areas of her life that meant anything to her?

Alone on the sidewalk, she made her way to the restaurant. It was an upscale bistro—Kendall's favorite. Jenny did her best to ignore the sidelong glances she received from some of the other diners. It felt like her face was burning, and if her eyes showed the wild panic roaring through her, she was surprised strangers didn't run screaming from her.

She tried to school her features as she approached Kendall, Chloe, and Sam laughing together in a quiet corner booth.

"We ordered for you," Kendall said as Jenny slipped in next to Chloe.

Sam leaned across the wood table. "Hey, Red, you don't look so hot. Is everything okay?"

"Not exactly." Jenny shook her head. "I need to convince Owen Dalton to be my fiancé for one night."

Chloe's mouth dropped open, and Kendall blinked several times.

"You need food now," Sam said. "I think your blood sugar is out of whack and it's making you talk crazy."

"It's not crazy."

Sam lifted an eyebrow. "It sounds crazy."

"Let her talk," Chloe said, nudging Sam. "I'm sure she has a good explanation." She gave Jenny a hopeful smile. "Don't you, honey?"

Jenny sucked in a breath around the tight ball of embarrassment clogging the back of her throat. "My high school reunion is this coming weekend. Cooper's father, Trent, is going to be there, and I just ran into the two women planning everything. They were . . ." She paused, bit down on her lip. "I let them get to me and ran my mouth."

"What did they say?" Kendall asked. Her voice was soft but not as gentle as Chloe's tone. Kendall was still close friends with Owen and hadn't quite forgiven Jenny for how she'd treated him. Jenny didn't blame her. She hadn't forgiven herself, either.

"They insinuated that Cooper was a mistake."

"Bitches," Sam muttered as Chloe gasped and Kendall's eyes narrowed.

"They brought up Trent and how tough it is for kids who grow up without a father figure. I got mad and started talking before I thought about what I was saying." Jenny cleared her throat. "I told them I was engaged."

"To Owen?" Kendall asked.

Jenny shook her head. "I didn't mention him by name, but they assumed . . ."

"You could hire an escort for the night," Sam suggested. "We'll find a guy who's hot and looks rich. It would save you the humiliation of having to beg Owen to take pity on you."

"It wouldn't be a pity date," Chloe argued. "It would be Owen doing a favor for a friend."

Sam snorted. "Is Kendall going to ask him? Because I don't think he considers Jen a friend at this point."

Jenny took a quick sip of water to try to calm the burning in her throat. She glanced at Kendall. "What should I do?"

"You *should* have held your head high and not let those women get to you in the first place," Kendall answered. "You're a great mom, Jenny."

"But they were right about a kid needing a dad, and it killed me to hear it said out loud."

There was a moment of silence at the table while the waitress brought their meals. Jenny's stomach rolled as she looked at her club sandwich with a side of sweet potato fries. It was her favorite, but at the moment she couldn't muster a bit of interest in eating.

"Maybe today happened for a reason," Chloe said, pushing a dark curl behind her ear. "You made a mistake with Owen."

"A *huge* mistake," Sam interjected, earning a glare from Chloe. "But if he says yes, this could be the start of a second chance."

Kendall shook her head. "That's a big if."

"Yes," Chloe agreed, "but it might be the opening Jenny needs."

"I don't expect a second chance," Jenny told her friends. "I know I hurt him." She let her gaze rest on Kendall. "Is it the worst idea in the world if I ask him?"

Kendall took a moment to answer, then sighed. "Probably, but you're going to do it anyway. Just don't screw it up this time, Jen. Owen is a good guy."

"The best," Sam and Chloe said in unison.

Which was exactly why Jenny felt like she didn't deserve him. But she'd do anything to protect Cooper.

"I promise I won't hurt Owen," she told Kendall.

Chloe stole a fry off Jenny's plate and smiled. "Then let's figure out exactly what you're going to say to convince him."

She stood in the lobby of Dalton Enterprises later that afternoon, taking in the impressive view of the Front Range from the floor-to-ceiling windows on one side of the space.

Owen had purchased the building on the south side of Denver a few years ago. She'd met him when Rocky Mountain Landscapes had been hired to create the landscape plan for the newly renovated building. The native grasses she'd planted waved in the warm summer breeze.

The project had been one of the first she'd managed, and she'd had a hand in every piece of the design. It had also given her the chance to get to know Owen, who was one of the kindest, most authentic men she'd ever met, despite his power and wealth.

He was way too good for someone like her, so she'd sabotaged their burgeoning relationship only months after they'd started dating. He'd remained friendly, if distant, when they'd seen each other at Ty and Kendall's wedding last summer, but how would he react to what she was about to propose?

Her stomach lurched. She was about to propose to Owen Dalton. She glanced down and almost groaned out loud at the realization she was wearing her work boots from earlier that day. She'd stopped at her house on the way from lunch to change into a casual denim dress and slap a little makeup on her face. She tried to smooth her wild hair, but most days it had a mind of its own, so she settled for a braid at the back of her head. The more time she took to get ready, the more nervous she'd become, until she'd given up on making herself presentable and rushed over before she lost her nerve. That had clearly led to her stuffing her feet back in the scuffed and worn boots instead of the pair of ballet flats she'd planned to wear.

She couldn't possibly go through with it, and she turned to flee just as a feminine voice called, "Ms. Castelli?" The older woman, with silver hair in a spiked pixie cut and wearing tailored pants and a fitted jacket, gave her an assessing look. "Mr. Dalton will see you now."

Jenny's gaze darted to the exit, then to the young woman staring at her from the receptionist's desk, then back to the secretary, who raised a brow as if daring Jenny to make her escape.

"Right," Jenny muttered. "Let's do this thing."

The woman pursed her lips, then turned and headed down a hall without another word. Jenny felt the eyes of the workers in the airy open-concept office boring into her as she hurried to catch up to the secretary.

"Employees here seem pretty curious," she murmured, wondering if she was imagining the disapproving energy that seemed to be surging toward her like the tide.

"We're protective of Owen," the woman told her.

Jenny was used to disapproval. Her knee-jerk reaction was to get defensive, but she couldn't muster a bit of temper. She'd convinced herself and her friends that she needed to do this for Cooper. Jenny would do anything to take care of her son. He was truly her one best thing in life.

Suddenly she wished she'd taken Kendall's advice and come clean about her story, or Sam's suggestion of hiring an escort. It would have been a lot easier than facing Owen.

But Jenny was there. With how jumbled the rest of her life felt, somehow she couldn't admit that she'd made up the story of her engagement. It might be the tiny push that sent her over the edge. If she could prove—even for one night—that she had things together, maybe she'd begin to believe it herself.

She turned to the secretary as they reached a closed door at the end of the work space. "I'm not going to hurt him," she said softly.

The woman only stared at her until Jenny added, "Again."

"I remember how happy he was with you," the woman answered with a slight nod.

"I don't think we ever officially met." Jenny held out a hand. "Jenny Castelli."

After a moment, the woman slipped her hand into Jenny's but pulled it away seconds later. "I'm Diane Bricker."

"Owen is lucky to have someone so loyal working for him." He deserved to be surrounded by people who would take care of him. He was too nice for his own good, and he needed protection from people who would take advantage of that. People like Jenny.

The secretary inclined her head toward the massive door of a corner office. "I don't like to see him sad."

"Me neither," Jenny agreed honestly, because although she'd broken his heart, she still told herself she'd done it for the right reasons. She let herself into Owen's office and closed the door behind her.

He glanced up from his computer as the door clicked shut but didn't rise to greet her, which was odd, because Owen Dalton was a gentleman. Yet she barely recognized the man staring at her from behind the massive reclaimed-wood desk. The Owen she knew wore sweater vests and wire-rimmed glasses, the faint hint of high school science club always surrounding him.

This man was dressed in a crisp white shirt that had to have been custom made for him. It fit perfectly over his strong shoulders and stretched across the hard planes of his chest. She could see his defined biceps as he lifted a hand to tap a key on his keyboard.

Wait a minute. When did nerdy Owen Dalton get biceps?

"What happened to you?" she asked without thinking. A muscle ticking in his jaw was her only answer. "You don't even look like . . . *you.*"

One corner of his mouth curved, but even that felt unfamiliar. Owen had a huge smile, sweet and a little goofy. Nothing like the man in front of her. "Did you come here to talk about my appearance, Jenny?"

She blew out a breath. His voice hadn't changed. It was still soft and rich like hot buttered caramel. The way he said her ordinary name like it was the most precious word he'd ever spoken made shivers run the length of her body. Her physical reaction to him was dangerous, a piece of the equation she couldn't control, and another reason the whole thing was a huge mistake.

It wasn't too late. She could walk away before she made herself the biggest fool in the history of fools. Instead she took a breath. "I came here to ask you to marry me."

CHAPTER TWO

A bomb landing on his desk couldn't have rocked Owen's world more than that one sentence.

"I don't mean get married for real," she added in a rush. "Just one night."

"One night," he repeated, nodding as if his body wasn't reeling in shock. "You want to marry me for one night?"

"*Marry* isn't the right word." Color rose to her cheeks, and he wondered if there was anything more appealing than watching Jenny Castelli blush. Her normally creamy skin flushed pink and somehow it was the perfect complement to her fiery red hair.

He hadn't seen her since Ty and Kendall's wedding last summer. While he relied on time to lessen the intensity of his normal reaction to her, his body hadn't registered the message.

Her hair was pulled away from her face, and she wore a faded denim dress and work boots. The combination of the soft fabric and the hard leather, with just the tiniest bit of leg peeking out at the hem, about did him in. He'd always been too inclined to let his heart lead him and still believed the combination of tech savvy and emotional intelligence had led to his company's success.

Owen had a gift for reading what consumers craved as far as daily use of technology and connectivity needs. His microprocessors and mesh networks had revolutionized the way personal devices communicated and how people used the Internet. But that reliance on emotions had proved disastrous in his private life, and he'd made a concerted effort to become the type of man who didn't let his feelings rule his life.

Jenny was the epitome of temptation standing in front of him. Her lush mouth pressed into a thin line as her caramel-colored eyes filled with uncertainty. He was used to watching her head-butt her way through life, bulldozing through anyone who got her in way. It couldn't be easy for her to come to him, and he wanted to believe the fact she had meant something.

Once upon a time, he'd wanted to slay all of Jenny's dragons. But she'd destroyed what had been between them, and this was his chance to exact a bit of retribution for the pain and embarrassment she'd caused him.

Yet even if he couldn't understand what the hell she was talking about, he wanted to answer yes to all of it, which made him the biggest fool on the planet.

It would be a hell of a lot easier if he could just design a fake heart for himself—something that would keep him alive like a machine without the need for messy emotions. His own version of Tony Stark's Arc Reactor glowing from his chest.

"What is the right word?" he asked slowly, forcing his heart to calm its frantic beating.

"A fiancé." Her lips curled as she uttered the word, as if it tasted rancid on her tongue. "I'd like you to pretend to be my fiancé." He must not have hidden his reaction because she added, "Like I said, it's only for one night. I'll pay you."

If his head weren't spinning, he would have laughed. "You'll pay me? Are we talking cash or favors of the sexual variety?"

She sucked in a breath and he saw her eyes flash. She clenched her fists to her sides as she took a step toward the desk. "Who are you right now?"

"I'd think you'd know that given you just proposed to me."

"I didn't . . ." She paused, drew in a breath. "You aren't the Owen I know." Moving closer, she studied him. "You cut your hair."

"Shall I tell my stylist you approve?"

"Where are your glasses?"

He lifted a finger to the bridge of his nose, as always surprised to find it empty. "I don't wear them anymore."

She opened her mouth, but before she could speak, he stood and shoved his hands into his pockets. He didn't want to talk to Jenny about his transformation and what—or who—had been the catalyst for it. "I still can't figure out why you're here. We're not getting married, fake or otherwise. If you need an escort, pay for one. I've got a day job that keeps me plenty busy."

"I need you, Owen."

The only time he'd heard her voice like that, strains of vulnerability coloring her inflection, was when she'd murmured a hushed apology after he'd discovered her in the arms of one of his business associates at a fund-raiser where he'd been thrilled to introduce her as his girlfriend. It was a moment he would never put himself in a position to repeat.

"No."

Her eyes widened a fraction, but Jenny was a fighter, and she only took another step closer. "It's my high school reunion. I . . . you . . . the women organizing it . . ." She bit off a harsh laugh. "God, they were the worst of the mean girls back when I was in school. They had no use for me and . . . once I infiltrated their ranks by garnering the attention of one of the boys who belonged to them . . . then they hated me."

"Don't go to the reunion," he told her, even though he should just keep his mouth shut. *No* was the only word Jenny Castelli deserved to hear from him.

"No shit, Sher—" she muttered, then bit down on her lip. "Sorry. I don't mean to be rude. I wasn't planning on going, and then I ran into them today and they were talking about Trent—"

"Who's Trent?"

"Cooper's father."

"The one who's never seen his own son."

She nodded and he tried to ignore the way her skin paled. She sighed and he felt the whisper of breath against his jaw. "You know my mouth, Owen."

He stifled a groan. Christ, how he knew her mouth.

"They started talking about Cooper, insinuating that he was bound for trouble because he didn't have a father." Her eyes drifted closed for an instant as she murmured, "That he was a mistake."

"Jenny."

"So I shot back that he has a man in his life who loves him."

"Cooper has lots of people who love him, Jen. He's a great kid and you're a great mother."

She stared at him a long moment, then said, "But that's my fear, you know? What if I'm not enough? It feels like I'll never be enough."

His heart stumbled at her admission. He knew. And he understood because, as different as their circumstances were, he and Jenny shared that deep, hidden wound.

"You are enough."

She snorted. "You sound like my mother. I'm not to the people I grew up with, and before you turn into my mother and start lecturing me on my self-worth, I know I shouldn't let their opinions matter." She met his gaze and what he saw in the depths of her light brown eyes slayed him. "But it's not about me. I can live with my shortcomings and all the mistakes I've made. We both know the list is long and creative."

He inclined his head.

"They went after Cooper. I couldn't let it go."

"You told them we were engaged?"

"Not exactly. I never mentioned your name, but they assumed it was you." She gave him a rueful half smile. "I might have mentioned my enormous engagement ring."

"I have deep pockets."

"You do," she admitted, looking vaguely embarrassed. "Before I knew what was happening, they posted about a celebrity guest coming to the reunion on Facebook."

"Ah, yes. Money makes me a bit of a celebrity."

"You're no Mark Zuckerberg," she shot back, then winked.

She was teasing him. His body hummed in approval as the glow returned to her eyes. Jenny was bold and brash, but more than anything, she belonged in the light. The scent of the sun warming the earth always reminded him of her and made him long for things that were never going to be.

Which was why he should stay far away. She was like quicksand from the old seventies TV shows—one false step and he'd sink into the abyss.

"I know I've given you plenty of reasons to hate me," she said after a moment.

"One in particular," he agreed.

Her lips compressed, but she nodded. "I'm desperate, Owen. It's one night, and I'll find a way to make it up to you." She crossed her arms over her chest as if preparing herself for the rejection.

He had every right to give it to her. It was a perfect opportunity to prove that Jenny Castelli was well and truly out of his system. He didn't owe her a thing. But as he opened his mouth to repeat his earlier no, his gaze snagged on a framed photo tucked into the corner of the bookshelf that lined the wall behind her.

It was a snapshot of Owen and Cooper, taken during the brief months of his relationship with Jenny. He'd helped Cooper with his science project, which had taken second place in the school district's competition. Owen felt they'd been robbed of the win, but Cooper had been thrilled with his red ribbon and had sent Owen a heartfelt thank-you note along with the photo.

He wasn't sure why he'd kept it, but seeing the boy's innocent face made a slow ache echo through Owen's chest. His parents were still together, but Owen understood what it was like not to have a father's support. It was a pain that lingered long after he thought he'd pushed it to the dark, shadowy places inside him.

Even though Jenny had hurt him once, he couldn't deny that her love for her son was fierce and pure. He hated to think of the jackass rich boy who'd walked away from her years ago having the last laugh.

"I'm curious to hear how you'll make it up to me," he said, and had the satisfaction of watching her jaw drop. Clearly she'd braced herself for another no. Which he certainly should have given her.

"What do you want?" she asked without hesitation. "I'll do anything."

"After what you did, do you trust me enough to make that offer without qualification? This could be my chance for payback."

"You can change your hair and your clothes," she answered, her dark eyes glinting, "but you're a good man, Owen. I know you."

"I'm not sure you do anymore." He shifted, the awareness sparking along his skin forcing him to move before it burned him with its heat. "I haven't decided what I'll ask in way of recompense, but it's part of the deal. You will agree."

She stuck out her hand. "Anything."

He stared down at her hand like it was a demon tendril come to ensnare him and pull him through the gateway of hell. After a moment she dropped it and muttered, "Thank you, Owen."

He gave a slight nod. "When is the reunion?"

"This coming weekend. They've rented out a ballroom at the Hotel Boulderado."

"Text me the particulars," he said, tapping a finger on the top of his desk. "I have another meeting this afternoon and we've wasted enough time together."

He saw her flinch before she straightened her shoulders. He had the sudden uncomfortable sensation that he'd just kicked a puppy.

"Are you going to be a dick the whole time?" she asked even as she took a step toward the door.

Not a puppy. More like a baby tiger, cute to look at but still with a mouthful of sharp teeth.

"I don't think you're in a position to complain if I am," he answered smoothly.

"You're right," she said after a moment. "I appreciate you doing this." With a last nod, she turned and walked out of his office.

One night, he reminded himself, ignoring the rapidly expanding knot of dread in his stomach. It was only one night.

"Do you get a real ring?"

Cooper asked the question around a mouthful of hamburger over dinner that night. Despite how crazy it sounded, her son remained as calm as if he were discussing whether to have strawberry or vanilla ice cream for dessert.

"No, sweetie." She pushed her plate aside, her stomach far too jumbled to think of eating. Cooper, at twelve, had the appetite of an NFL linebacker, and she'd made his favorite dinner, grilled burgers and sweet potato fries. Maybe she was trying to prove to both of them that she was still a decent mother, despite getting herself into such a mixed-up situation.

"I know this whole thing seems strange but—"

"I get it, Mom." He dunked a fry in enough ketchup to soak it from tip to tip. "It's like when Aidan went to Hawaii for spring break."

Jenny frowned. "Aidan spent most of spring break sleeping over at our house."

"Yeah," Cooper agreed with a grin. "But he got sick of everyone bragging about their vacations. So he told them his grandparents took him to Hawaii. He Photoshopped pictures of himself at the beach and sent them to the group text. It was awesome."

Jenny had certainly been through enough of feeling "less than" growing up, but until six months ago, she and Cooper had lived in a middle-class subdivision on the north side of Denver. The ramshackle property they'd moved to so she could open her garden center had been near enough to the old neighborhood that Cooper hadn't needed to switch schools. As far as she'd known, her son had been safe from the trappings of status and kids who were all too aware of who were the haves and the have-nots.

She worked hard to provide for their tiny family but lived simply while she saved for something more. They'd taken a trip to Disney World a few years ago with her mom, but other than that, most of their vacations were spent camping throughout Colorado.

She had thought all the sacrifices were worth it when a family friend had offered to sell her the house, which was solid even if it needed work. She'd always dreamed of having her own garden center but never thought it would become a reality. But the property had come with a barn that she'd converted to a retail nursery and a greenhouse on the edge of the yard. She'd been so close to finally making it on her own, until life had thrown her a curve ball in the form of her mother's illness and the fallout from the disastrous financial decisions her mom had made in the confusion of rapidly progressing dementia.

"Do your friends brag about vacations?"

"Sometimes." He dipped another fry. "But I've got bragging rights on the loudest burp on the planet. Wanna hear it?" he asked, then swallowed a huge gulp of air.

She rolled her eyes as he let out a huge belch. "Impressive," she told him. "Just keep it under wraps when Grandma's around. Let me make sure I understand. You're equating me asking Owen to be my pretend fiancé to Aidan creating a fake vacation?"

Cooper nodded. "Kind of. If Owen gives you a ring, you should sell it, then we can go to Hawaii for real and take Aidan along."

"Owen isn't giving me a ring." She lifted the glass of water to soothe her suddenly dry throat.

It had been both amazing and agonizing to see Owen again. As changed as he was physically, there was still something about him that soothed the disquiet inside her, even when he clearly wanted no part of her latest crazy scheme. "Does it upset you at all, Cooper? The fact that I got myself into this mess? Because just say the word and I'll—"

"Mom, it's fine." Cooper shrugged. "Will my dad be at the reunion?"

She nodded. She'd gone onto Facebook to check the reunion's event page. The post hinting at her engagement to Owen already had over a hundred likes. There had barely been that many people in her graduating class.

Trent had been tagged on a post about the golf tournament, and she'd barely resisted clicking on his name to check up on him again. She'd quickly signed out of her account so she didn't have to add "Facebook stalker" to the list of stupid things she'd done that day. "I've heard he's coming to town to play golf. But I don't think he normally spends much time in Colorado, so maybe it's not true. I'm sure—"

"Don't say he'll want to see me. He won't."

"I'm sorry, Coop." She picked up a fry and dipped it in his ketchup. "Your father is missing out by not being part of your life."

"He has his own family," Cooper answered quietly. "My half siblings."

Jenny wanted to cry at the faint note of pain in her son's voice. For years, Cooper was satisfied with her explanation that Trent simply wasn't cut out to be a father. That's the excuse he'd given her when he'd dumped her a week after she refused his request to have an abortion.

Then last year, Cooper had searched for him on Jenny's Facebook account—Trent Decker. He lived in Madison, Wisconsin, and from the photos Cooper had found, he had a pretty blond wife, twin girls who were in second grade, and a toddler son.

A family for the man who couldn't handle being a father.

Jenny had immediately blocked Trent from her account. She'd thought of explanations and excuses to give Cooper for why his father wouldn't have tried to see him at any point during the past dozen years, yet proudly displayed photos of holidays, vacations, and school events for his other children.

Did Trent's wife even know Cooper existed? Cooper had resisted her attempts to talk about what he'd seen, telling her it didn't make a difference one way or the other. But that seemed impossible.

It had made a difference to her. She'd also been raised by a single mother and had never known her father. She'd never said it out loud, but there had always been a constant, niggling question in her mind as to why he would have walked away from her and never looked back.

Her first inclination after seeing Trent's Facebook profile had been to track him down and call him out on his deadbeat status. Yet there was a small selfish part of her that was afraid she could lose her son if his father ever did take an active interest in him.

Cooper had been her whole world since the moment the nurse had placed him in her arms. She couldn't imagine a scenario where he wasn't with her. But . . .

"Do you want to meet him if he comes to the reunion?" she asked softly. She forced a smile when Cooper glanced up at her from beneath dark lashes any woman would envy.

Green eyes—so like those of the first boy she'd loved—stared into hers, as if searching for a way to answer the question without hurting her feelings. From the time he was a baby, her son had been an old soul, watchful and content. While she ran on instinct, so often leaping before she looked, Cooper held back. He was her rock, and sometimes it felt like he was the only thing that kept her moored to the ground. She'd been a kid with a kid, and in many ways the two of them had grown up together.

Except she was the adult, so it was her job as a parent to dig deep and do the right thing.

"It's okay with me, Coop. I won't freak out. Promise."

"He probably doesn't want to. Why wouldn't he have contacted us before this?"

"I don't know, buddy," she answered, hating the tears that clogged her throat. The pain in her son's eyes was ultimately her fault. She'd been stupid enough to fall for the lies of a spoiled teenage boy. Cooper would spend his whole life paying the price. "But if you want to ask him that for yourself, I swear I'll find a way to make it happen."

He idly swirled a fry in the ketchup but eventually dropped it to his plate. "I like Owen," he said, and Jenny's throat tightened for an entirely different reason.

"He's a good person," she answered softly. "And really nice to do this for me. But it's pretend. You understand that, right? Owen and I are just friends."

"I know, Mom." He took a long drink of milk and wiped his mouth with the back of his hand. "Do we have any ice cream left?"

Jenny popped up from the table. Finally, a question she could answer. "We sure do. Cookies and cream. Let's eat it straight from the carton and watch *Life Below Zero*."

She ruffled Cooper's hair as he got up to clear his plate. Her baby was already an inch taller than she was, but he was still the sweet boy who meant the world to her. There was nothing she wouldn't do to take care of him.

Jenny vowed to handle her night with Owen and the possibility of seeing Cooper's father with caution and care, even though neither of those words was a normal part of her vocabulary.

CHAPTER THREE

"This was a mistake. I don't need a new dress." Jenny reached out one finger to touch the rack of beautiful, delicate fabrics in the Nordstrom dress department, then snatched back her hand, expecting some sort of "you don't belong here" alarm to sound.

Sam Carlton only laughed and continued to examine the clothes. "Don't think of it as a dress. It's like battle armor or a version of magic bracelets you can use to deflect incoming mean-girl bullets." She picked out one and held it up for Jenny. It was silver satin with a lace overlay above the waist. "This would be gorgeous on you."

"It's strapless," Jenny said in the same way Indiana Jones might mutter *It's a snake*. "What if I go to punch Trent, and I pop out of the top when I swing?"

"Kick him in the family jewels instead," Sam replied without hesitation, reminding Jenny why she'd invited Sam on this shopping excursion instead of Kendall or Chloe, both of whom were far gentler souls.

A saleswoman approached, then gasped when Sam turned to face her. "Oh my gosh," the woman breathed.

Sam held one finger to her lips. "We're just browsing, so I don't want extra attention today. Sound good?"

The woman let out a little squeak as a reply. "You're on a huge poster in the cosmetics department."

"Then we'll avoid cosmetics," Sam answered. "Thanks for letting me know." She handed the dress to the woman. "Could you start a fitting room for us?"

"Of course." The young saleswoman took the dress as if it were Sam's firstborn child. "If you need anything, I'm Marcy."

"Thanks, Marcy."

When the woman walked away, Jenny rolled her eyes. "Does being beautiful and famous get tiresome?"

Sam smiled. "You're the star today, Red."

While she knew her friend meant it, Jenny didn't care about being the center of attention. She was comfortable with her grubby jeans and work boots. That was her armor, and the thought of abandoning it, even for a night, made her skin feel like it was a size too small for her body.

Sam was normally just as casual in how she dressed, and up until a few years ago she'd also been one of the most famous models in the world. She was still a household name, and with her gorgeous mane of honey-blond hair and her statuesque figure, she could wear a potato sack and look gorgeous. But she knew how to rock designer clothes, while Jenny felt as awkward as a pig shoved into an evening gown when she tried to dress up.

"Seriously," she muttered when Sam held up a sequined number. "Why did I suggest this? I can wear my bridesmaid dress from Kendall's wedding."

Sam scrunched up her perfectly upturned nose. "Um, no. You are going to this reunion as a big F-you to your past. You are going on the arm of one of the most powerful technology businessmen in the country. You are going to be so smoking hot that the whole place goes up in flames." Her blue eyes widened and she plucked another dress off the rack. "This is the dress you're going to wear."

Jenny couldn't help the small whimper that escaped her lips. Even on the hanger, it was the most spectacular gown she'd ever seen. The sleeveless sheath was made of a shimmering green fabric that gave it an iridescent quality. There was lace and leather detailing around the scooped neckline, making it a perfect mix of elegant and edgy.

"I can't," she whispered automatically. A dress like that deserved a woman who was confident and ready to work it. A woman who could shimmy and sashay and walk in heels without falling on her face.

"Hell, yes, you can." Sam grabbed Jenny's wrist and dragged her to the fitting room, lecturing with every step. "It's your ten-year reunion. Half the women have gotten fat and another quarter of them are probably so Botoxed their eyebrows skim their hairline. You are naturally gorgeous, and you have a body to die for." She glanced over her shoulder. "Your legs are killer, and they'll look a mile long with where this hemline hits your thigh."

"It will look like I'm trying too hard."

"It's a high school reunion." Sam gave a little wave to the saleswoman as they entered the dressing room. "Everyone is trying too hard."

She shoved Jenny into the stall where the gown she'd first chosen had been hung. "Forget the other one." She held out the hanger. "Start with this. I'm going to get the saleswoman to bring up shoes."

"I hate heels," Jenny argued.

"Not as much," Sam said, raising a brow, "as you're going to love Owen's reaction when you're wearing them."

Jenny bit down on her lip. "I'm not choosing an outfit based on what Owen might think of it," she lied. "He's doing me a favor, nothing more."

"You know you want him back."

"He's never going to take me back." Jenny hugged the dress closer to her chest. "I cheated and publicly humiliated him."

"I'll agree with the public humiliation," Sam answered. "And it was monumentally awful on your part. But we both know you only made it look like you were cheating."

"Perception is reality," Jenny countered. "Owen doesn't realize that I purposely sabotaged what was between us."

"Because you refused to tell him."

Jenny shook her head. "I'm a bad bet, Sam. He deserves better . . . more than I could give." Her feelings for Owen had made her feel crazy and out of control. At the time, it seemed like the only way to regain her sanity was to force him to realize she didn't deserve him. But as soon as she'd seen the excruciating pain that filled his gaze, she'd realized what a horrible mistake she'd made.

Once again her doubts and fears had gotten the best of her and she'd acted without thinking. She was nowhere near worthy of a man like Owen. It had seemed easier to force the inevitable breakup than to prolong the relationship when she'd found herself falling more in love with him every day.

She didn't trust love. Love had screwed her over and left her out to dry. Thanks to both a father who hadn't wanted to know her and the boy who'd callously broken her heart, it was difficult for her to separate love from pain.

"Even if I wanted him," she told Sam, "I don't want a relationship. I'm not cut out for committing to anyone except Cooper."

"Bullshit," Sam muttered with a fake cough.

Jenny snorted. "You were the same as me not too long ago, Cover Girl. Don't act like you're an expert on love just because you've managed to pull your head out—"

"Ask Trevor," Sam shot back, a mischievous grin curving her lips as she mentioned her husband of almost a year. "He'll tell you all the ways I'm an expert."

"I just threw up a little in my mouth," Jenny said, and swung the fitting room door closed.

She was glad for the happiness Sam, Kendall, and Chloe had found in love, but it was sometimes difficult to be the third wheel three times over. It wasn't that she was envious of her friends. Jenny knew she wasn't built for falling in love.

Until Owen, she'd been content with her simple life, working and raising her son. Owen had been different. They'd started as friends, but somehow he'd slipped by her defenses and become more. The "more" was what scared her. She'd made a life on being satisfied with "enough," training herself not to want or expect more. Unwilling to risk any more of the deep hurt she felt from being rejected by the father she never knew.

She stood there a moment, staring at herself in the mirror. Pulling out her ponytail holder, she shook her head so that her thick copper waves fell over her shoulders.

She leaned closer and searched for additional freckles across the bridge of her nose, but the sunscreen she wore religiously seemed to be doing the trick. While she was nowhere near Sam's level of beauty, Jenny knew she was pretty enough in a pixie-cute kind of way.

But she'd worked hard to be taken seriously in her career, and much of that had involved downplaying her femininity. Now she thought of herself as one of the guys just as much as anyone else she knew did.

She turned away from the mirror, undressed, and then slipped into the sparkly gown, its silky lining soft against her skin. Adjusting the zipper, she turned back around and drew in a shallow breath.

For a moment she saw herself the way a stranger might. Sam had been right—the dress was incredible. Although her curves weren't generous, the fabric clung to them in a way that was downright provocative. As she pivoted in the small fitting room, the fabric shimmered, radiating shades of luminous greens depending on how the light caught on it. The hemline stopped just above her knees, showing off her toned thighs and calves, strong from years of hauling landscaping materials.

If the men on her crew saw her walking down the street in this dress, she doubted any of them would recognize her. She barely knew herself, and suddenly, it made perfect sense that this was the dress she had to have for the reunion. Call it armor or her F-you outfit, wearing it made her feel different. Stronger.

Hell, it made her want to shop for a whole new wardrobe, and that was quite the accomplishment.

She walked out into the hallway and found Sam waiting for her.

"Holy shit," her friend murmured. "I knew it."

The saleswoman stepped up behind Sam. "You look like that mermaid princess from the movie."

Jenny fidgeted, feeling color rise to her cheeks. "I'm not a princess. Not even close."

"You could be," Sam said with a wink. "And Owen can be your fairy-tale prince."

"Shut. Up." Jenny looked between Sam and the saleswoman. "Both of you. Before I come over there and—"

"Okay," the young woman answered nervously. "I'll just leave these shoes with you." She shoved several boxes into Sam's arms. "Let me know if you need anything."

Sam pulled the first set of shoes out of the box. "You have a bad habit of threatening physical violence."

Jenny shrugged. "People have a bad habit of pissing me off."

"I bet you've never even been in a real fight."

"Maybe not, but I'm scrappy. I could kick some ass."

"You're all bark and no bite," Sam said, handing over the strappy heels.

"I can't wear those. I'll fall on my face."

"Practice this week," Sam told her. "You need some badass shoes to go with that dress." She shimmied her hips. "We're gonna make Owen want some make-up lovin'."

Jenny slipped her feet into the heels and turned to the three-way mirror at the far end of the fitting room. She had to admit they were fantastic. She took a hesitant step forward and her ankle wobbled only a tiny bit. Maybe heels were doable.

"We would have to have had some lovin' to start with in order to try the make-up variety," she answered, continuing to move forward, slightly mesmerized by the woman she saw before her.

"You've never had sex with Owen?" Sam asked, stalking up behind her.

Jenny cursed as her ankle rolled and she tumbled into the fitting room wall. She pulled off the heels and handed them to Sam.

Sam continued to stare at her, clearly waiting for an answer. "You dated for like three months."

"We were just friends for most of that time before it turned romantic," Jenny said, embarrassed at how old-fashioned her relationship with Owen had been. At the time, his willingness to wait had seemed chivalrous. But she realized it was just one more way she'd manipulated the situation, too scared to move forward with a physical commitment. Not that she'd admit that to Sam. "I wanted to take it slow because of Cooper and—"

"And?" Sam prompted.

"Because I liked him," Jenny admitted. "Really liked him. So much that I screwed it up. We've been through this. Old news."

"This dress is going to kill him."

Jenny took another look at herself. "If spending an evening with him as my fake fiancé doesn't kill me first."

"Are you getting married?"

Owen massaged two fingers against his forehead at the note of accusation in his sister's voice.

"No."

Gabrielle breathed out a labored sigh over the phone. "Then why did someone I know from the ski team text that her older sister saw your engagement announcement on Facebook?"

"I hate Facebook," he muttered.

His baby sister, who wasn't such a baby, laughed. "You just wish you'd thought of it."

"Maybe," he admitted. "I'm pretending to be engaged as a favor for a friend. Don't mention it to Mom and Dad."

"An engagement is a pretty big favor," she murmured.

"Or Jack," he added, ignoring her comment as he thought of his younger brother, the consummate middle child. "I definitely don't want Jack to know."

"Jack and Kristin are way too busy planning their wedding," Gabby answered. "You know they're the first couple in the history of the world to get married? Or at least in Kristin's mind they are. Honestly, Owen, I know Kristin broke your heart, but you dodged a bullet with that one. I hope you're not that big an idiot with all women."

He let out a small laugh. "Thanks for the vote of confidence." He wasn't about to admit that he'd allowed another woman to make a fool of him. In some ways, Jenny reminded him of his boisterous sister—both of them willing to say whatever came to mind with little thought for the consequences.

"Tell me about your fiancée," Gabby prompted. "Are you sure I can't mention it to Kristin? She's having a bridal shower this weekend, and there's already another scheduled for when the out-of-town guests arrive. That one is a lingerie shower, which . . . blech." She made another noise of disgust. "I swear, Owen, it would kill her to know you're engaged if only because it would take some of the attention off her and Jack."

"I'm *not* engaged, Gabby."

"Whatever," she shot back. "She could *think* you are, and that would be enough. Plus Mom is online all the time. Just last week she had me help her set up an Instagram account. You can't keep this a secret forever."

"It will be a non-issue when I arrive for the weekend alone."

Gabby let out a cackle. "Bring along your friend. Come on, Owen. When was the last time we had some fun with Jack?"

"I doubt Jack would consider this fun."

"Every party needs a pooper . . ."

Owen smiled despite himself. Even though he and his younger brother were only separated by eighteen months, he'd always been closer to Gabby, who'd come along as a surprise five years later. Jack was the favorite, Gabby was the baby of the family, and Owen was . . . the son who'd never fit in.

So the fact that his little sister had adored him from the moment their parents brought her home from the hospital had been a beacon of light in Owen's otherwise shadowy childhood. It also meant he'd been wrapped around her little finger for just as long.

"Please," she pleaded in her sweetest tone. "I've been stuck listening to this for a month and—"

"How's your leg?"

There was an abrupt silence on the other end of the line. "Fine."

"Liar."

When she didn't respond, he said quietly, "It's going to get better, Gabby. My offer still stands to fly you to the Steadman Clinic in Vail. It's one of the best orthopedic centers in—"

"I said it's fine," she snapped. "I'm not a kid with a skinned knee. You don't have to fix me."

"I understand that." He sighed, knowing it was useless to have the conversation over the phone. He could barely manage his own life. He had no right to insert himself into Gabby's. But he hated hearing the underlying twinge of melancholy in her tone. "Are Jack and Kristin really that annoying?"

"The worst." There was a pause before she added, "I can't wait for you to get here, Owen."

He heard in his sister's voice all the things she wasn't saying out loud. Every last one was like a score across his heart. "I'll be there a few days before the wedding, kiddo."

"Maybe the week before?" she asked, her voice pleading.

"I'll try," he promised, and heard her deep release of breath.

They disconnected and Owen tossed the phone onto his coffee table and stood. He walked to the bank of windows that looked over both Union Station in Lower Downtown Denver and farther toward the Front Range to the west beyond the city.

When he'd bought the penthouse loft five years ago, he'd had walls torn out and opened up the space. Windows were installed across one full wall, similar to the ones he'd had designed for his office building. Growing up in West Virginia, Owen had only seen the gentle sloping Appalachian Mountains before venturing west to Colorado.

The rugged peaks of the Rockies were massive in scale, and Owen took inspiration from them every day. His childhood had been a series of disappointments—or more accurately, he'd continually disappointed his parents because he wasn't the son they wanted or expected him to be. Even with all of his professional success, his mom and dad still seemed baffled by why he was so interested in technology. It had always been that way. There was no room for who he was in his family.

He watched the sun dip below the highest peak as streaks of pink and purple moved across the sky. He'd felt stifled as a boy, constantly having a ball of one sort or the other shoved into his hands. He was fairly certain he was the only kid in history who had been punished by being forced to stop reading. He'd loved the science of taking things apart and putting them back together. Old radios, broken computers, whatever little pieces of machinery he could find.

Still, his father had insisted that he sign up for every sport his elementary school offered. By junior high, it had become clear that Owen had little athletic ability and even less inclination. His father had stopped trying with him. Stopped . . . everything. At least that's how it had felt to Owen. None of his academic accomplishments had mattered compared to the athletic prowess of the other two Dalton children.

Jack had been the quarterback for the high school football team, pitcher for the baseball team, and star center for the basketball team. Then he followed in their father's footsteps as a marine.

His sister had taken a different, if equally bright, path. From the time she'd first been on skis as a toddler, Gabby had loved speed. She'd mountain biked in the summer and skied all winter, eventually being the youngest girl to qualify for the US Olympic alpine ski team in the downhill event.

Fast-forward to now and both of his siblings were back in Hastings, Jack on leave from the marines and Gabby sidelined with a fractured knee from a crash at the World Cup.

Owen had recently been named one of *Time* magazine's top one hundred most influential people in the world as part of their Person of the Year issue, for the seventh year in a row. But none of it mattered. Owen might be rich and powerful, but back in his childhood home, he was simply the geeky son who hadn't fit the Dalton mold.

He'd planned to spend as little time as possible in Hastings for the wedding. But Gabby needed him, and he had a difficult time denying his sister anything.

He walked to the kitchen and grabbed a beer from the fridge, popping the top and taking a long pull. Before he could even think about his brother's impending nuptials, he had to get through a night with Jenny on his arm.

Just like with Gabby, he couldn't seem to deny Jenny Castelli, and he wondered how much of a thrashing both his willpower and ego were going to take.

CHAPTER FOUR

The doorbell gave a second, more insistent ring as Jenny stood in the entry of her cozy house the following Saturday night. She was frozen in place, unable to move forward to answer it, her heart pounding double time against her ribs, and her whole body stiff with panic.

What the hell had she been thinking?

A million answers raced through her mind, none of them helpful. Most included the words *fool, idiot, reckless, rash, stupid.* And those were the ones she could include without owing money to Cooper's swear jar.

Cooper.

He was at a sleepover with a friend, arranged so he wouldn't be at the house when Owen arrived. After their initial conversation over dinner, she'd tried to avoid the topic of the reunion, both because she didn't want to deal with it and because she hated the pain of discussing a father who wasn't interested in having a relationship with Cooper.

It was a more difficult absence to ignore once they knew about Trent's family. Over the years, she'd used every excuse she could think of to avoid Cooper internalizing Trent's rejection in the way that Jenny had always felt the absence of her dad.

The idea that her father had walked away because something was wrong with her—that she hadn't been enough—was a deeply embedded part of her identity. It killed her to think Cooper might ever believe he was less than amazing.

The opportunity to confront Trent at the reunion both propelled her forward and made her want to run in the other direction. Her first priority was to protect her son, but there was no right answer for how to safeguard his heart when dealing with a deadbeat father.

But she needed to do *something*, and the fact that she would be on Owen's arm tonight made her brave enough to face an army of petty, judgmental women or the man who had walked away from her and her unborn son so many years before.

Pulling in a deep breath, she yanked open the door only to see Owen heading down the front steps. He turned back around, his eyes widening as he took her in from head to toe.

"Hey," she whispered, then cleared her throat. All that panic from a minute ago seemed to take flight in her stomach as she met Owen's dark gaze, her nerves swooping and diving like an eagle over a mountain lake. "Sorry it took me a minute to get to the door."

He moved toward her slowly. "I thought I was being stood up."

She shook her head. "I wouldn't . . . I'm just . . ."

"Having second thoughts about our engagement?"

"Sort of. Although my doubts have nothing to do with you." She let out a breathy laugh and tugged at the fabric of her gown. "Or this dress. Sam picked it out. It's supposed to be my armor for the night."

One side of his mouth quirked. "Are we going into battle?"

"I'm not sure yet," she admitted. "Maybe."

His eyes turned dark and his body went stiff, like there was some sort of internal battle waging inside him. For a moment she thought maybe he was going to walk away. Then he muttered, "The dress is gorgeous and the shoes are amazing, but they're just icing on the cake, Jenny."

It was obvious he didn't want to give her the compliment, but he offered it anyway. This man was so much more of a threat than any former high school bully. His innate kindness allowed him to slip past her defenses, and there was nothing she could do to stop it. She'd erected those walls for good reason, and the fact that he could so easily breach them made her even more nervous. It had also led to her hurting him, a decision she would regret for the rest of her life.

"You look pretty good, too," she said, trying to make her tone light. He wore a charcoal-gray suit with a pale blue shirt and a burgundy tie. Without his oversize desk separating them, there was no doubt that he was different than before. His edges were sharpened, and an air of something less "goofy tech nerd" and more "powerful corporate scion" swirled around him.

Whatever it was, her body was reacting in a way that left her feeling wholly out of control, especially when he stared at her as if he could read every thought ripping through her mind.

"I just need to grab my keys," she mumbled, then stepped back into the house. Her heel caught on the threshold, and she started to pitch back before strong arms reached for her.

A moment later she was plastered against Owen, her hands instinctively wrapping around his shoulders. He smelled like a delicious mix of mint gum and spice that sent her senses reeling. She was suddenly off balance for an entirely different reason than her silly heels.

His eyes darkened as he gazed down at her, but then he set her away from him with a soft laugh. "High heels are tough."

She nodded, still in a daze, and stepped into the house to grab her small clutch from the table in the entry. She swallowed as her gaze caught on the ring sitting next to it.

"Um . . ." She turned and gestured to Owen, who moved to stand next to her. It was the first time he'd been to her new house, and she couldn't help but wonder what he thought of the property and all the work that needed to be done on it.

Although her friends had supported her plan for the nursery, she suspected they thought she was a little bit crazy to take on such a huge project, especially with her limited financial resources. Hell, there were many times over the past six months when she'd thought she was crazy. Somehow she knew any type of disapproval from Owen would carry more weight in her heart, and the last thing she needed was another reason to doubt herself.

She was full up on doubts.

She tried to concentrate on the present moment, even as his presence next to her made nerves dance along her skin.

Or maybe it was what she was about to say.

"I went ahead and got a ring," she muttered, picking it up and holding out her flattened palm for him to examine. "It's paste, of course, but I had to get one that was kind of gaudy because . . ." She glanced up at him from under her lashes. "I kind of bragged about the size of the diamond."

"You mentioned that," he answered.

But when she went to slip the ring onto her left hand, he plucked it out of her fingers.

"I know it's weird," she told him, "but I have to wear it."

He slipped the ring into his jacket, then pulled out a black velvet box from his pants pocket. "I think it's customary that the man present his fiancée with a ring."

Before she could argue, he opened the box to reveal the most beautiful engagement ring she could imagine. The center stone was princess cut and surrounded by three tiny diamonds on either side, all set in a simple platinum band. Even in the muted light of her entry, she could tell that the main stone was flawless.

"Tell me you didn't buy that." Her voice sounded raspy. Jenny had never let herself imagine getting married, but if she had, this would be her perfect ring. The fact that Owen was standing in front of her with it made her heart squeeze in ways she didn't care to examine.

He shrugged. "Let's say it's on loan from a jewelry designer I know."

She continued to stare, not trusting herself to respond.

"Do I actually need to get down on one knee?" he asked with a wry smile.

"I can't wear the ring. It's too much. It's too beautiful. It's all—"

"It's all part of tonight's farce," he told her. "We're doing this to make a statement. No one would believe I'd let my fiancée settle for anything but the best." He removed the ring from the box and took her hand in his. Her fingertips were freezing and his skin almost burned as he touched her.

She tried not to react as he slipped the ring onto her finger. It caught for an instant on her knuckle, then he twisted, and it slid into place. The solid weight felt so right on her finger that a piece of her never wanted to take off the band.

"So the ring is about you?" she asked as she stared at it.

"You're basically using me, Jenny." His tone turned chilly. "But it goes both ways. Tonight you're a reflection of me." He lifted her hand to examine the ring. "Plus, you'll owe me, and I like the thought of that."

At the rough timbre of his voice, another shiver passed through Jenny. When they'd previously been together, she'd had the upper hand with Owen and they'd both known it. She was the one who set the pace and the one who'd made a mess of things when her feelings for him had become too much for her.

But now she was off-kilter—left of center and out of her element. She didn't like being in the position of owing anyone, but there was a sexy note of promise in Owen's voice that a secret part of her reveled in.

When she didn't immediately answer, he crouched down so he was at eye level with her. "I think you like the thought of it, too."

"Nope," she answered, grabbing her purse, then pushing past him and shoving a key in the front door. "But I will admit, Owen Dalton, you give good diamond."

Owen pulled onto the interstate a few minutes later, trying not to let his gaze fall to the expanse of Jenny's bare leg visible on the other side of the console.

"If you ever want a second career," she told him, "you should hire yourself out as the perfect revenge date. A diamond ring and a Porsche? Hell, I don't even need to show up at this reunion to prove to everyone that I hit the jackpot."

He chuckled despite himself and kept his eyes on the highway, maneuvering the sports car through weekend traffic. "I'm probably not necessary to the equation. I can just hire out the car and jewelry."

"You're necessary," she murmured, and those two words made his heart stumble a beat. He was used to people wanting him for what he'd created and built with Dalton Enterprises—his reputation or connections. The way Jenny said it made him think she found him necessary for something more.

At one point, he'd wanted to be her something more.

Of course, he knew better than to read too much into it. He wasn't going to allow himself to be a fool for this woman ever again.

"How's Cooper doing?"

"Awesome, as usual," she answered, and he loved the note of pride in her voice. "He's at a sleepover tonight. It's weird with him not in the house, though. He's going to sleepaway camp the last week of June, for the first time ever." She made a face that was both cringeworthy and adorable. "It's going to kill me not to have him around. I don't know how the universe managed to bless me with such an amazing kid. He studies when he's supposed to, does chores without asking, and manages not to freak out about anything life throws at him."

"Like his mom being fake engaged?"

"I prefer the word *pretend*, but you're exactly right. He even gave me a rationale for how I got myself into this in the first place."

"Maybe he'll have a career in politics. I met with the US Senate Committee on Commerce, Science, and Transportation last week. They could use someone to help them come up with more convincing arguments for some of their plans."

She didn't answer for several moments, and he finally glanced over. "You were on Capitol Hill? You say that like it's no big deal."

He tapped his fingers on the steering wheel. "It's what I do, Jenny. You know most of my work now is focused on the foundation. We have a chance to make a real difference in using technology in both the environmental and public health sectors, but the amount of red tape and bureaucracy is mind boggling."

"You should sound more impressed with yourself, Owen."

He chuckled.

"I mean it," she insisted. "You're impressive. You're a catch. You're smart, handsome, funny, and—"

"Stop. You sound like my grandmother." He shook his head, not sure what to think about Jenny reminding him of the woman who had shown him the meaning of unconditional love when he was a kid. "I'd spend weekends at her house when the rest of the family went on camping trips. She was an aging hippie and used to make me stand in front of the mirror and recite positive affirmations to myself before I went to bed. She was very much the school of 'if you can believe it, you can achieve it.'"

She held up a hand. "I want to talk about your awesome-sounding grandma, but first tell me why you were left behind when your family went on vacation."

Damn. He hadn't meant her to pick up on that part. "They weren't exactly vacations. They were camping trips around the area—state parks and over near the New River Gorge. Mostly long weekends."

"Which still doesn't explain why you didn't go with them."

"I wasn't much of a hiker," he admitted. "I had allergies and asthma as a kid."

"But you run and bike now, right? Kendall mentioned that you and Ty did a triathlon last year."

"I've grown out of most of my symptoms, but back then I was . . . sickly. I wouldn't have been able to keep up. My dad was a marine, and he set a grueling pace."

"Did you ever try?"

"Not really."

"Did you want to?"

He felt his fingers tighten around the steering wheel and forced himself to relax. "It wasn't an option." He held his breath, hoping she didn't press him for more information.

"How often did these trips take place?"

Damn.

"My parents liked to camp," he said, slanting her a glance. "So they went at least once a month in the summer. I was fine at my grandma's. She was an amazing cook and baked the best pies."

"You shouldn't have been left behind," she murmured.

Owen took the exit off the interstate into Boulder faster than necessary, pushing the sports car in a way that had Jenny gripping the door handle. He wanted to be done talking about his family, hating how much not fitting in as a boy had shaped who he was as a man. "I don't know how we even got on the topic of childhood vacations."

"Me giving you a compliment reminds you of your grandma." She bit down on her lip as if she was resisting the urge to say more, then asked, "Is she still alive?"

He shook his head. "She passed away a few years ago, but before that lived in an assisted living facility in Hastings and practically ran the place."

"I wish my mom was adjusting so well to the memory care unit in the nursing home."

He stopped at a red light near the hotel and turned to her. "How is she doing?"

Jenny smiled, but it was strained. "Some days are better than others. She still knows Cooper and me, but she occasionally thinks he's her younger brother who was killed in Vietnam. It makes it a challenge when we visit, although Coop is a trooper, like always."

She took a small breath, then added, "The worst times are when she's aware of what's happening. My mom's whole identity was based on taking care of other people. The fact that she's now dependent and understands that the disease is stripping away not only her memory but also the very fabric of who she is as a person is difficult to handle. Alzheimer's sucks balls."

"Succinctly put." He reached out a hand and traced one finger over the delicate bone of her wrist. "How are you holding up?"

Her gaze dropped to her lap. "My mom has always been the strongest person I know, and that's still true. She's taken care of me for my whole life. I hate watching her slip away, but now it's my turn to take care of her. I'm going to make sure she has the best care and her life is as easy as I can make it. But things progressed more rapidly than I thought they would, and she made some bad decisions before I realized what was happening."

"What kind of decisions?"

Her head rolled back against the seat and she closed her eyes. "It was her retirement savings. Somehow a scam artist got a hold of her and she didn't mention it to me. He convinced her he was setting up long-term care insurance and a way for her money to be put into a trust for me and Cooper. Not that she had a lot, but my mom was a saver. Then it was gone."

"All of it?"

She gave a bitter laugh. "The majority. I'd just bought the new house and was working a ton of hours to set up the nursery. I wasn't paying enough attention, and by the time I realized what was happening and got a power-of-attorney authorization, he was long gone. I should have realized—"

"It's not your fault, Jen." Owen knew how close Jenny was to her mom and the toll Mona's illness must be taking. He wanted to gather

her into his arms and wipe away the deep sorrow etched across her delicate features.

"Thanks," she whispered. "Sometimes it's hard to remember that."

A horn honked behind them, and Jenny immediately shifted in her seat, lifting her hand and jabbing two fingers toward the rearview mirror.

Owen took another turn as he glanced at her. "Did you just give that car the peace sign?"

Jenny rolled her eyes. "Cooper wanted me to stop with the one-fingered salute in traffic."

"So now you do a very enthusiastic peace sign?"

"Exactly."

He smiled. The car ride had not been what he'd expected. He'd thought it would be difficult to be with Jenny again after how things had ended. He'd spent most of the week mentally flogging himself for not refusing her request in the first place.

Instead it had been easy to fall back into friendship with her. Their day-to-day conversations had always been one of his favorite things. Of course, he hadn't planned to let that bit about his grandma and the camping trips slip. But he was glad that it had led her to telling him about her mom. There was so much more to Jenny than she let anyone see.

Owen got that—he was a master of sharing himself without really letting anyone in. Now he realized tonight might actually be fun. There were people in his life he would have liked to have recognize that he'd turned out better than they expected. It just so happened that most of those people were related to him.

Jenny sucked in a quick breath as the hotel where the reunion was taking place came into view. The Hotel Boulderado, with its redbrick exterior and green awnings around the ground floor, was an iconic landmark near downtown and the popular Pearl Street Mall. Owen had been to several events at the popular and well-respected hotel, but never had one seemed more important than Jenny's reunion.

"Crap," she muttered, "we were so busy talking I forgot to get our stories straight about wedding plans."

"You talk," he told her. "I'll follow your lead."

"What if someone gets us alone?"

"Are you planning to ditch me again?" he asked mildly. "It's still in the midseventies, so I doubt they have a coat closet at the event."

She sucked in a breath. "That's not what I meant."

"We'll be fine, Jenny." He pulled the car to a stop under the hotel's deep green awning and climbed out when the valet opened the car door. After giving the man his information and accepting a few gushing comments about his car, he moved toward the entrance, then stopped when he didn't see Jenny waiting for him.

"Sir," the valet called, and Owen turned. "I . . . uh . . . your date is still in the car."

Another young man in the hotel's valet uniform of a white shirt, red vest, and black pants stood next to the passenger's-side door. "She's locked herself in," he said as Owen stepped closer.

Even though he couldn't see her through the tinted glass, he could feel the weight of her stare. Owen looked at the window and raised a brow. So much for thinking the night was going to be easy.

CHAPTER FIVE

Jenny felt Owen's eyes on her as she watched another group of her former high school classmates walk into the hotel.

A tap on the glass made her roll down the window. "Get in the car," she said on a panicked hiss of breath. "We're getting the hell out of here."

"I think you need to get *out* of the car," Owen responded calmly. Damn him for his quiet composure.

"I need a cigarette," she muttered.

"You don't smoke."

"I might start." She nodded to herself. "Hell, maybe I'll try some of those marijuana gummy bears that are so popular on Colfax Avenue. I bet I'd feel a lot better now if I was stoned."

"You don't need an excuse for more paranoia," Owen answered with a slight smile, and leaned closer. "Let's go into the party, Jen."

She shook her head. "None of it matters, Owen. The dress . . . the car . . . even arriving on your arm. All of that is my own personal version of smoke and mirrors. It's still me underneath it all."

"Thank God," he murmured, and she glanced up at him. "I wish you believed that all you have to be is who you are. Ten years changes a lot of things for people."

"Easy for you to say." She grabbed her small purse off the floor and clutched it to her chest. "You must have been the returning king at your reunion." She knew Owen was a year older than her and assumed—

"I didn't go back for my reunion," he answered.

"Why not? It's not like Steve Jobs was from your hometown. Who else could hold a candle to your success?"

"Why am I always on the losing end of comparisons with other tech company founders?" He shrugged. "You know it's not always about success."

"Of course it is."

"Sometimes it's about having the guts to take the first step. In this case, the first step out of the car."

"Is that your nice-guy way of calling me a chickenshit?"

He flashed a wide grin. "I don't think I need to call you anything. I can almost see the words bouncing around inside your head."

It was true. There was nothing bad Owen or anyone inside that hotel could think about her that she hadn't—at some point—believed about herself.

Often when fear got the best of her she played a "what's the worst thing that could happen" game. She'd run through worst-case scenarios in her head and figure out how to handle them. If she prepared for the worst, anything else would be a cakewalk.

This felt more like walking the gangplank, but she climbed out of the car anyway.

Instead of moving back to give her room, Owen crowded her a little. His hands lifted and he cupped her cheeks, his coffee-colored eyes so intense that for a moment, she forgot all about her nerves. She couldn't remember why they were standing there. She practically forgot to breathe. All of her senses were filled with him, strong and steady. The feeling of being safe was the biggest turn-on she'd ever had.

Then he brushed his lips over hers. The kiss was gentle but somehow still commanding, as if his easygoing image was only a mask and he'd

48

been the one in control all along. She wanted to wrap herself around him and never let go, never lose that feeling.

He pulled away and took her hand. She followed him up the stairs in a daze. "Hope you don't mind the improvisation," he said as a doorman held open the door. "There was a group watching us, and it seemed like a good idea to start the evening with a display of our affection for each other."

She blinked, then glanced over her shoulder. Sure enough, a handful of her classmates stood at the edge of the sidewalk in front of the hotel. A woman who she recognized as Brenna Holt took a long drag on a cigarette and waved in Jenny's direction.

Right. The kiss had been fake, a convincing bit of pretend chemistry. The entire date was a favor. Owen might have been in control of the kiss, but there was no denying at his core he was the nicest person she knew.

"Warn me next time," she muttered, touching a finger to her still-tingling lips, "so I can make it seem real."

He chuckled. "Things get any more authentic than that, and we're going to need a room."

She stumbled a step. "Stupid shoes." Owen placed his hand on the small of her back and her body grew heavy in response. "You can't say things like that. It's distracting."

"Can't you tell?" he asked, leaning so close his breath tickled her ear. "I'm trying to distract you."

Owen Dalton might be trying to kill her.

Jenny splashed water on her face in the hotel bathroom, then dabbed at her cheeks with a crisp paper towel. She wasn't sure jumping headfirst into a snowbank would cool her down at this point.

To the outside observer, the evening must look like a complete success. Owen had stayed at her side, attentive and affectionate as they made their way from the registration table to the bar. Even though Jenny understood that affection was not the same as love, and sexual chemistry meant even less when it came to true emotions, she had felt herself leaning into his touch and coming to rely on his presence at her side.

They mingled with various classmates who had never given Jenny the time of day but were now acting like they'd been her high school besties.

But the longer they stayed at the event, the more anxious Jenny became. It felt like her skin was a size too small again, which had more to do with Owen than anyone else. She hadn't been thinking when she'd made the comment about having a fiancé, but she would have never guessed in a million years that a night spent pretending to be in love with Owen could make her so crazy.

Each brush of his fingers along her shoulder, every time he wrapped an arm around her waist, the way he smelled so good she wanted to bury her nose in his neck . . . the whole of it was driving her into a frenzy of need and want that she could not seem to control.

"You definitely traded up," a cool voice said, and she turned to where Dina Sullivan, one of the former mean girls she'd seen last week in Denver, stood in the doorway between the bathroom and the lounge area.

"I don't know what you're talking about," Jenny muttered, even though she knew exactly what Dina meant. "But I can guarantee you have more Botox than brains in your head at this point."

Dina sniffed and took a step closer. "Not everyone can rock the 'rugged mountain girl' look. Natural and outdoorsy might work for you, but some of us need a little help."

Jenny opened her mouth to make a retort, then snapped it shut again. Was that some kind of weird, backhanded compliment?

"Trent hasn't shown up yet," the other woman said crisply. "But he played in the golf tournament this morning, so I know he's in town."

"I couldn't care less." Jenny swallowed at the outrageousness of her lie. She was feeling like such a phony, which she'd worked most of her life not to be. Surely she was so bad at it that everyone around her could see through her act.

She moved past the other woman before she lost her mind once again and did something stupid like throw out an invitation to the wedding.

"Did he give you the line about wanting to be inside you without anything in the way?"

Jenny sucked in a breath and turned back to Dina. Memories of her own foolishness flooded through her, a thousand hours of condemning herself for believing the lies of a selfish teenage boy.

"He did," she answered. "I was a fool to fall for that bullshit." She'd been so dazzled by the most popular boy at school noticing her she hadn't even realized she was being played. Ty had tried to warn her, but there was nothing that would have stopped her from giving Trent anything he wanted. The thought of how desperate she'd been made her stomach turn even after so many years.

"Did you—"

Dina shook her head. "He was my first," she said quietly. "But my mom was a nurse at the university's student health service. It was her mission to make sure I practiced safe sex." She gave a mock shudder. "I still have nightmares from the things she described to me. I was in love with Trent, but that didn't change the 'if you want to ride the bike, you have to wear the helmet' rule. Then he broke up with me to date you."

"How could I forget?" Jenny shot back. "I'd managed to fly under the social radar until then, but you made sure everyone hated me."

"I didn't hate you," the other woman clarified. "I was jealous. He made it clear that, unlike me, you weren't a prude."

"Because I was an idiot."

"All I knew was you'd stolen my boyfriend."

"That isn't how it happened."

"Does it matter?"

Yes, Jenny wanted to scream. It mattered because it had changed her whole life. She couldn't imagine her sweet, soft-spoken mother ever talking about safe sex—or any kind of sex. Mona never quite knew what to do with her fiery, argumentative, outspoken daughter. As close as Jenny had been to Ty, she'd resented her mother's second-class status in the Bishops' house and in the larger community.

All Jenny had ever wanted was to be loved—to be the most important thing in someone's life. Mona loved her, but she was also dedicated to the family that employed her. It had been difficult for Jenny to share her mother's attention, so when Trent first noticed her, it had felt like stepping into the sun after a lifetime of gray skies. Need had made her believe he loved her when she was really only an easy conquest for him.

"You're right." She took a step toward Dina. "It doesn't matter because I've 'traded up' as you put it."

"Owen Dalton seems like a really nice guy."

Jenny leaned forward. "Are you saying that because you're trying to figure out what he's doing with someone like me?"

Dina shook her head, her voice gentling. "I'm happy for you. I know it wasn't easy for you in high school, especially after . . ." She shrugged. "It sounds like you've made a great life for yourself and that you deserve it. I've seen Ty Bishop at a couple of charity functions in Denver. He sings your praises to anyone who will listen, and Owen dotes on you. You're surrounded by people who love you."

Jenny clamped shut her mouth. How was she supposed to respond to a statement like that?

"A lot of people get stuck in the patterns they developed when they were teens." Dina gave a small laugh. "No names mentioned," she said, and pointed a finger at herself, "but real life isn't high school. It's nice to know you understand the difference."

"Why are you being nice to me?" Jenny asked, narrowing her eyes as she glanced over her shoulder. "Is your posse rigging up a bucket of pig blood to dump on my head or something?"

Dina's eyes widened, except not a lot because her face was frozen. Jenny wondered what it was about certain women that made them terrified of aging. Jenny had plenty of issues, but at least worrying about wrinkles wasn't one of them. "I don't have a posse anymore," she said, and dabbed at the corner of her eye.

"I saw you a week ago," Jenny argued. "No offense, but you were the same petty girl from a decade ago. You insinuated my son was a mistake."

"I . . . it wasn't . . . I've been under a lot of stress lately." She looked to the floor. "My husband is screwing our nanny."

"Asshole," Jenny muttered, an unexpected burst of sympathy flashing through her.

"That's putting it mildly." Dina drew in a shuddery breath. "She's nineteen and has the body of . . . well, a nineteen-year-old."

"I saw you here with him tonight. Why didn't you kick him to the curb?"

"I don't know what I'm going to do, so I haven't done anything yet." Dina rolled her eyes. "Except cry a lot. I also bought some new lingerie because . . . well, he says part of the reason he did it is because things haven't been exciting between us lately."

Jenny stepped forward and wrapped both her hands around Dina's tiny, toned arms. "What he did wasn't your fault."

She knew this because what she'd done to Owen had nothing to do with him. For a married man to have sex with the girl who watched his children . . . what a scumbag. She might not like Dina very much, but no one deserved that.

"I don't know why I'm even telling you this. None of my friends know, and John wants to pretend like nothing happened." She sniffed.

"Although I'm not sure he wants to stop sleeping with her. I think he hopes I'll pretend like nothing is wrong."

"You need to stand up for yourself," Jenny told her.

"We have a good life."

"Your life is a lie." Jenny said the words on a hiss of breath, then squeezed shut her eyes because her life was a lie she'd purposely created for just that reason. She wanted to stick it to the people she'd known in high school. She wanted them to believe she was better than they were, but all of it was based on a lie.

Shit.

"How do I live it any other way?" Dina was watching her as if Jenny had all the answers. "I'm not you. I'm not brave or independent . . ."

Double shit.

Jenny swallowed. "I'm going to tell you something," she whispered. "Then you'll know—"

The bathroom door burst open at that moment. "Dina, what are you doing?"

Three women piled in and Jenny heard a chorus of strangled gasps behind her.

"I'm sorry for this." Dina shrugged off Jenny's touch. "Get your hands off me," she shouted. "This is a reunion, not a biker bar. If you have a problem, grow up and use your words."

"Are you okay, Dina?" Brenna reached out to pull Dina away from Jenny like she was rescuing her from the hounds of hell. "They're about to announce the reunion king and queen. You and John are sure to win," she gushed. "You're the perfect couple."

Jenny saw the other woman's slight flinch, as if the words sliced through her. But a moment later Dina smiled that high school prom-queen smile, fluffed her blond hair, and said, "Of course we'll win. Who else can hold a candle to us?"

Would the real Dina—bitter mom bully or emotionally shattered wife—please stand up? Jenny opened her mouth to take down the whole troop of them, then stopped. What purpose would it serve, and who was she to cast stones?

As much as Dina was perpetrating a lie, so was Jenny. She wasn't in a position to sit in judgment of anyone.

"Good luck to you," she called, earning an apologetic smile from Dina and a round of glares from the other women.

They bustled Dina out of the bathroom. Jenny followed a few moments later. She had a headache the size of the Oklahoma Panhandle and wanted nothing more than to disentangle herself from the fresh hell she'd created with her stupid mouth.

What she really wanted was to track down Owen, pull him from this event, and plaster her mouth to his. She wanted to make his throwaway comment about getting a room a reality and stay in that room all night long and find out if he could truly live up to the promise of his touch.

It might not even matter. If he was willing, she was ready enough for both of them.

The thought of getting naked with Owen did wonders for her headache. Who cared if it was a horrible idea? The whole night had been a cluster sundae. Why not put a big fat cherry on top?

Before heading back to the reunion, she veered off to the reception desk and booked a room. She hadn't ever wanted to be with a man as much as she did Owen. When the woman behind the counter set the plastic key card in her hand, a thrill of anticipation rippled along her spine. Clasping the small piece of plastic between her fingers, she turned and—

"Trent."

"Hello, Jennifer."

Trent Decker stood in front of her, a grown-up version of the overly confident boy she remembered. He was still handsome, although his chiseled features seemed almost like a caricature to her. His dark hair had thinned slightly, but he still wore it gelled in front. With his pale eyes and tanned face, he could have been the cover model for a cheap dime-store novel.

Anger replaced the anticipation, swift and sure like a kick to the gut. He'd always called her Jennifer, as if the three syllables would elevate her regular name and her common background to levels worthy of his opinion of himself.

As a sixteen-year-old girl, under the mesmerizing spell of first love, she'd imagined changing her name to Vanessa or Jacqueline—something sophisticated that would make her fit into his world. As if her name mattered. As if any piece of her was important to him, other than the fact that she was an easy piece of ass.

"Are you here to talk about your son?"

So much for being cautious. She might not want Trent in her son's life, but Cooper had a right to know his father. Especially when Trent had clearly gotten over his purported aversion to the role.

He gave a strangled laugh, color rising on his cheeks. "You always were blunt."

"You always were a jackass," she replied. "I've seen your perfect family on social media."

He raised a brow. "Checking up on me?"

She ignored the question. "What happened to not being cut out for fatherhood?"

"I grew up. Give me a break, Jennifer. We were kids. I was in no place to raise a child."

"And you think I was?"

His green eyes narrowed. "I gave you a choice."

"Shoving a couple hundred bucks at me wasn't a choice. It was an insult."

They glared at each other for several long seconds, and then he sighed. "How is he?"

"Do you even remember his name?"

"Cooper. How is Cooper?"

"Smart, sweet, perfect," she answered automatically. "Nothing like you."

He inclined his head. "I suppose I deserve that, but you—"

"Is your wife here with you?"

His shoulders stiffened under the tailored suit he wore. "No. It would have been complicated."

"Because she doesn't know you have another son," she guessed.

"She knows. But our kids are young and it might—"

Oh, hell no. She would not stand there and listen to him tell her that Cooper's very existence could be a burden to his other children. "Save it, Trent. You're not really his father anyway." Satisfaction burned in her gut when his head snapped back.

"What the hell does that mean?"

"A father is a man who cares for his child. A man who makes an effort to be a part of his son's life." Anger continued to thunder through her, obliterating the wispy tendrils of shameful regret she often felt when she thought of how much of herself she'd given to Trent. Fury seemed to clear her mind, allowing her to feel confident in her belief that the man did not deserve a place in her son's life.

She jabbed a finger into Trent's chest. "You're nothing more than a sperm donor. Don't talk to me, Trent. Don't ask about *my* son. Go back to your picture-postcard family and leave me alone, the way you have since the day you walked out of my life."

"My name is on the birth certificate," he countered. "If I wanted to be a part of his life, I could. I have rights, Jennifer." Contempt burned in his eyes, and suddenly she realized she'd done it again. Ran her mouth before thinking about the consequences of what she was saying.

"It's fine, Trent," she told him, trying to change her voice to a placating tone. "Cooper is fine. He's a good boy. He's happy. There are plenty of people in his life who care about him. He doesn't need you."

"A boy needs his father." He adjusted his tie as if his collar was too tight. "Maybe I'll stay an extra day and meet him."

"You don't want that. You just said your other kids don't even know he exists."

"Maybe it's time they learn. If we handle it the right way, they'd be happy to discover they had an older brother, especially little Mikey."

"Stop acting like you care." She prayed he didn't recognize the edge of desperation in her voice. So much pretending. So many lies.

"The last time I checked," he said, "you weren't privy to my feelings. I only agreed to come to the reunion once I heard you'd be here. If you'd given me a chance before jumping down my throat, I—"

"No."

He had to be manipulating her again. There was no way Trent truly wanted to be a father after all these years.

But doubts quickly quashed her anger, leaving her adrift in the familiar sea of second-guessing herself. What was she trying to accomplish? Despite shrugging it off, there was a good chance Cooper truly wanted to get to know his father.

He'd been hurt by Trent's tacit rejection, but her boy had the biggest heart of anyone, capable of rivers of forgiveness. What if he wanted to meet his half sisters and baby brother? As far as she knew, Trent had a stable home, a solid job. He hadn't given her a thing for twelve years, but if he chose to step back into Cooper's life, did she have the right to stop him?

He didn't answer, and she forced her lips to remain pressed together, afraid of antagonizing him further.

"I was wondering where you'd gone."

She whirled around to find Owen standing behind her. She pressed a hand to her chest, her fingers still clutching the card key. His gaze clouded over as if he saw something he hadn't expected. Something that disappointed him.

As if she'd disappointed him.

The last time he'd had to come looking for her at an event, he'd found her in the arms of another man. Surely he could feel the tension crackling between Trent and her? Hell, she'd been reserving a room to share with Owen.

His gaze dropped to her hands as she shoved the plastic card into her purse. Of course, he didn't know why she had the key, and she wasn't exactly a sure bet. For a moment she ignored the tumult of emotions running through her and focused on the way she'd felt the moment she heard his voice.

Relieved. Safe. Happy.

In a move so out of character as to be ridiculous, she threw her arms around his neck. "I missed you," she murmured against the base of his throat.

While she'd only been away from the party for fifteen minutes or so, the words were true. They were also more—an acknowledgment of what she'd willingly thrown away because of her fears and doubt.

His hands came around her waist, although his shoulders remained stiff. "You shouldn't have been gone so long," he murmured into her hair. His gentle admonishment made her knees go weak because it gave her hope that he was also talking about more than the reunion.

He shifted her away from him, and she had to force herself not to cling to him like a barnacle.

They both faced Trent, who held out his hand. "Trent Decker," he said, pumping Owen's fist. "I heard a rumor you were going to grace us with your presence tonight. I couldn't pass up the opportunity to meet you."

"Owen Dalton. I'm . . ." Owen paused, glanced down at Jenny, then said, "I'm here with Jenny."

She released the first easy breath she'd taken all night. Owen was there with her. That wasn't a lie, even by omission. She was done with lies.

"Jennifer and I knew each other in high school," Trent offered smoothly.

Owen didn't react, although he understood how she'd known Trent. "I've heard."

"I own a little stock in your company," Trent told him, flashing an ingratiating smile. "I'm pretty sure you paid for my last vacation. A Disney cruise." He gave a small chuckle. "That's one expensive mouse, you know?"

Jenny sucked in a breath as she felt the sudden change in Owen. He'd been reserved before, but now a quiet fury radiated from him. Did he have something against Walt Disney?

"Did you take your whole family?" Owen asked Trent.

"Yeah, man. Even the in-laws. I figured—"

"All of your kids?"

"Sure," Trent answered. "My son was only—" He stopped, swallowed as if suddenly realizing the mistake he'd made. He changed tack. "You know I'm in the technology business, too." He dug in his pocket and pulled out a business card that he held out to Owen. "I work for a company that brokers relationships between civilian companies and the military. Word on the street is Dalton Enterprises is looking to extend their reach into new markets. I'd love to buy you a drink or grab a bite before I head back, to talk about how we might be able to facilitate things for you."

"Maybe another time," Owen said, keeping his hands firmly in his pockets. "I think I'm going to be busy planning a vacation for *my* family. Who knows, I might even rent out a theme park for the day." He reached out and pulled Jenny close against his side. "Wouldn't that be fun, sweetie pie?"

Jenny's stomach lurched at the thought of her and Cooper making a family with Owen, even if it would never happen. Trent wasn't going to believe—

"Wow," Trent murmured. "That sounds great. Sure beats standing in line with the masses."

"Sure does," Owen agreed, sending Trent a scathing look that clearly communicated *he* was the masses to which Owen referred.

Jenny's heart tripped at the knowledge that Owen was, in his own quiet way, defending her. And by the look on Trent's face, he knew he'd been thoroughly put in his place.

Trent studied the business card in his hand as if he wasn't sure how it had gotten there. He glanced between Owen and Jenny as he stuffed it into his pocket. "Congratulations on your engagement."

"Thank you." With Owen as a steady presence at her side, she was able to keep the lid on her temper. "As far as what we were talking about just now . . ."

"I've actually got an early flight," he interrupted. "I'll be in touch on that front." He turned to Owen. "We'll get that drink next time I'm in town," he told him.

When Owen didn't respond, Trent continued, "Or maybe I'll give you a call at the office."

Owen inclined his head. "You can try that."

"Right," Trent agreed. "That's a plan. Okay, you two kids have fun. I'm going to head back to my parents' house. I've had enough of people trying to relive their glory days for one night."

Jenny watched him walk away, then turned to Owen with a small smile. "Thank you for rescuing me there. I don't know how I ever could have been fool enough to think I loved that jackass."

A sliver of unease snaked through her when Owen's gaze remained fixed on the hotel's front entrance. "Tell me," he said, "about the hotel key in your purse."

CHAPTER SIX

Owen kept his voice neutral as he watched Trent Decker walk out the hotel's main entrance.

He'd never wanted to punch a man as much as he had a few minutes ago. That was saying something since he'd once discovered his then fiancée on her knees in front of his brother.

He almost laughed at the absurdity of his life. He didn't put much stock in his personal reputation as a tech-industry visionary and mogul. He'd always loved technology and he'd wanted to help more people use it. It was a mix of luck and talent that, in the year his fledgling company had brought it to market, the mesh router he had designed became the biggest game changer since the birth of the Internet. He'd hit the sweet spot in the wave of the world's demand for better networks that would enable personal devices to communicate without relying on Internet service providers and a few centralized access points.

From there, it seemed like he had a Midas touch when it came to innovations. He employed the best people he could find and made sure to treat them well so they remained loyal. Loyalty was paramount to Owen, so it was ironic that he'd been betrayed in his personal life by some of the people closest to him.

He'd been on edge for the past two hours as a result of working to keep up the charade of his engagement to Jenny. The woman might be gorgeous, but she was a horrible actor. Every emotion she had played across her delicate features, so he'd upped his game, continually touching her or murmuring in her ear to keep her distracted enough that she didn't give away the whole farce.

The pretend intimacy had taken its toll on his nerves as well as his libido. When she'd excused herself to the bathroom, he'd headed straight for the bar and done a round of shots with her high school class's starting football lineup. The liquor had burned his throat but hadn't done anything to quench his need.

The way the dress shimmered over her curves, the scent of her lingering in the air, the way she unconsciously pressed a little closer to him every time someone approached them. All of it thrummed through Owen until his desire was so intense it felt like it might bring him to his knees. An evening with Jenny, and the previous two years spent shoring up his defenses disappeared like no time had passed.

He knew she was freaked out, and when she hadn't returned, a thread of panic had snaked its way through him. Jenny Castelli wasn't great under stress, and he didn't know if he could keep it together if she once again turned those emotionally destructive tendencies on him.

He'd recognized Cooper's father immediately, and the angry sneer on the man's face as he looked at Jenny made Owen want to wipe it right off. Then she'd turned and he'd glimpsed the hotel room key clutched in her fingers. There was no way she planned to use that key with Trent, which did nothing to explain why she had it.

Every time he'd touched her tonight she'd bristled like a feral cat. Although the arrangement had been her idea, it was clear she regretted it. She could barely stand to have any contact with him. So what the hell was she doing with a room key?

She blinked up at him, as if she didn't know what he was talking about. "I did it again, Owen," she said, her voice miserable. "I pissed off Trent and he threatened to make contact with Cooper." She shook her head. "Which maybe is good because he's the father, but he hasn't ever been a father to my son. What if he breaks Cooper's heart?" Her eyes filled with tears. "I don't know whether it's worse to never know your dad, or to have one who says he'll show up to take you out for your birthday and then never comes. Trent could do that to him. He could hurt Cooper more than he already has."

Christ, he'd never seen Jenny cry. The vulnerability of it wrecked him. She was gulping in air, and he took her hand, leading her to an empty corner of the lobby.

"But what if," she continued, "he's a good dad and Cooper has sisters and a brother and a real family where the mom stays home and bakes cookies and shit?"

He laced his fingers with hers. "And shit?"

"You know what I mean." She swiped under her eyes with her fingers.

"You are an amazing mother, Jen. Cooper has people who love him."

"That's what I told Trent," she answered. "But it's not the same, you know? A single mom who works a hundred hours a week and a grandma who is slowly losing her mind are not the same as a real family."

"Stop." He cupped her face between his palms. Even though she'd crushed him once before, a part of him wanted to do whatever it took to wipe the pain from her eyes. "Cooper knows how much you love him and understands how hard you've worked to build a good life for him."

"You're right. I know you're right." She bit down on her lip and gave a shaky nod. "I'm pulling it together. And the key is for us."

It felt like his heart stopped beating inside his chest. "I'm going to need you to clarify that statement," he said, unable to believe what he hoped she meant.

"You and me," she answered, pointing a finger between the two of them. "Done with the reunion and going upstairs. All night." She frowned. "Tell me you don't need me to draw you a diagram."

"No diagram." He dropped his hands. "But are you sure? Because in there"—he pointed to the ballroom where the reunion was in full swing, the strains of an old-school dance song spilling out from the open doors—"it felt like I was driving you crazy every time I touched you."

"Uh, yeah," she agreed.

"I mean drive you crazy as in 'don't lay a hand on me, or I'll break every one of your fingers.'"

She raised a brow. "More like driving me crazy as in 'I'm going to rip off your expensive suit and have my down-and-dirty way with you.'"

"I like your version better," he said, ready to worship this woman, whether it was the smart choice or not.

He leaned in to claim her mouth for a deep kiss. Not a brush of their lips for an audience. Owen kissed her as he'd been dying to all night, like she was the only thing he'd ever needed in the world. That's how he felt at the moment, and even the thought of how dangerous that could be didn't stop him.

He wanted her. All of her. He'd been a gentleman before, taking it slow because his feelings for her had overwhelmed him. He ignored that now and simply focused on how right she felt in his arms. She moaned and he slid his tongue into her mouth, his whole body lighting on fire as she met his need with her own. She reached her hands under his coat and wrapped them around him, her nails scratching lightly through the thin fabric of his crisp cotton shirt.

How the hell had he ever managed to rein in his need for her?

After another moment he lifted his head, a deep satisfaction rumbling through him at the dazed look in her bourbon-colored gaze. "Shall we use that key?"

She nodded and stuck close to him as they hurried across the lobby toward the bank of elevators on the far end. But just as they passed the reservation desk, another couple came around the corner. He recognized them from the reunion, and Jenny abruptly stopped. She and the woman eyed each other for several long moments, as if engaged in a silent conversation.

The woman was rail thin, as if she lived on nothing but lettuce and air, with long blond hair and overly feminine features. It looked like she'd spent half her life with a Barbie doll as her style role model. But as he looked closer, he could see that her hair was mussed and her lipstick slightly smeared. She adjusted her dress and dropped her gaze from Jenny's as the man with her chuckled.

"I guess we're not the only ones taking advantage of an evening out," he said, drawing the woman closer. "Gotta keep the sparks flying after five years of marriage, and it sure beats line dancing with a bunch of losers from high school. Right, pook?"

The look of smug satisfaction in the man's grin made Owen's stomach turn. Thank god he and Jenny could finally get out of there.

He'd been the keynote speaker at a conference in Geneva the weekend of his own ten-year high school reunion. At the time, he'd been almost sad to miss it. Despite being the outcast within his own family, no one at his local public high school had seemed to care about Owen's propensity toward geekdom, and there were a few fellow former members of the school's science club that he still counted as friends.

But tonight made him thankful he'd missed the event if his graduating class had turned out anything like Jenny's.

The woman tucked a stray lock of hair behind one ear. "It was good to visit with you, Jenny," she said, "earlier in . . . you know . . ."

"While I was turning the hotel into a biker bar?" Jenny shot back.

The woman cringed, then looked between Jenny and Owen, her gaze apologetic. "I hope you both have a good night. Thanks for attending the reunion." She offered a wan smile to Owen. "You were quite a draw."

She grabbed the man's hand and hurried past them back toward the party.

Owen placed his palm on the small of Jenny's back and started toward the elevator. "I don't think I want to know about the biker bar comment."

The elevator door swished opened as they approached. They walked on, and Jenny punched a button for their floor, then bolted to one corner of the small space. Owen reached up a hand to massage the back of his neck. He was getting whiplash from trying to keep up with her mercurial moods.

"Is everything okay?" He crouched so they were at eye level. Even in heels, she was several inches shorter than him, and the combination of her tiny size and her bigger-than-life attitude was one of the things he'd always liked best about her.

"Fine," she mumbled, then crossed her arms over her chest. "We're another happy couple, just like Dina and her husband."

There was something she wasn't saying, but he had a feeling if he pushed her, she'd only shut down more. He had to remind himself that this woman had just been playing an enthusiastic game of tonsil hockey with him. The atmosphere in the elevator had chilled to temperatures found around Christmas in Siberia.

When the elevator stopped, she stalked down the hall, not seeming to care if he followed. As soon as the hotel room door opened, she grabbed the front of his jacket and dragged him into the room. She launched herself at him, and he dug his heels into the plush carpet to keep from stumbling back.

Enthusiastic was one thing, but this was downright aggressive. After attempting several times to slow their pace, he finally took both of her arms in his hands and held her away from him.

"What the hell, Jenny?"

"What the hell, Owen?" she mimicked, and his frustration ratcheted up another notch.

He closed his eyes for a moment, trying to bite back his temper. His even-keeled reputation flew out the window when he was around Jenny. She pushed his buttons like no one he'd ever met.

"Apparently there's a fine line for you between seduction and assault."

She gasped and tried to wriggle free from his grasp.

"I'm sorry," he said immediately. "I didn't mean that. But I can't figure out what changed from five minutes ago to now."

"We're in the hotel room," she snapped. "What did you think was going to happen?"

"Something that didn't feel like angry sex when we're not actually fighting."

"What does it matter how I act?" she asked, her shoulders slumping. "Who cares what kind of sex we're having? It's all a lie. The whole night is a lie."

He shook his head. "Me wanting you isn't a lie."

"Then why did you stop?" She reached for the zipper on her dress. "You want me. I owe you. Let's—"

He held up a hand. "That's not what this is," he said with a growl. "You're not having sex with me as payment for tonight."

Her chin notched up an inch. "The reason you want me is because you bought into what we're pretending to be here. It's not me you want. It's Jenny your fiancée."

"It's you."

She pulled the diamond ring off her finger and held out her hand, palm open. "This isn't me."

"Keep it."

"Owen, no. This ring costs a fortune. I don't—"

"You're going to need it. I've decided what I want as payment for tonight." He glanced at the bed and back at her, his conviction to stay careful and in control disintegrating in the heat of the moment. "And it isn't as simple as a roll in the sheets."

"What are you talking about?"

His sister's voice pounded through his head. He didn't have anything to prove to his brother or the rest of his family, but he couldn't deny that he wanted to. He needed to show them that he'd moved on, past the slights and betrayals of his childhood.

"I need a date to my brother's wedding." He pinned her with a stare that told her exactly how serious it was to him and pitched his voice low. "I want a fiancée."

Her eyes widened. "We agreed to one night."

"We agreed that you owe me."

She looked around wildly, as if searching for an excuse. "Where's the wedding?"

"West Virginia. The town where I grew up."

"No way," she answered immediately. "I can't leave Cooper, and don't even ask me to bring him. It's bad enough he knows about tonight, but to be witness to—"

"Cooper doesn't have to know. The wedding is the last weekend in June."

It took her a moment to react. "When he's at camp," she muttered with a scowl.

He hated himself for wanting to kiss the frown off her face. "I think your exact words were 'I'll do anything.'"

"Can't you just be into kinky sex like a normal guy?"

"Maybe I am."

He took a step closer and she moved away until the backs of her knees hit the bed. Her eyes had darkened to the point that they looked like melted chocolate, and he wanted to sink into them—into her—until nothing else mattered. She didn't fool him. Desire was obvious in her gaze. Hell, it was coming off her in waves.

"But you won't find out tonight. Enjoy the hotel room, Jenny." He took a step back. "I hear room service has fabulous cookies on the late-night menu."

Before his desire obliterated the willpower he was holding on to like a lifeline, he walked away. It was the most difficult thing he'd done in years.

"Don't eat that."

Jenny paused with the cookie halfway to her mouth. She was sitting in the dining room at her mother's assisted living facility the next morning. The breakfast dishes had just been cleared, but she'd snagged a chocolate-chip cookie from the plastic container shoved under the counter. They must have been left over from a family member visiting another patient in the memory care unit the day before. Jenny definitely hadn't taken Owen up on his suggestion to order late-night room service after he'd left, but somehow she couldn't suppress her craving for a cookie right now.

She examined the round cookie she held between her fingers. "Why shouldn't I eat it?"

Mona Castelli wrinkled her nose. "They're store bought." Her tone made the words sound blasphemous. "I made a batch yesterday after school and pulled a few out for you and Claire before Ty and Charlie get to them." She gave a soft chuckle. "I can barely keep enough food in the house for two growing boys. I'm going to need to ask Mrs. Bishop to raise my grocery budget for the month."

Jenny set the cookie on the napkin in front of her. Her mouth was suddenly filled with sand. "How old do you think Ty and Charlie are now, Mom?"

Mona looked at Jenny as if she were crazy. "We just celebrated Charlie's birthday last week," she said, her tone mildly disapproving. "How can you not remember the lasagna dinner I made? It's his favorite. One more year and he'll be allowed to vote, which makes Ty fifteen. You have a milestone birthday coming up, too. Double digits."

"Ten years old," Jenny said dully. It was hard to believe that just six months ago her mother had still been living in the cozy condo she'd retired to after working as the Bishops' housekeeper for most of her adult life and acting as a surrogate mother to Ty and his siblings for much of that time. Ty was Jenny's best friend, but his older brother, Charlie, and younger sister, Claire, had loved to remind her of her status as the daughter of hired help. Ty's parents, Eric and Libby Bishop, were kind—if condescending—and Jenny had chafed at the rules and restrictions placed on her, living in the strict Bishop household.

Her father was never in the picture. He'd divorced her mother while Mona was still pregnant with Jenny. A musician and a gypsy at heart, according to her mother he wasn't meant for sticking around. That had left Mona to raise Jenny while also taking care of the wealthy family that paid their bills.

"I'm not going to be ten," she said, reaching out to gently clasp her mother's fingers. "Do you remember what year it is?"

"Of course I do," Mona snapped, snatching away her hand. "Do you think I'm stupid?" She pulled at the ends of her short bob as if that would help her dislodge the jumble of memories in her brain. Her dark hair had gone silver in the past few years, and there were fine lines fanning out from the corners of her eyes, but Mona's olive complexion was still enviable. Jenny had lost count of the times she'd wished she favored her Italian mother instead of the redheaded Irishman from whom she'd inherited her hair and her temper.

"No, Mom. Tell me what year it is."

Her mother gazed at her hands and began to worry her thumbs together. Jenny could imagine the synapses in her brain firing away and the tiny gaps and holes where the disease had worn away the connections. It broke her heart when a single tear spilled from her mother's gentle eyes. "You're not a child," Mona murmured. "You have a child. Cooper. My grandson."

She ticked off the words as if reading a list. In her room there were framed photos on the nightstand and dresser, images of family and friends with labels naming them and their relation to Mona. It had seemed almost offensive to Jenny when she'd first typed out the little slips of paper, as if Mona could ever forget the grandson she adored.

Now Jenny realized that no number of labels could stop the relentless march of Alzheimer's, flattening everything in its path and stealing her mother one brutal step at a time.

"He loves you so much, Mom." She leaned in again, and wiped her thumb across the paper-thin skin of her mother's cheek. "I love you, too."

"I'm sorry." Her voice was shaky. "You can eat the cookie." She sniffed. "You can do anything you want, of course. You're all grown up."

"I've only made it this far because of your support, Mom," Jenny answered. "I wouldn't be anything without you."

"Nonsense." Her mother patted Jenny's cheek. "You have always been the very best part of me."

Jenny snorted.

"I mean it. You are strong and brave. I know how much you hated not having a father."

Jenny rolled her eyes and tried to look like she didn't care. "I never even knew him." But she had felt the lack of the father she'd never met like a deep, integral part of her was missing. She knew kids whose mom and dad were divorced and a couple of classmates who'd had a parent die. But she was the only one who'd never even had a father.

It upset her mother to talk about the man who'd abandoned them both, so Jenny had learned not to mention it. But from what she had pieced together, her parents had been deeply in love until Mona discovered she was pregnant. Jenny's father, a bass player in a touring jazz band, left them for a life on the road and never looked back.

"Things weren't easy for you as a girl," her mother said, "and living with the Bishops wasn't what you wanted. But it was the best I could give you, sweetie."

"It was fine," Jenny lied, and because emotion knotted in the back of her throat, she took a small bite of the cookie, then made an exaggerated choking sound. "That's horrible. Nothing like what you used to bake."

She was going for humor, but Mona's smile was sad. "I wish I still could bake for you."

Oh, crap. The wistful expression on her mother's face did nothing to help Jenny regain control of her emotions. As awful as it was losing her mother in tiny, painful bits, the times when Mona was aware of what was happening were even more difficult.

"How about you come over this weekend and we can have a day of baking? I'm finally getting settled in the new house." That was another lie, and the truth was Jenny wasn't even sure if the oven worked correctly. It could heat frozen pizza, but anything beyond that was definitely questionable.

"You hate being in the kitchen."

"Not when your caramel pecan cake is my reward."

Mona clapped her hands together, her smile broadening. "It's been so long since I've made that cake." She ticked off ingredients. "Two cups of flour, a cup of sugar, two sticks of melted butter, three eggs, a teaspoon of cinnamon, a half teaspoon of both salt and baking powder, and a cup of chopped pecans."

"Sounds about right," Jenny agreed, although she'd never baked a cake that didn't come from a box mix.

"How come I can remember recipes and I forget how old my only daughter is?" Mona's eyes welled with tears.

Jenny sighed. The doctor had warned her about depression as the disease progressed. She'd made it her mission to keep her mother's spirits up, but some days were harder than others, especially after a night like the one she'd had.

She'd sat on the bed in the hotel room for hours after Owen had left, replaying all the things she'd done and said wrong over the course of the night—throughout the entire time she'd known him, really.

Was kindness so disconcerting that she had to screw it up every time?

Yep.

Running into Dina and her husband so soon after that bizarre encounter in the ladies' room had thrown Jenny for a hell of a loop. How could a woman pretend everything was fine and fake that kind of affection with her husband? Jenny couldn't help but compare it to the lie her current relationship with Owen was based on. She hated that what was between them was for show when it felt so real to her. But, once again, she'd let her doubts overwhelm her and ruined their night together.

Eventually she'd curled into a ball and fallen asleep for a few fitful hours. She'd woken in the middle of the night and called down to the front desk for a taxi to take her home. No sense staying in a hotel alone with no change of clothes or when the whole purpose for booking it had been to be with Owen. To finally be with Owen.

The desk clerk had informed her that there was a car waiting. That was the kind of gentleman Owen was at his core. As pissed as he'd been when he'd left, he'd arranged a car to drive her home.

"My high school reunion was last night," she told her mother.

"Assholes," her mother muttered, and Jenny's jaw dropped. Mona Castelli did *not* swear.

"What?" Mona raised a brow. "You think I don't know how they treated you, especially after how that boy left you with no support?"

"You never said anything."

Her mother shrugged. "What good would that have done? I wanted you to have a good education and the Summit School was the best."

"A lot of good it did me."

"Life happens," her mother said, and Jenny choked back a laugh. "Tell me about the reunion. Did *that boy* attend?"

Since high school, her mother had only referred to Trent as "that boy." The news of Jenny's pregnancy had caused a huge rift between

Mona and Libby Bishop, Ty's mom. Libby, who Jenny had never liked, was friends with Trent's mother. The fact that she was unwilling to support Jenny in making Trent do the right thing was something Mona had never forgiven.

In the end, Jenny had been the one to convince her mother not to quit working for the Bishops. Despite her distaste for their lifestyle, they were a sort of family to her mother, and Jenny didn't want her mistakes to affect her mom.

Instead, her mother had moved out of the cozy carriage house on the Bishop property that had been their home and rented a tiny bungalow outside Boulder. It had been cramped and a struggle, especially when Cooper was a baby. Mona had supported the three of them with her salary from the Bishops while Jenny worked odd jobs that allowed her to spend days with Cooper. She owed her mom more than she could ever hope to repay.

"He was there," she said, and Mona's eyes narrowed. "But he's not a kid anymore, Mom. Neither of us is."

"Did you ask him if he ever plans to do right by you and Cooper? It's not too late."

Jenny shook her head. "Trent has a family in Wisconsin."

"He has a *son* in Colorado," Mona said through clenched teeth.

"I don't want him in Cooper's life." Jenny broke off another bite of cookie. "Not really. We're doing fine on our own."

Her mother didn't respond, but one of her brows arched. Mona Castelli could communicate more with a raised brow than most career politicians did during a well-rehearsed campaign speech.

"Owen came as my date," Jenny said, needing to change the subject.

Mona smiled. "He's a nice boy."

"He's not a boy, either." She thought about pressing her fingers against the hard cords of muscle on Owen's back as he kissed her into oblivion. She'd once thought of him as boyish. Boyishly handsome. Boyishly charming.

Last night he'd been one hundred percent man.

It totally freaked her out.

Especially after finding out what he wanted from her in return for attending the reunion. She couldn't possibly go to his brother's wedding, and he wouldn't really expect it, right? It was something he'd said in the heat of anger. He wanted to make her uncomfortable, and he'd more than accomplished that.

"Owen would make a good husband," her mother said absently.

"I'm not marrying Owen." Jenny's heart thrummed out of control. She'd taken off the ring that morning and slipped it back into the velvet box he'd left on the entry table. She touched a finger to the bare space on her left hand.

Despite the fact that she'd only worn the ring for a couple of hours last night, her finger felt weirdly empty without it.

"I didn't say you were," her mother clarified. "You've made it quite clear that you aren't interested in having a man in your life."

Jenny paused with a piece of cookie halfway to her mouth. "I have?"

"I understand, sweetie." Her mother's smile was gentle. "After your father left, I knew I'd never have relations with another man."

"Mom." Jenny felt her mouth drop open. Her mother's face was as familiar to her as her own reflection, but a part of her wondered who this woman was sitting across the table. The Alzheimer's had altered her mom's personality, bringing forth aspects that had been hidden Jenny's whole life. Where was the sex talk when Jenny had needed it back in high school? Mona had never once spoken about anything remotely related to men with Jenny.

Based on how her mother had acted, Jenny's pregnancy could have been the second immaculate conception, even though she'd wanted Trent to marry Jenny. Hearing Mona mention "relations" with anyone was as foreign to Jenny as walking hand in hand with her mother into a strip club.

"Well," her mother prompted. "When was the last time you had—"

"Do not say 'relations,'" Jenny said before her mother could finish the question. "I'm not talking about that with you."

Another arched brow. "I do understand how babies are made, Jennifer." Mona let out a little sigh. "There are some things a woman doesn't forget."

Jenny hadn't forgotten, either, although she hated to admit even to herself how long it had been since she'd been with a man. Trent had been her first, and for several years after Cooper was born, she'd been too busy, stressed, and chronically sleep-deprived to even consider finding a man.

When she'd finally gotten the itch again, she'd had a string of casual boyfriends and, to her humiliation, one-night stands that had meant little and left her feeling like less than nothing. It had seemed easier not to try.

Until Owen.

Of course, that had been a disaster. She'd sabotaged their relationship before they'd gotten to the bedroom, and last night she'd pushed him away once again.

Surely his demand that she go to West Virginia had been an idle threat. Why would he want to spend any more time with her than he had to? She acted like a lunatic bitch-on-wheels whenever he was around.

"You're right, Mom. I don't want a man in my life. Cooper is it for me."

At the mention of her grandson, Mona relaxed even more. "I miss him," she said softly. "I miss seeing him every day."

"I know," Jenny said, a sharp ball of emotion clogging her throat. The most difficult thing she'd ever done in her life had been to move her mother into a facility. Even though she knew it was for the best, it never got any easier.

"Mona." One of the young nursing aides, Jessa, approached the table where they sat. "We're about to start today's craft project. We're making beaded bracelets. Will you join us?" She leaned in closer and added, "Bernie Wilcox was asking about you."

A faint hint of pink colored Mona's cheeks. "I loved to make jewelry and little trinkets when I was a girl."

"I remember," Jessa answered gently. "You told me about collecting soda pop cans to earn money for colored string."

Jenny straightened as her mother smiled. She'd never heard the story of the soda pop cans. How was it that the paid aide knew something about her mother that Jenny didn't? Mona stood, then leaned down and kissed Jenny's cheek.

Tears sprung to Jenny's eyes as she was enveloped in the soft scent of lavender. She would forever associate that fragrance with her mother.

"I'll see you next time, sweetie. Give Cooper a hug for me."

"I love you, Mom," Jenny said, and watched her mother make her way down the hall, allowing the aide to take her hand. No matter what Jenny had to sacrifice in her own life, she would always make sure Mona was safe and happy.

This facility was the best in the city for Alzheimer's patients, and although it was almost double the monthly cost of the others Jenny had visited and didn't take insurance, the fact that Mona was finally settling into a routine left no doubt in Jenny's mind that she'd made the right choice.

If only the other doubts she harbored were so easily erased.

CHAPTER SEVEN

"To your engagement." Ty Bishop lifted his beer bottle in mock salute as Owen choked on the drink he'd just taken.

He grabbed a napkin from the center of the scratched wood high-top table where they sat. It was just after six on Monday night, almost forty-eight hours since he'd slipped that diamond ring onto Jenny's finger.

He'd met Ty for a drink at one of Denver's ubiquitous local brew-pubs, but hadn't expected the conversation to so quickly turn to his sham engagement.

"If you've heard about it, then you've also heard it's fake."

"Kendall mentioned that," Ty told him, keeping his deceptively casual gaze on the baseball game being broadcast on the bank of flat-screen TVs hanging on the far wall.

Owen knew he and Ty made an unlikely pair, even as friends. Ty was tall and blond, with the chiseled features and movie-star blue eyes that made women fall all over themselves to have him notice them. He looked like he'd just been on set at a photo shoot advertising clean Colorado mountain living. He wore cargo pants and a faded T-shirt with the image of the large red-and-yellow *C* from Colorado's state flag printed on the front.

Owen had just come from a meeting with the Dalton Enterprises board of directors, so he still wore his suit and tie. Yes, he'd upped his game in the style and wardrobe department, but he was still a computer nerd in expensive clothes.

Ty's blue eyes shifted to him. "But she couldn't give me a plausible explanation for why you agreed to it. You and Jenny don't exactly have the best history."

"Maybe I was just being nice."

"I thought you gave that up around the time you started gelling your hair and dating bimbos."

"What the hell is it with people and my hair?" Owen loosened his tie and undid the top button on his custom dress shirt. "Was it so damn bad before?"

Ty flashed a grin. "Not if you're into the classic bowl cut."

"Go to hell, Bishop."

"I'm having too much fun here with you." Ty had started working for Owen's namesake foundation, leading the environmental initiatives, around the time things had gotten serious with him and Kendall. It should have been awkward since Owen had actually gone on a couple of dates with the woman who would later become Mrs. Ty Bishop as part of an on-air dating show that Kendall starred in at the time. Instead, Owen counted Ty as one of his best friends.

But Jenny had been Ty's friend for much longer, so Owen had no doubt where Ty's allegiance would lie if things ever went sideways. That was one of several reasons Owen had kept things civil with Jenny after she'd crushed his stupid soft heart into a million pieces. He made light of their breakup, partly because it kept things harmonious within their tight-knit group of friends, and partly because his stubborn pride wouldn't allow him to admit how much her betrayal had hurt. But the biggest reason had been the fact that he couldn't bring himself to totally cut her from his life.

When Owen was younger, his father had tried a lot of methods to encourage him to "grow a pair"—one of Hank Dalton's favorite catchphrases. After Jenny's betrayal, Owen had gone to work on reinventing himself. Clearly, despite his wealth and power, the man he was couldn't hold a woman's attention. He'd loved two women in his life, and both of them had cheated on him.

He'd gone about changing every aspect of who he was—from his hair to his wardrobe to working out to the point of exhaustion. The transformation had been successful on the outside, but based on the situation he found himself in now, he remained a pansy-assed pushover on the inside.

Ty took another long pull on his beer. "Kendall told me Jenny's mouth got her into a whole bunch of trouble with some of the ladies from high school. That wasn't your problem. So what's the real reason you agreed to help her?"

"What did Jenny tell you?"

"She's gone radio silent."

"Tell me about it," Owen muttered. Ever the fool, Owen had both texted and called Jenny yesterday to check in. He knew she'd made it home safely thanks to the report from his driver, but that pansy-assed part of him couldn't settle after things had been left all blown to hell between the two of them. Apparently, she had no such issue.

"Do I need to give you the lecture about her being like a sister to me and what she went through raising Cooper on her own and the toll her mom's illness has taken and if you hurt her I'll—"

"Back 'er down," Owen interrupted, lifting a hand. "If you remember, Jenny was riding the horse that left the barn and trampled me to the ground on its way out."

Ty lifted a brow. "You're different now."

Not really, Owen thought. He was still a sucker for a certain brash, beautiful redhead. But he didn't admit it out loud.

As much as he still wanted Jenny, he told himself his heart wasn't in danger any longer because he'd locked it up tight. He had no plans to ever expose his soft underbelly to a woman again, because love and need were nothing more than an outward display of his inner weakness. If he'd learned one thing from his father, it was that weakness meant pain.

"Jenny can take care of herself," he answered.

A muscle ticked in Ty's jaw. "That's what she wants everyone to think."

Owen put his beer on the table and turned fully to Ty. "I'm not going to hurt her." Even if he wanted to, he didn't think he had it in him to purposely hurt Jenny. Too bad she had no such qualms when it came to him.

Ty studied him a moment longer, then nodded. "That wasn't actually the reason I asked you to meet me here."

Owen sighed. "I figured as much."

"There are rumblings around the foundation office," Ty told him, "about the financial state of Dalton Enterprises."

"Did you show them our first-quarter earnings?" Owen asked, picking up his beer bottle and wishing it was a shot glass.

"So things are good with the company?"

A simple yes would have sufficed, but Ty was a friend. Owen wouldn't lie to a friend. "They're stable. We've got a couple of new projects that aren't getting off the ground as quickly as I'd hoped."

"Is one of them the Labyrinth Web technology you're developing for the military?"

Owen bit off a harsh laugh. "I thought the foundation was supposed to concern itself with spending my money, not worrying about how I make it."

"You built the company on networks that can be used in communities. Owen Dalton brings people together."

"Are you saying the men and women who fight for our country aren't worthy of my time?"

"Hell, no," Ty clarified, tipping back his beer. "But from the little I understand, military technology is a whole different beast than bringing another device to market or improving the way mesh networks function. There are plenty of companies that do it well. I'm wondering why you're risking so much to make yours one of them."

Shit. A sinking feeling gripped Owen's chest. If enough details had leaked to the foundation about the risks he was taking, then the whole company must know. He'd already fielded calls from two members of his board of directors about the funds he was funneling toward the Labyrinth Web project.

On the surface it made sense. The Internet was based on a few centralized access points or Internet service providers, which left it weak and ripe for disruptions. Sometimes those came in the form of natural disasters or deliberate attempts to shut it down.

Mesh networks, which Dalton Enterprises had championed and refined for individuals and communities, wirelessly connected devices without the need to pass through a centralized organization. This gave the mesh infrastructure far more flexibility and strength than a regular Internet connection. However, the mesh network initiatives were difficult to translate effectively during a combat situation. They were simply too limited, and the security challenges presented a huge obstacle.

Owen had conceived his Labyrinth Web after Jack's marine fire team lost communications during an attack. Jack had made it out, but his fire team lost two marines. The Labyrinth Web would be unbreakable while still retaining the speed and flexibility of mesh networking.

But it was easier said than done. Owen needed a breakthrough on the technology so that he could quiet his critics. "My family has a long history of military service," he said as an explanation. "The Labyrinth Web is a way that I can give back to my country. I understand it isn't the same as fighting on the front lines but—"

"I'm not doubting your patriotism," Ty told him. "You give back plenty. I should know since it's my job to spend your money. Between the wing at the hospital, the acres of forest you're preserving through the land trust, and all the other community projects you support with foundation funds, you don't have anything to prove."

The words ricocheted through Owen's brain, and he only wished he could believe they were true. He still had plenty to prove. Whether or not he admitted it out loud, the goal behind everything he did was an attempt to demonstrate that he deserved his father's approval. He would have liked to think he'd outgrown his foolish need for validation. Hell, he could practically afford to buy his hometown in its entirety. But it wasn't enough.

The technology he was working on could change the way military forces stayed connected during heated battles. It had the potential to revolutionize military communication. No one could deny his success then. Not his former-marine father or his active-duty brother.

"I'll get the Labyrinth Web working, and then the board and share-holders will understand the risks I took were worth it."

Ty set down his beer. "Are you working so hard to prove something to the shareholders, or to your dad? I've been down that road, Owen. It leads to nowhere."

"My situation and yours aren't the same." Owen ran a hand through his hair. In the Dalton family, the fault was squarely on Owen's shoulders for simply being born outside the mold of what his father valued. "Can we boil this conversation down to 'don't screw up Jenny's life and don't screw up your own life'?"

Ty inclined his head. "That about sums it up."

"Then we can move on to the 'drink a beer and enjoy the game' portion of the evening?"

"I believe it's past time for that," Ty agreed with a grin.

They stayed at the bar for one more drink, then Ty headed home to Kendall, and Owen started toward his loft in the LoDo district downtown. It was a perfect early summer night in Colorado, the air beginning to cool and the sun starting to make its way behind the mountain range to the west of the city.

Owen loved the mix of the urban vibe and Wild West sensibility that made Denver unique. His neighborhood would be alive with hip millennials and city dwellers catching dinner or a drink after work. As if on cue, his cell phone chirped, and he read a text from a woman he'd gone on a few casual dates with in the past month, asking if he wanted to meet at the bar around the corner from his building.

Since his disastrous attempt at a relationship with Jenny, he'd had a series of short-term girlfriends. One of them had been a personal stylist at a high-end department store in nearby Cherry Creek, and he had her to thank for the revamping of his wardrobe. He didn't want to be the nice, goofy tech genius any longer. That guy was a pushover.

The fact was he cared little about what he wore or how someone cut his hair, so it was easy to change his style and become the type of man to crack the list of *Forbes*'s most-eligible bachelors.

But none of it truly mattered to him, and without allowing himself time to second-guess the decision, he returned the text, saying he had plans, and turned his Toyota 4Runner onto the northbound ramp of the interstate.

Fifteen minutes later he pulled down the gravel driveway that led to Jenny's property. Last Saturday night, he'd been unable to concentrate on anything but the ring in his pocket. Now he took a moment to study the land she'd purchased to create her dream nursery and garden center.

He knew she had five acres, which was fairly unheard of so close to the city. He guessed the reason she'd been able to afford it was because the house needed some work. A lot of work, now that he saw it in the waning daylight.

The yard in front was tidy, and there were big clay pots on each of the porch steps filled with bright flowers, trailing vines, and a host of other plants he couldn't identify. From working with her on the landscape design for his office, Owen knew Jenny had an encyclopedia-like knowledge of plant and flower varieties and a great eye for how to place them.

Gray wood siding, which at one point had probably been bright white, covered the house, and the roof had been patched in several places. He tipped his head as he gazed through the SUV's windshield, trying to figure out if the front porch sloped slightly, or if he'd parked the truck on a hill that messed with his perception.

Looking past the outward appearance, he could almost see Jenny's vision without her even having to share it. Maybe it should disturb him that he so completely understood the way her mind worked, but he smiled as he thought of how perfectly the space would fit her when it was done.

A figure came around the side of the house and headed straight for his car. It had been close to two years since Owen had seen Jenny's son, and it looked like Cooper had grown at least four inches in that time. He was all elbows and gangly legs, his hair overlong and hanging in his eyes. It made Owen's chest tighten to realize that the boy was quickly growing into a young man and Owen wouldn't have the opportunity to watch it happen.

"Hey, Coop," he said, climbing out and shutting the door.

"Hi, Owen." The boy held out his hands to reveal a jumble of plastic. "Do you know anything about remote control planes? Mine slammed into a tree and the wing broke."

"A little," Owen answered, marveling at the fact that Cooper could pick up their relationship right where it had left off during the time Owen and Jenny dated. "We'll need packing tape, popsicle sticks, pliers, and an X-Acto knife."

The boy definitely had an interest in engineering and figuring out how things worked, much like Owen had as a kid. In addition to missing Jenny, not seeing Cooper had left an empty place in Owen's life. He could act the part of the eligible tech bachelor, but in his heart he would have preferred to remain a boring homebody.

"I've got all that in the workshop at the back of Mom's barn," Cooper said, and led him across the gravel driveway toward the faded red barn that sat on the edge of a fenced field.

"Are you sure it's okay for us to be in there?" Owen asked doubtfully.

Cooper laughed. "It's fine. Mom got a barn cat to take care of the mice."

Owen didn't have a problem with mice, but he wasn't real interested in Jenny biting his head off for inserting himself back into her life. Still, he followed the boy, thinking about what it would take to mend the broken wing as they walked. "What's new with you?"

Cooper shrugged. "Mom's making me do one of those stupid summer workbooks to make sure I'm ready for seventh grade."

"Bummer, but I bet you'll thank her later."

The boy rolled his eyes. "I've been doing chores to save up for the expansion pack for my Magik of Myth game."

"It released last week, right? I heard it has the latest virtual reality and cloud gaming technologies."

Cooper glanced up at him, a small smile playing around the corner of his mouth. "It's kind of weird that you're an adult and you like video games."

"Do you mind weird?"

"Nah." The barn's wide-plank wood door creaked as Cooper pulled it open. A rich, loamy scent greeted him and he could almost feel how much plant life was growing inside the barn's walls. "Did you come over to take back Mom's ginormous diamond?" Cooper asked.

"Um . . ." How much had Jenny told her son? "Not quite yet."

Cooper paused in the act of laying out the pieces of the broken airplane on the counter above the built-in cabinets along one side of the barn. "I bet a ring like that could pay for a better barn," he said casually.

Owen hid his smile. He'd forgotten about Cooper's mercenary streak. Maybe it was a result of growing up with a single mom, but the boy had an almost unnatural fixation with figuring out ways he could make a windfall to benefit his mother.

When Owen and Jenny had dated, Cooper had shared his list of potential inventions with Owen and how much he thought he could get in investment dollars on a show like *Shark Tank*. At that point, Cooper had seemed certain that Mark Cuban was the financial answer to his prayers.

Apparently, he'd gotten more realistic in his goals.

"My friend Aidan's sister got engaged at Christmas," Cooper continued, handing Owen the items he'd asked for.

Owen began to repair the plane. "When's the wedding?" he asked.

"She decided not to get married," Cooper answered, "but her fiancé let her keep the ring. She said that's what's supposed to happen. I guess this was her second engagement, so now she has two rings."

"Maybe she wants a diamond bracelet," Owen suggested, trying not to laugh.

"Maybe she should just buy one for herself," a voice called from the barn door.

He turned to see Jenny stalking toward them, and judging by the look on her face, she wasn't happy to see him.

"You're in trouble," Cooper whispered.

"What did I do?"

"I don't know," the boy said, "but it would probably help if you let her keep the ring."

Jenny tried to keep the lid on her temper as she pointed a finger at her son. "We talked about the ring," she said, making her voice level. "Owen did me a favor, but the engagement wasn't real."

Cooper's chin tipped up, and she hated to admit how much of herself she saw in the stubborn set of his jaw. "He said he didn't come here for the ring."

She counted to ten in her head. "Dinner is ready. Go wash your hands."

"Owen is helping me fix the plane."

"Listen to your mother," Owen said calmly, placing a hand on Cooper's shoulder. The gesture was so innately paternal, it made her breath hitch. "We'll have time for the plane later."

Cooper turned to look up at him. "Promise?"

She saw Owen's shoulders stiffen, but he kept his eyes on Cooper. "I promise."

All the air whooshed out of her lungs, but she managed a smile as Cooper moved past her.

As soon as he was out of the barn, she surged toward Owen, jabbing a finger into his chest. "You can't do that. Don't make promises to my son that you can't keep."

He wrapped his hand around her finger. "I can help him fix the plane, Jenny. It's not a big deal."

"Promises," she hissed, "are a big deal." She tugged at her hand, but he didn't let go.

"I know," he told her gently. "I know."

That was why Owen Dalton was so dangerous to her. He understood her better than anyone other than her mother. And probably even more than Mona since Alzheimer's had taken a hold on her mind.

She couldn't stop her reaction to Owen any more than the earth could stop turning on its axis. The more she tried to fortify her defenses, the more easily he seemed to maneuver past them.

He lowered their hands and slowly released hers. "I'm surprised he knew about the ring," he said.

"I was afraid he'd hear about it through the grapevine."

"It moves especially fast in the age of social media," he said, turning to place the screwdriver on the workbench again. "My sister called to talk engagements even before we'd gone to the reunion."

"Is that why you made the joke about me attending your brother's wedding?"

Owen took a moment to survey the barn's interior before answering. He wore another fitted collared shirt, and she guessed he'd taken off his tie on the way over. A hint of stubble darkened his jaw, making him look a bit like a pirate. Where had that somewhat awkward geek she'd first dated gone? She could handle that guy. But this Owen . . .

Oh, who was she kidding? She could never handle Owen. The nerdy tech mogul might not have appealed to everyone, but she'd loved his innate gentleness and the way he'd made her feel like she was the most important thing in his life.

But believing she was important, much like trusting in promises, was a path that led into the deep, dark forest of heartbreak for Jenny. She'd learned the hard way not to trust anyone, especially herself.

"It wasn't a joke." Owen's voice was so soft in the quiet of the old barn that she almost didn't register the words.

Almost.

"I'm not going to your brother's wedding," she said, and turned away.

Before she'd taken two steps, he spoke again. "You said 'anything,' Jenny. One might even call it a *promise*."

Damn him for using her words against her. Damn herself for being foolish enough to have said them in the first place.

Instead of answering, she called over her shoulder. "We're having spaghetti tonight. You can stay or not, but I need a glass of wine before I can have this conversation."

He was at her side as she reached the barn door, holding it open like the gentleman he was to his core.

"Thanks for the invitation."

She sniffed. "After dinner I expect you to fix that airplane."

Without actually touching her, he leaned so close she could feel his breath against her hair. It sent shivers of awareness running down her spine.

"After dinner," he murmured, "we'll discuss the wedding *and* I'll fix the plane."

CHAPTER EIGHT

"Mom, we fixed it." Cooper burst through the back door an hour later, excitement lighting his sweet face. "Owen helped me smooth the lines to give the plane less drag. It flies so fast now. You've got to come and see."

Jenny dropped her checkbook to the kitchen table and stood. "I can't wait," she said, and with a last glance at the pile of bills she didn't have the money to pay, she followed him into the backyard.

Cooper skipped over the stair with the loose board on the back steps, and she did the same. It hadn't been her plan to be forced to delay fixing up the house and instead spend every bit of extra time and energy she had to make her dream of opening the garden center a reality. She thought she'd been smart, saving enough over the years to buy a property that would fit her vision for a neighborhood nursery.

But all of that money had been put into an account for her mother's monthly bills. There was enough left over to pay her mortgage and buy enough stock to open the nursery each weekend. She had a steady stream of customers who had found her, thanks to the contacts she had through the landscape company. But she was nowhere near the point when running the garden center full-time could support her, Cooper, and her mother.

Something whizzed by her head, and she dropped to the ground with a muttered curse.

"Too close," Owen shouted at the same time Cooper called, "Sorry, Mom."

A moment later, a pair of expensive-looking dress shoes appeared in her vision. "You're fine," Owen said, and crouched in front of her. "Need a hand?"

She pushed off the patchy grass and hopped to her feet. He straightened and reached out to touch a finger to her cheek. "You have a little dirt," he said, glancing from her face down the front of her body. "Everywhere."

Narrowing her eyes, she brushed her hands down the front of her shirt. "He could have taken my head off with that thing. Are you teaching my kid to build some sort of military secret weapon? It's supposed to be a toy."

His shoulders stiffened, as if she'd said something to offend him. That was hard to believe when she'd been the one to be almost mutilated by the streamlined airplane.

"It's awesome now. Right, Mom?" Cooper ran up to her, holding the small airplane in one hand. "My friends are going to freak out over it."

"Until someone loses an eye," she muttered.

"Remember what we talked about," Owen said to Cooper, turning to face the boy. "When it's flying that fast, you need to keep control over it." He pointed to the field beyond the barn. "Plan on sticking to open spaces until you're an expert pilot, okay?"

Cooper nodded, a huge grin still plastered across his face. It had been months since she'd seen him so happy, and a gentle ache expanded in Jenny's chest. Once upon a time, she'd been able to make him smile like that.

"I'm going to practice flying it," he said, "so I'm an expert before Aidan comes over tomorrow." He gave her a quick hug. "At least all the land is good for something this summer."

She pressed her fingers against her chest as he ran off across the driveway. "That was a direct hit."

"He'll appreciate it at some point." Owen looked from her shabby house to her shabbier barn. "It's a great property."

"Cooper liked our suburbia tract home," she answered. "Living in a garden paradise is my dream, not his."

"Kids like open spaces to run around."

She rolled her eyes. "Some kids like video games and a fast Internet connection."

"I might have been that kid, too," he said with a laugh.

"You certainly seem to be an expert at relating to my son. Come into the kitchen," she told him, turning for the house. "We need to talk."

At the top of the porch steps she grabbed the screen-door handle, which came loose in her hand, the door remaining firmly latched. "Shit," she mumbled. "Stay here. I need to go around to the front door. I can get it to open from the inside." She placed the broken handle on the windowsill and jogged down the steps and around the front of the house.

Embarrassment heated her cheeks. Owen Dalton, who could afford to stay in the finest hotels in the world and owned a penthouse loft in one of the most expensive buildings in downtown Denver, was waiting on her back porch with the wonky step and the peeling paint on the rails for her to force open the broken screen door.

A busted latch might be minor, and the house was basically solid, but with every step she took toward the front of the house, her feet seemed to grow heavier. Why had she ever thought she could make it on her own?

She forced herself to keep moving, yet by the time she got to kitchen, Owen was letting himself in the back door.

"How'd you get in?" she asked.

"I fixed the handle," he said, slipping what looked to be some sort of multiuse tool into his pocket. "It just needed to be tightened."

"Since when do you wear a tool belt along with your pocket protector?" she asked, cringing almost as soon as the words left her mouth. Owen made her feel off balance, which made her defensive. But he didn't deserve her attitude. "I'm sorry. What I meant to say was 'thank you.'"

"I've never been a fan of pocket protectors," he said casually. "Although they certainly serve a valid purpose."

"I own a tool belt," she said for no reason. Then he smiled and she realized that was reason enough.

"Thank you for that mental picture," he murmured, and pulled out a kitchen chair.

She sniffed. "I'm always dressed while wearing it."

"Not in my mind," he answered, and suddenly there was a charge between them, an invisible snare of energy that made her skin tingle. Her head spun and other parts of her body shimmied into the light he cast. The way she wanted him was like walking a tightrope—such a clear path to the other side, but it would be far too easy to lose her balance and plunge into the depths of her need.

"The ring is upstairs," she told him. "I'll get it for you."

He shook his head. "I don't want the ring back, Jenny. Not yet."

"I can't do what you're asking, Owen."

"Sit down." He tapped a finger on the stack of bills she'd been working on before Cooper called her to witness the miracle of the remote control dive bomber. "Tell me about all of this."

She hadn't meant for him to see any of it and quickly pushed the stray papers into a neat pile in the center of the table. "Just paperwork," she said, picking up the stack and flipping it facedown.

"A lot of red ink," he commented.

Panic streaked across her belly, leaving a trail of fire in its wake. She breathed against the familiar burn. "Nothing you have to worry about. Do you want a beer or a glass of water?"

He studied her. "Must be worse than you're letting on if you're using decent manners to distract me."

"What do you want me to say?" She crossed her arms over her chest and leaned against the kitchen counter. For sanity's sake, she needed a little distance between her and Owen.

"I know you had a solid plan. Even when we were together, you had the idea mapped out. It seems like this property is perfect for what you wanted to do with the business. What happened?"

She bit down on her bottom lip. "Like I told you the other night, life happened. Alzheimer's happened. My mother signing over her bank account to the grifter who tricked her into believing she was buying long-term care insurance happened. Paying for a private room at an amazing assisted living center happened." She shrugged. "Me being stupid enough to believe I could make it without handouts from the Bishop family happened."

He shook his head. "Ty considered you his equal at the landscaping company. He trusted you with everything, and I know he's happy to have you still working there, even in a consulting role."

"He's a good friend, but Rocky Mountain Landscapes is *his*, Owen. Is it so wrong of me to want something of my own?" She held up a hand. "Don't answer that. It doesn't matter now. I've got a fixer-upper house, bills to pay, and Ty has been generous enough to let me come back to work on a contract basis. A Bishop has stepped in once again to save some Castelli ass."

"I doubt Ty sees it that way," Owen murmured. "He's your friend."

"But he's also my boss again. For once, I wanted to be the one calling the shots." She shook her head. "I'm going to make the garden center a reality. It'll just take more time than I'd planned."

"I could help."

"Because we're such good friends?"

"Because what I want from you is more than one night."

Oh, God. Her knees threatened to give way and she pressed harder into the counter so she wouldn't melt to the floor. The intensity in his dark eyes shook her to her core.

"I need to be in West Virginia for a week."

Jenny blinked. Wait. What? Did he just call her a virgin?

West Virginia. He'd mentioned West Virginia. Payback for acting the part of her fake fiancé at the reunion.

"It's more than you asked of me, and I'd like to pay you."

"Like I'm a hooker?" she blurted.

"No," he answered immediately. "There would be no . . . expectations. But thanks to the wonders of social media, my family now assumes I'll have a fiancée accompanying me to the wedding."

"You could find a willing date."

"I want you."

Those three words were like a blade across her heart. "Why?" she asked.

"I need whoever is with me to understand that the relationship is completely fake."

"Are you afraid another woman might want to keep the ring for real?"

"There are benefits to marrying a man like me."

Jenny could think of a few. The way he kissed, how patient he was with her son . . .

"My bank account to be precise," he said casually.

"There's more to you than your money."

He didn't answer but the way he studied her made her mouth go dry.

"I can't go with you, Owen."

"I'll pay you twenty grand for the week."

"Are you fucking crazy?" The words were out of her mouth before she even realized she'd spoken. She moved to the table, gripping the back of a chair. "Take that back. You don't mean it."

"I do," he said. "If the money feels too crass, keep the ring at the end of the week. It should fetch even more at any jeweler's."

"You told me the ring was on loan."

"It was for that night. Now I own it."

"I won't take your money and—"

"She'll settle for the ring."

Jenny whirled at the sound of Cooper's voice. Her son stood in the doorway, fists clenched at his sides, staring at Owen.

"Cooper, you aren't part of this conversation," she said, moving toward him as if she could block him from Owen's view. It was a silly instinct, because Owen would never do anything to hurt her son.

But Cooper could easily look over her shoulder. "And we want to borrow your Gulfstream to go to Hawaii at the end of the summer."

"Cooper," she shouted, squeezing his thin shoulders. "Stop that right now," she told him in a lower tone. "This isn't open for discussion."

"You can use the plane," Owen said from behind her.

"We're not using the plane," she told both of them, her teeth tightly clenched. What business did she have going to Hawaii, let alone on a private plane?

About as much as her son had negotiating the terms of an arrangement that was not going to happen.

"You can use the plane even if you don't agree to West Virginia," Owen offered.

"Agree to the week, Mom." Cooper's normally even-tempered gaze turned mutinous. "It's not a big deal."

Oh yes it was a big deal. It wasn't just the thought of taking money to be Owen's pretend fiancée that had her on edge. The night of her reunion had been torture with Owen so attentive at her side.

She knew he'd never be hers, and the knowledge had been like little tacks shoved under her fingernails. How could she even consider spending a week in that state? She'd drive herself and everyone around her crazy. And there was the distinct possibility she wouldn't be able to walk away from him again with her heart intact.

"I can't, honey. It isn't right."

"You need money for Grandma and to renovate the house and for the nursery." Cooper paused, his bright green eyes boring into hers. Then he went in for the final knockout blow. "What about the college fund you've never started?"

"I'm going to," she said, but they both knew it was a pipe dream. At the rate things were going, she'd have the extra money to save for college around the time Cooper was ready to retire.

"The ring would make a solid start for a college account," Owen offered quietly.

She'd been so intent on her son she'd almost forgotten they had an audience for the humiliating tableau of maternal failure.

"It's just like Aidan Photoshopping spring break," Cooper told her.

A fissure of self-recrimination threatened to split her apart. How had all her years of planning brought her to this moment?

But just as quickly, the yawning gap was filled with affection for her son. She'd do anything for Cooper. Her love for him was the one thing she'd never doubted in her life. She might fail in so many areas, and had made more than her share of parenting mistakes, but her love never faltered. If he wanted this . . .

"Are you sure?"

"We're playing pretend," Cooper answered, smiling again. "It's only for a week. And you owe a dollar to the swear jar."

She traced her finger along the skin between his eyes, where a shallow crease had formed in the past few months.

He was too young to be worried about anything beyond grades and finishing his chores on time. If a week with Owen—no expectations—would erase that fine line, she'd swallow back her pride and make the best of it.

"Okay."

Cooper stepped around her then, and she turned to see that Owen had stood from the table. The boy and the man shook hands, and her heart took another direct hit.

"We have a deal," Cooper said, like he was an old-fashioned match-maker, brokering a contract between the two of them.

"I'll take good care of her," Owen said solemnly.

I can take care of myself, Jenny wanted to shout. But who was she kidding?

Apparently satisfied, Cooper stepped toward the refrigerator. "Hey, Mom," he said over his shoulder. "I'm going to get dessert and play Magik of Myth with Aidan. He said he'd be online by eight."

"Take a napkin," she said, "and only one round. You need to shower before bed tonight."

The instructions rolled off her tongue like it was any other normal night in their house. Like she was the mother and in control, setting limits for her growing boy.

Cooper nodded, grabbing an ice cream bar from the freezer. "See ya later, Owen," he said with a small wave.

"See ya, Coop."

"Throw the wrapper in the trash," she said as he walked by.

"Got it," Cooper answered, and disappeared around the corner, as if nothing out of the ordinary had just happened. A moment later she heard his footsteps pounding up to the second-floor attic, where he had a bedroom and TV set up. The walls in the old farmhouse were paper-thin.

The uneasy quiet that descended in the kitchen reminded her that nothing about this night was normal.

Her eyes resolutely trained to the scuffed linoleum floor, she heard rather than saw Owen take a step toward her.

"Jenny."

She held up a hand. "Grab two beers from the fridge. I'll meet you on the front porch, and we can work out the details of this . . . arrangement."

Turning on her heel, she moved through the house that was filled with a mix of the secondhand furniture she'd collected and refinished over the years and the pieces she'd saved from her mother's condo. In the soft light of the descending evening, everything looked cozy, if a little worn around the edges.

A lot like her.

In the bathroom off the front hall, she splashed cold water on her face and studied herself in the mirror above the porcelain sink.

Her skin was looking particularly pale against her bright hair, the freckles that dusted her nose and cheeks standing out in stark relief. Maybe if she hadn't been born with red hair, and the tumbling emotions that went with it, she would have made better decisions in her life. She'd read a quote from Aristotle where he described redheads as *emotionally unhousebroken*, and it had always made her smile. But she suddenly detested the lack of control that seemed to prevent her from learning to lead with her head instead of her heart.

Maybe it wouldn't be too difficult. She could handle anything for a week, right?

CHAPTER NINE

Owen tipped back his head, eyes closed, and listened to the sounds of a quiet night outside town. Crickets chirped and a car engine hummed in the distance. The sprinklers from a nearby property sputtered on, then settled into a gentle cadence that reminded him of his childhood and long summer evenings in the small town of Hastings, West Virginia.

The noise he was used to in the city was different, a manic cacophony of traffic, late-night revelers, and the occasional homeless person heckling a group of tourists.

How had he gotten there so suddenly? One quick turn onto the interstate instead of his usual route into downtown, and he'd once again made Jenny Castelli an integral part of his life.

But not his heart. He was smarter than that this time around.

It was difficult to remember he even had a brain when Jenny dropped onto the porch next to him, snagging the beer he held out to her.

She smelled like fresh citrus and looked like a beautiful woodland fairy come to life in the dusky shadows of approaching night. In spite of all the places he'd seen in the world and all the views he'd enjoyed, nothing compared to looking out over the ramshackle property with Jenny's leg just brushing the fabric of his pants.

"Are we good?" he asked softly.

"My son seems to think so."

"He's like your own personal soldier of fortune," he said. He knew he should be a gentleman and give her a way out of the deal Cooper had insisted she take, but he couldn't force his mouth to form the words. Instead he said, "It won't be too bad, and you'll have your garden center."

"Don't forget the start of a college fund." She bit off a laugh. "I can't believe he played that card." She turned to study him. "Why is a date for your brother's wedding so important? Are we revisiting the pain of being left behind during family vacations?"

He drew in a breath. It wasn't an admission he wanted to make, but she'd find out soon enough. "I have a history with the woman my brother is marrying."

"A history like you two used to play doctor when you were kids?"

"We were engaged."

Beer shot out of Jenny's mouth as she choked and sputtered. "Your brother is marrying your old girlfriend?"

"Yep."

"How long after the two of you broke up did he start dating her?"

He ran a hand through his hair, long-suppressed bitterness rising in his throat. "To the best of my knowledge, it was about six months before we broke up."

She grabbed his arm. "She cheated on you with your brother?"

"Apparently I have bad luck discovering the women I'm dating having sex with other men."

She jerked back as if he'd slapped her. "I wasn't having sex."

"Neither was Kristin, officially. But she was on her knees in front of Jack with his pants around his ankles so—"

"Owen." She squeezed his arm, but he shrugged off her touch.

"I was in my senior year at MIT, a nerdy kid with nothing to my name. I had a lot of ideas, but even more student loans. Jack is a year and a half younger than me and had joined the marines right out of high school. He was a big deal in Hastings—high school football star, military hero." He took a long pull on his beer. "Kristin figured he was the better bet. Most people did."

"But if you were engaged, she was supposed to be in love with you." She poked his arm with the tip of one finger. "With *you*, Owen. Not some bullshit small-town reputation."

"You're right," he agreed. "But that isn't how it worked out."

"What about—"

"After my first mesh router hit the market and I was a success?" He shrugged. "Like I said, I don't get back to Hastings often. I'm sure Kristin is happy being a big fish in a small pond. She and my brother are a good match. They both like the spotlight."

"Do you still have feelings for her?"

"No," he said, although it wasn't exactly true. He had feelings about being betrayed by the woman he'd thought he loved and his brother. Plenty of bitterness that everyone in his family except Gabby had swept Kristin's faithlessness under the rug. They'd welcomed her into the family as if she and Jack were meant to be. Anger that his brother had never once apologized or given any indication of recognizing that he'd done something wrong in appropriating Owen's fiancée as if she'd belonged to him all along.

He nudged Jenny's shoulder. "I let her keep the ring, but it wasn't worth anything compared to yours."

"Don't say that," she hissed. "Don't compare me to her. I hate her for what she did to you."

Owen sighed. The funny thing was how easy it had been to fall out of love with the woman he'd planned to spend his life with. As opposed to the relentless drumming of need he continued to feel toward Jenny despite the way she'd betrayed him.

"Tell me about your plans for the nursery," he said, wanting to change the direction of the conversation.

"I'll go with you," she answered instead, "and you don't have to pay me." She shifted again, set down her beer, and grabbed his shoulders. "We'll make them think we are the happiest couple since Meg Ryan and Tom Hanks starred in their last rom com."

He tucked a stray curl behind her ear, his whole body reacting to the conviction in her tone. He knew Jenny was a warrior and that, despite her hard shell, she had a tender heart. Her willingness to help him without taking the money she so desperately needed made his defenses crack like shifting ice after the first spring thaw. That was treacherous territory.

"Cooper would be so disappointed. He has plans for the Aloha State."

A corner of her mouth curved. "His best friend is obsessed with Hawaii, and now Cooper thinks he's going to grow up to be a video-game programmer slash professional surfer."

"Not a bad way to make a living." He rolled a strand of her fiery hair through his fingers, loving the silky feel of it. "But you'd be happy to spend your days digging in the dirt?"

"Something like that," she agreed. "My mom was the Bishops' housekeeper, but they also employed a gardener for their property. His name was Roy, and he was one of the sweetest men I ever knew. Mom and I lived in the carriage house, so I was around all the time. Ty and I were close, but his brother and sister didn't like me. I didn't fit in with their friends."

"Idiots."

Her smile grew wistful, and his chest ached. He knew all too well what it was like to be the odd man out.

"I started hanging out with Roy and pestered him to put me to work just so it would look like I was busy." She shrugged. "Turns out I loved 'digging in the dirt.' I probably owe a thank-you to Charlie and Claire, because if they hadn't made me feel like a second-class citizen, I might never have discovered how much I love plants."

"Why do you love them?"

She searched his face as if she couldn't figure out why he was so interested in her history. He couldn't explain it, but he wanted to know every detail about this woman and what made her tick.

"I don't know if you've noticed," she said, wrinkling her nose, "but I have a bit of a temper."

"Really?" He inclined his head. "I'll remember that."

"I spent a lot of time as a kid wanting to kick people in the shin."

"Is that the youthful version of wanting to punch them in the throat?"

Her eyes narrowed and went dark at the edges. "How do you know I use that expression?"

"Use or overuse?" he asked.

She snorted. "Point taken. Anyway, being outside has always calmed me down. It gave me something useful to do with my hands besides wrapping them around the necks of all those snobby girls who were Claire's friends and wanted nothing to do with me."

He watched her chest rise and fall as she turned to look out to the yard beyond the house. "It's more than that, though. From the time Roy handed me that first seed packet, I was enthralled. There's something about being a part of the act of creation, you know?"

Her shoulders relaxed, and he could almost feel the tension from earlier tonight seeping out of her.

"I could make something," she said quietly, "from almost nothing. My hands and the attention I paid to the earth and the water helped to create beautiful flowers, gorgeous herbs, and hardy plants. We could take a tiny tomato seedling and by the end of the summer it would be a huge plant bursting with vegetables." She made a face. "I know it wasn't really me doing the work. It's Mother Nature and all that. But I was a part of it. I still am."

"Working at the landscaping company isn't enough?"

She tugged at the ends of her long curls. "I'm grateful to Ty. Really I am. He started Rocky Mountain Landscapes in the summers while he was still in college. He always found a place for me, even when I had to bring Cooper to work. As the business grew, so did my responsibilities."

"And when he came to work for me, you took over," Owen commented.

"Yes, but it was his dream. Not mine. I like working with regular people on choosing the right kind of plants, flowers, pots, vegetables . . . whatever floats their boat."

God help him, there were so damn many ways the woman floated Owen's boat.

"I know it's selfish to want something for myself, when I had . . ." She paused, cleared her throat. "I *have* a job that pays good money and gives me flexibility to be with Cooper."

"It's not selfish, Jenny. You're working hard to make your dream come true, and Cooper will see the value of that. Maybe not now, but he'll recognize it as he gets older."

She bit down on her lower lip. "I hope going through all this is worth it in the end."

"Is a week with me such a horrible prospect?"

She rolled her eyes to the night sky, then met his gaze once more. "I don't want to hurt you, but I don't trust myself not to."

He leaned in and claimed her mouth, unable to stop himself. He didn't want to hear her fears or think about how foolish the arrangement was for both of them.

All he wanted was Jenny.

Everything else fell away as he tasted her sweetness and she moaned softly. He focused until the world was a pinpoint, with his desire for Jenny at the center.

Nothing mattered except that moment and pulling her even closer. He threaded his fingers through her hair, angling her head to deepen the kiss. She wound her arms around his neck, and somehow he maneuvered her so she was straddling him.

It felt like batting a thousand home runs and Christmas and the answer to every prayer he'd ever whispered in the dark.

He wasn't sure how long they stayed like that, all hands and mouths and seeking need. But just as quickly as the moment began, Jenny wrenched away and out of his arms. She scrambled several feet away on the porch, her knees gathered in to her chest and her fingers pressed to her mouth.

"You can't do that," she said, her breath ragged. "Ever again."

That pricked his temper, which was no easy feat. "Give me one reason why not?"

"Because . . ."

"Don't tell me you didn't enjoy it, Jenny."

She shook her head. "I liked it way too much. That's the problem."

"Then we've got one hell of a problem."

"I can't be your date for the wedding." She dropped her forehead to her knees. "You can see why, right?" She lifted her gaze to his. "You can *feel* why, Owen."

"It will be fine," he answered immediately, shifting closer, then stopping when she inched away. "We'll make sure things don't get out of control. There are no expectations. I told you that. You don't have to do anything that makes you uncomfortable."

She laughed. "You want me to be *comfortable*. I haven't been comfortable since . . . well, I can't remember the last time."

"Except when you're in the garden."

She stared at him for several long moments, her eyes blazing with whiskey-colored sparks. "Yes," she admitted, and he could tell it took something out of her to share that one word with him.

"We need rules," she said after a moment.

"You don't really seem like the rule-following type."

"And it gets me into trouble every time." She dropped her knees to one side and tucked her feet closer to her body. "Which is why we need rules."

"Have you started a list?" He smiled when her eyes narrowed. She was concentrating so hard on ways to prevent the spark between them from flaming out of control.

He should be grateful. She might claim to be destructive, but Jenny had a stronger instinct for self-preservation than he could ever manage.

"No kissing," she told him, her mouth pulling down at the corners. "Or touching each other."

No way in hell was he adhering to either of those rules. "What about in front of my family and friends? That won't be very convincing."

"Fine," she breathed. "Only in public." She flipped her hair over one shoulder. "But no tongue."

"Anything else?"

"Where are we staying?"

"Not with my parents," he muttered. "I'm not that much of a masochist. I'll rent a house in town."

"I want a separate bedroom."

"Done."

"With a lock on the door," she added.

He chuckled. "Do you think I'm going to sneak in to have my wicked way with you?"

"To be honest, I never thought you had a wicked way."

That was a prick to his ego, although not a surprise. He knew his reputation.

"But now . . ."

A sliver of awareness sharpened the air between them. "Now?"

"Let's just say I'm not taking any chances."

Oh, yeah. No matter what a week with Jenny cost him—and he had a feeling he'd be paying with way more than his bank account—it would be worth it. The way she was eyeing him right now, like she was torn between bolting into the house and throwing herself at him, made everything worth it.

"Are those all the rules?"

She tipped up her chin. "Until I think of more."

He didn't bother to hide his smile as he placed the empty beer bottle on the porch rail. One way or another, he would find a way to make this woman his. "Keep me updated," he told her and started down the steps. "Good night, Jenny."

"Good night, Owen."

Jenny was alternately relieved and disappointed when she didn't hear from Owen over the next three days.

But she did receive discreet inquiries from three local jewelers regarding a piece of jewelry she might be interested in selling. Apparently the engagement ring was not only beautiful, but also once owned by an infamous Russian princess, making it worth far more than she'd ever imagined. She'd immediately texted Owen insisting that he take back the ring and to stop having jewelry stores hound her.

He'd sent back a winky-face emoji. A flippin' winky face.

She was busy managing a big installation for the landscape company during the day while spending every evening working in the barn. She shouldn't have had the time to worry about anything else.

Cooper seemed strangely more content since she'd made the arrangement with Owen, and while she assumed it had to do with the money, a part of her felt like there was more to it.

He was upstairs online when a knock sounded on the door around nine, and she assumed it was Owen, since she'd texted him a pile-of-poo emoji and a message that they needed to talk.

It was a lame excuse. She should be embarrassed by how much she wanted to see him. Instead, certain parts of her body were singing the "Hallelujah Chorus" and all she felt was a thrill of anticipation.

Until she opened the door.

Dina Sullivan stood on the other side, looking twenty kinds of a hot mess. Her normally long and shiny blond hair was greasy and dull and had been cut into a bob so uneven it looked like a pre-schooler had wielded the scissors. She wore no makeup and, although her cheeks were dry, her nose and eyes were both swollen and red as if she'd been crying for days. A young girl with two long braids and frightened blue eyes clung to her leg and a toddler boy was asleep in her arms.

"I left John," Dina said, her voice catching on her husband's name. "And I didn't have any other place to go."

Jenny swallowed and ushered the three of them into the farm-house's tiny living room. "It's going to be okay," she said automatically, although she had no idea how to make that statement true.

She turned as Cooper bounded into the room. "Go make up the pullout couch in my office," she told him. "A friend of mine from high school is going to stay the night with us." She felt a rush of love and pride when he didn't bat an eye at the crazy-looking stranger standing in their house.

"I'll get out the air mattress, too," he answered, and headed back toward the stairs.

"He looks like Trent," Dina said, her voice vacant. "My Dylan . . ." She placed a hand on the sleeping boy's brown curls. "Looks just like his daddy, too."

Jenny forced down her reaction to that comment when Dina let out a muffled sob.

"Okay," Jenny repeated like the word was her new mantra. "We're going to figure this out."

Dina wiped the back of her hand across her nose and started to follow. The girl was practically strapped to her leg. Dina looked about as substantial as dandelion fluff, and with the two kids weighing her down, Jenny wasn't sure she wouldn't crumple into a heap on the floor.

"I'll make it," Dina said, as if reading her thoughts. She sank into a chair at the kitchen table and shifted Dylan in her arms so she could wrap the other one around her daughter.

Jenny crouched down to eye level with the girl. "What's your name?"

The girl glanced at Dina, who nodded. "You can talk to Jenny, sweetie. She's Mommy's friend."

Crap. Dina must be in a particularly bad place if Jenny was now considered a friend.

"Emma," the girl whispered.

"Are you hungry, Emma? Cooper and I baked my mom's chocolate-chip cookies today. They're a great pre-bed snack."

"I wanna cookie," the sleeping boy mumbled, his eyes still closed.

Emma nodded. "I'll have one, please."

"Did you use organic flour and non-GMO chocolate chips?" Dina asked.

"It's my mother's recipe. They're the best you'll ever have." Jenny managed to smile at Emma while giving Dina a look that communicated exactly where she could shove her non-GMO chips.

"Sorry," Dina mumbled. "John feels passionately about the kids eating organic."

"Maybe John should think about how his passions affect the rest of your family," Jenny answered, keeping her voice soft.

She took the carton of milk from the refrigerator and got two glasses down from the cabinet. "It's organic," she said to Dina as she poured.

She placed one glass on the table in front of Dina and the other at the next chair. "Emma, you sit here, and I'll get your cookie."

The girl stared at the milk for several seconds and then released her mother and climbed onto the empty chair.

With a small sigh of relief, Jenny opened the container of cookies. Emma took a long time to choose, given that the cookies were all the same.

By the time she did, Dylan had turned and was facing forward in his mother's lap.

"I'm going to check on Cooper's progress," she told the sad little trio. "We'll have beds made up for you soon."

"I didn't pack bags," Dina muttered, her voice trembling. "We don't even have toothbrushes."

"I'll find you some," Jenny told her and placed a hand on the woman's slim shoulder. "It's going to be okay."

As she walked up the steps, she wondered how many times she could utter that sentence before she believed it.

CHAPTER TEN

It was close to ten before Jenny heard soft footsteps padding down the stairs. A moment later Dina appeared in the doorway of the kitchen.

"Sit down," Jenny told her. "I'll pour you a drink."

"I shouldn't—"

"You're going to have at least one," Jenny said, uncapping the bottle of scotch. "There's no way I'm going to risk you telling the other ladies that I sit in my darkened house at night and drink alone."

Dina flashed the ghost of a smile but nodded. "I think you're the one with fodder for the gossip mill after taking us in tonight."

When the other woman slipped into the chair across the table, Jenny pushed the glass of amber liquid toward her. "Gossip isn't my thing. How are the kids?"

"Finally asleep. I can't stay down here long. Sometimes Dylan has night terrors. I don't want him to be scared if he wakes up in an unfamiliar bedroom."

"Lucky for you, the walls are paper-thin. If he wakes before you get up there, we'll hear him."

"It's a cute house."

Jenny gave a soft laugh. "Don't start blowing sunshine just because I let you stay. The house needs work."

"Don't we all," Dina said. She wrapped her fingers around the tumbler and threw back the entire contents, then immediately began to choke and cough, her eyes watering.

"Holy hell, woman." Jenny shoved a napkin toward her. "This isn't spring break with watered-down tequila. That's a two-hundred-dollar bottle of scotch. You're supposed to actually take the time to taste it."

"I wanted the burn," Dina said through clenched teeth, her voice hoarse. "I need to feel *something*." She set down the glass next to the liquor bottle. "Another."

Jenny poured another two fingers of scotch. "Drink this one slower."

Dina nodded. "Thank you for taking us in. I know you don't owe me a thing."

"Tell me how you ended up here."

"I had to go someplace John wouldn't think to look for me," Dina said, sipping at the scotch.

"Mission accomplished." Jenny's heart squeezed at the hollowness in the other woman's tone. "But why? I have a friend who runs a domestic violence agency. If your husband—"

"It's nothing like that. He would never hurt me. But I know if I saw him, there'd be no way I could keep up my resolve. He's too damn charming for his own good, and I still love him. I wish I didn't, but . . ."

Jenny thought of herself as a wide-eyed teenage girl and how charming Trent Decker had been while pursuing her. She hoped she had become smarter than that.

"I thought the two of you were working it out."

"He wants us to have a threesome with his nineteen-year-old girlfriend." She grabbed her chest with her free hand. "I've nursed two kids with these things. Do you think I'm going to stand naked next to some . . . perky teenager and let my husband compare me to her?"

Jenny shook her head. "Are you saying you'd do it if you liked your boobs?"

"No." Dina gulped down her scotch and choked again, this time a little less forcefully. "At least, I don't think so. But John is really persuasive when he wants to be."

"So you left because you don't want a ménage à trois?"

Dina sniffed. "I left because my husband won't give up his girlfriend. My young, nubile, recently fired nanny. Now I'm at home raising our children, and can I tell you something?" Before Jenny could answer, Dina said, "It's hard with no help. I don't know how women manage this stuff. I've had to give up tennis and now I do yoga from YouTube videos. Half the time someone is hanging off me when I'm trying to get into downward-facing dog position. Not exactly mindful and relaxing."

Jenny shrugged. Dina was out of touch with reality, but no one deserved a cheating spouse. "Welcome to the real world. I hate to be the one to burst your bubble, but parenting doesn't exactly lend itself to mindful and relaxing."

"That's why I need your help. You're raising a son on your own and doing a great job of it." Dina didn't bother to refill her glass. She took the bottle of scotch Jenny had been given as a thank-you from a big client at the landscaping company and brought it to her lips, taking a deep swallow.

"Whoa, there, thirsty gal." Jenny took the bottle and twisted the cap back in place. "Your newfound respect for me is lovely, if unwarranted." She stood and placed the scotch on the counter, then filled a glass with water and returned to the table. "One thing I can tell you from personal experience is that single parenting doesn't get any easier with a hangover."

Dina's mouth pressed into a thin line. "I don't want to be a single mother." Tears spilled down her cheeks.

"It's not really the kind of thing little girls dream of when they imagine a perfect life." Jenny handed over another napkin. "Don't romanticize my life, Dina." She held up a hand when the other woman would have argued. "I'm not saying you were wrong to leave. Your husband is taking advantage of the situation and of you, but you have to get strong if you're going to do this." She blew out a breath. "I had my mom's help the whole time, and even with that, I've made plenty of mistakes. Cooper is a fantastic kid, but a lot of that is because of who he is, not what I've done."

Dina hiccuped. "You don't give yourself enough credit."

"You give me too much."

"I don't want to be married to a man who doesn't think I'm enough." Dina met Jenny's gaze. "This isn't the first time he's cheated. It happened when we were engaged, too."

"Why did you marry him in the first place?"

"We'd sent the invitations and I had the dress and . . . he told me it was just the stress of the commitment."

"Which might have been a huge red flag?"

"He promised it would never happen again. He told me we'd have the perfect life together. As far as all of my friends are concerned, we do. That's another reason I can't go to any of them now. Trust me, when it comes down to choosing sides, they'll pick Team John every day of the week."

"Then they aren't truly your friends," Jenny murmured. She inclined her head. "Do we need to talk about your hair?"

Dina grimaced. "I wanted to make a statement. John liked to use my hair to tickle—"

"Stop," Jenny hissed, covering her ears with her hands for a moment. "There isn't enough bleach in the world to scrub my eyeballs clean if you finish that sentence."

"I shoved the hair I cut off into the gas tank of his Porsche"— Dina gingerly combed her fingers through the butchered ends—"after I found a thong in the glove compartment."

"One classy dude," Jenny muttered.

"I want to find a guy like Owen," Dina told her. "Filthy rich, hot as hell, and head-over-heels in love with me."

It was Jenny's turn to choke.

Owen was rich and handsome but as for being in love . . .

Dina needed to hear the truth of Jenny's arrangement with Owen immediately. But she couldn't bring herself to say the words. "If you're leaving your husband," she said instead, "it can't be because you're looking to find a sugar daddy to take his place."

"I'm not looking," Dina answered, desperation clear in her tone. "But I wouldn't mind if one found me." Her voice quavered again and she covered her face with her hands, shoulders trembling as she cried softly. "How am I going to take care of my babies?"

Jenny hated the woman's tears and her scumbag husband. An undercurrent of guilt ran below the anger Jenny felt on Dina's behalf. She couldn't help but feel partially responsible for Dina's current predicament. Not the philandering spouse, but the fact that she'd had the nerve to leave him.

Would Dina have walked out the door if she hadn't viewed Jenny as a role model?

The woman's respect was a joke, based on a fictionalized image of Jenny's life that had little to do with reality. Jenny had only made it through life thanks to help from other people—her mother, the Bishops as a whole, and Ty in particular. Now she was going to be several steps closer to realizing her dream of opening the nursery full-time thanks to Owen.

Of course, she was giving him something in return. Another reason she didn't mention the truth to Dina. Jenny might not have turned away Dina and her kids, but that didn't mean she trusted the woman to keep her secret. The less people who knew about her pretend engagement the better.

"You'll find a way," Jenny said, and she believed it was true. Despite her own unsavory history with Dina, there was no doubt the woman loved her children. "You can stay here as long as you need," she added, then snapped shut her mouth.

There was guilt talking, and then there was plain old crazy.

"Thank you," Dina whispered. At least she'd stopped crying. "I should go to bed. My head feels kind of spinny."

"Bathroom's first door on the left out of your bedroom," Jenny said. "In case you have some night terrors of your own." She stood as Dina did. "Do you need help up the stairs?"

"I can manage." Dina gave her a quick hug. "You're a good friend, Jenny. I'm sorry I didn't realize it back in high school."

Jenny forced a smile. It was still difficult to process this delicate, broken woman in front of her as the girl who'd been the biggest queen bee in their high school. "Good night, Dina. Things will seem better in the morning."

Dina gave a sad smile. "They certainly can't get worse."

Jenny washed the glasses they'd used, then turned off the lights and locked up the house. She grabbed her phone from the counter on her way upstairs. A text from Owen had come in while she was talking with Dina.

Nice emoji. I'm assuming the poo is an abbreviation of pook. Sweet dreams, pookie.

She wanted to be annoyed at his flirtatious humor and the obnoxious term of endearment. A moratorium on flirting needed to be added to the list of rules. But her stomach did a little dance at the underlying affection in his message. She was heading to bed with thoughts of Owen at the forefront of her mind and heart.

Sweet dreams indeed.

Owen pressed his ID card to the keypad and the doors to the research and development lab within Dalton Enterprises whooshed open.

He walked down the muted gray hall lined with framed photos of the various technological innovations his company had brought to market. Even now, it sometimes still felt like a daydream that all of it belonged to him.

Although not exactly to him.

Since the initial public offering on the stock market almost four years ago, shares of Dalton Enterprises had increased in value by almost a third. Owen understood the need for public capital and exposure but still missed the fun and flexibility from the company's early days.

It had changed something for him. He was no longer the leader of an innovative tech company. Instead, he'd reluctantly become a traditional CEO. He spent way too much time dealing with his board of directors, plus analysts and journalists, constantly being judged by the company's share price performance, to the exclusion of almost everything else.

He'd lost some of his drive and the fire that had pushed him to become a success. He told himself it was because he couldn't recreate the feeling of generating something every day that he'd had in the early years of the business.

There was more to it than that. The stock offering had made him rich beyond belief, and he'd gone back to West Virginia shortly after being added to the famous *Forbes* World's Billionaires list. He'd gone with the intention of finally convincing his parents to allow him to buy them a new house and with the idea of taking a family vacation to . . .

He laughed softly, thinking of Cooper. Owen had wanted to take his parents to Hawaii.

But before his mother had a chance to respond, his father had made a comment about the house he'd worked hard to pay for being good enough and not wanting his son showing off his wealth to their hometown.

Owen had looked at his mother for support, but other than a sympathetic smile and the murmured words "he means well," she hadn't said a word to challenge his father.

She never did.

Instead of arguing, Owen had sat down for another awkward dinner where he alternately heard about Jack's military accomplishments and Gabby's success on the ski slopes. He'd left the next morning, tossing the magazine with his face on the cover into the recycling bin outside the airport.

It would have been simpler to ignore his father. God knew Owen had tried. He had world leaders clamoring for his attention, but at his parents' home, he remained persona non grata. Then, shortly after the incident with Jack's fire team coming under attack, he'd read an article about difficulties with security and interference in the connectivity of military mesh networks around the world. And a plan had been hatched.

He'd put his work with both his namesake company and foundation to the back burner in order to devote a huge portion of Dalton Enterprises' financial and intellectual capital to a new venture. Owen's goal was to create a completely hack-proof, one hundred percent reliable network, which he'd named Labyrinth Web, that could be utilized exclusively by the US military. It would be his contribution to the armed services—not quite the same as serving his country the way his father and brother had, but something they couldn't ignore.

The board had been skeptical, as had his management team. No one could deny, however, that Dalton Enterprises had been built from Owen's instincts and expertise with innovation. The board had approved his funding request and he'd assembled a top-notch R&D team. Two years later and they were no closer to bringing a viable product to market than when he'd first conceived of the technology.

He stepped into the main lab and waved to his chief scientist, Charles Kenkel.

"It's Saturday morning." The soft-spoken man, who looked like he used the same hairstylist as Albert Einstein, smiled at Owen. "Since when do you frequent the lab on weekends? Don't you have a photo shoot for some magazine's 'Fifty Sexiest Technology Geeks' to get to?"

Owen shook his head. "Never going to live down that *People* article, am I?" Charles had been at MIT with Owen, and he was the first employee Owen had hired. Several of Owen's other early hires had moved up the ranks as the company grew and were heading his senior management team. Charles had chosen to remain in the comfort of his lab.

"I thought I'd check in and see if you were any closer to having a prototype ready to go live."

Charles shrugged. "We're closer, but as it looks now, Labyrinth Web isn't any more secure than a regular mesh network. We still need a secure vehicle, and it's likely soldiers in combat situations would outrun the technology more quickly than connection speed could keep up."

"That isn't going to justify the money and resources we've put into this project for the shareholders," Owen said, trying to keep his voice level. That was only one of the reasons he needed the Labyrinth Web to succeed. Of course, he'd hoped to have a launch date for the product confirmed before his brother's wedding so he could share the news with his dad. But the truth was, he could not keep stalling the board and shareholders.

"However," Charles added, and Owen perked up a bit, "the technology is infinitely more stable than any other mesh network that's come before it. It could be a game changer as far as remote or economically challenged communities gaining consistent access to the web. And it would be a huge benefit during a natural disaster–type situation, when other traditional networks are cut off."

"That's not what it's designed to do," Owen said through gritted teeth. It was not the first time he and Charles had engaged in this conversation.

The scientist held up his hands, palms out. "You're the boss," he said, "but Dalton Enterprises is known for revolutionary products. Labyrinth Web could revolutionize the way certain sectors of the population communicate. It can't be ignored."

Watch me, Owen thought. To Charles, he said, "Keep working on the security angle. Text me when you have something."

Charles sighed but nodded, and after a few more minutes of uncharacteristically awkward conversation, Owen left the lab.

He drove away from the building, his stomach churning. Dalton Enterprises had once been his outlet, the place he channeled all of his frustration and desires into building something that would prove his worth.

To anyone on the outside and even most of his employees, he'd been successful beyond belief. But he'd saddled his company with the burdensome baggage of his paternal relationship and it no longer was a sanctuary for him.

Everywhere he turned he had reminders of how he wasn't capable of making a success in the one way that would count to his father.

Once again, instead of heading directly home, he drove northwest of downtown and turned in at the turquoise-and-yellow mailbox that stood on the edge of Jenny's property.

There was no reason he needed to see her again so soon. They had an arrangement for the week of his brother's wedding, nothing more. She'd made that clear. For two years he'd done his best to not think about her.

He'd dated a string of women who were cultured, educated, and wildly appropriate for the arm of a man like him. They spoke in modulated tones about charities and fund-raisers and giving back while spending thousands on designer purses, weekend spa getaways, and monthly trips to the dermatologist. But Jenny, who had so little, was risking everything to pursue her dream of sharing with people her love of gardening.

As he steered his 4Runner down the gravel driveway, he saw a half dozen cars parked near the fence line. In the bright morning light, the place looked different—cozy and charming with tables of plants and flowers lined up on either side of the barn doors. There were clusters of oversize clay pots and a display of wind chimes hanging from a clothesline that had been strung above the plants. Couples and a few young families milled around the open space of the driveway, wandering in and out of the barn to the different flower groupings.

He parked and headed toward the building, watching as people carried out various plants and herb arrangements in colorful pots. Scanning the interior, he stopped, heart clenching, as he saw Jenny bent over a flat of tomato plants, speaking to a middle-aged woman. She reached out her fingers to gently touch the leaves of the plant as she spoke, the other woman nodding and smiling at something she said.

Owen had thought he knew Jenny, had spent what felt like hours memorizing every nuance of her features, but that morning she was a revelation to him. All the wariness and worry that she normally carried were gone, replaced by a look of contentment he could feel like a tangible force from across the space.

Wearing a pair of faded, low-slung jeans that hugged her small frame perfectly, she bent to open the cabinet below the shelf and took out a bag of potting soil. She dipped her hand in and pulled out a clump of rich brown dirt that she held with all the reverence of a priest carrying a chalice. The woman standing with her pinched a bit of the soil between her fingers, then nodded. The smile that Jenny gave her literally took away his breath.

"She's in her element," a voice said next to him. "It doesn't take being in love with her to see how happy she is around all these plants and flowers and whatnot."

He glanced down into the blue eyes of a rail-thin blond who looked vaguely familiar.

"Dina Sullivan," the woman said, holding out her hand. "We met at the reunion."

Owen blinked and tried to figure out why the woman who had seemed to be Jenny's mortal enemy was standing in the garden barn, wearing the same green apron as Jenny, a smudge of dirt on her nose like she was on the job.

"I got my hair cut," the woman said, tugging at the ragged ends. "That could be why you don't remember."

"Probably," he agreed, even though he hadn't noticed her hair.

"But Jenny's talked about me, right?" Dina seemed to be studying his reaction far too closely. "She told you my kids and I are staying with her for a little while? She said you thought it was a good idea."

So he and Jenny had talked about the tiny woman with the butchered blond hair? Good to know. Of course, it would have been better to hear it from Jenny, who looked up from her conversation at that moment. Her eyes widened as they darted between Dina and him, and she gave a slight shake of her head.

"I'm an expert at planning parties," Dina was saying. "Better than I am at helping at a nursery." She held up her fingers for him to inspect. "My nails are wrecked. But it was nice of Jenny to give me a job." She laughed softly. "Jenny Castelli has a huge heart. Who would have guessed it?"

Owen had known it the first time he laid eyes on the redheaded spitfire. A huge heart along with the ability to crush his into a million pieces.

"Anyway," the woman continued, "if you need help with the wedding . . ." She broke off with a small laugh. "Not that you can't afford to hire the best wedding planner, but I'm available if you two need it. I also cook. Jenny said you might be coming to dinner tonight if your schedule allows it? I think it's cute that you two have standing date nights, like you're already married."

Standing date nights? Already married? What the hell . . .

"Hey, Owen," Jenny said as she approached them. "This is a surprise. I didn't expect to see you here this morning." She grasped his arm and squeezed, a little tighter than necessary. The sense of contentment was gone, replaced by a cord of tension he could feel despite her bright smile.

"Of course he's here," Dina said. "You have a man who loves and supports you. Go ahead and kiss him." She pointed to Jenny. "It won't bother me, and everyone can see how much you want to."

Owen's gaze shot to Jenny, who bit down on her lower lip as color crept up her cheeks. "You know you want to," he repeated, keeping his voice teasing even as his whole body went tight.

She lifted onto her toes, aiming for his cheek with her mouth. At the last second, Owen turned so that their lips met. As always, it felt as if sparks lit the air between them. Such a chaste kiss, totally appropriate for a Saturday morning in full view of the garden center shoppers. It was clear Jenny hadn't expected it because for a moment her mouth was soft against his. The next, she pulled back, and her cheeks had gone bright pink.

Dina sighed. "I remember when it was like that. I'm going to check on Cooper and my kids. Make sure they don't have him tied to a chair."

"Are you sure you weren't involved in sports?" Jenny muttered as the other woman walked away. "You've got pretty quick moves."

"Total nerd," Owen told her. "I excel at science. Motion and reaction time are all about physics."

She rolled her eyes.

"I hear I support your one-time nemesis as a houseguest."

"She walked out on her rat-bastard cheating husband."

"And ended up on your doorstep?"

"Yes," she said on an exasperated breath. "I told her to leave him and she did. What was I supposed to do?"

He couldn't stop his mouth from curving at one end. The woman acted so tough, but she had a heart as soft and sweet as a pile of kittens.

"I guess you were supposed to take her in, offer your son as a babysitter, and put her to work."

She narrowed her eyes. "It's temporary."

"Will she go back to him?"

"I don't know." Jenny gave a mock shudder. "The guy is slicker than an oil spill. He came out here last night and took the kids to dinner. Flowers arrived this morning. He wants her back, but he's not going to stop hurting her. I want her to understand she has options."

"Can I help in any way?"

She crossed her arms over her chest. "I haven't told her about our arrangement," she said quietly.

"I gathered that. You don't plan on it?"

"Not now. I don't trust that it wouldn't get out and then you'd be at the wedding with no date and everyone knowing you tried to hire a fiancée for the week."

"So you're doing this for me?"

"And the ring," she added, although it wasn't true.

"Ah, yes. The ring that is soon to make all your dreams come true." He glanced down at her empty finger. "Does this mean you'll start wearing it again?"

With another exaggerated eye roll, she reached up and pulled a chain from under the top of her faded denim shirt. The diamond flashed in the sunlight as she held it against the pale skin peeking out where she'd left the shirt unbuttoned at the top. "Dina was freaking out that I didn't have it on. She thinks it's bad luck, so I had to do this."

Seeing the ring he'd bought on the chain around her neck was like a kick to the gut. He had to remind himself that their arrangement was temporary. This woman had hurt him, betrayed him, and he'd made the choice to walk away. He didn't want her in his life beyond the weekend of Jack's wedding. It was a business transaction. Nothing more. He cleared his throat. "We're engaged until the end of the month."

"Yep."

He nodded. "I'm also coming to dinner for our standing date night?"

"Sorry about that," Jenny said with a grimace. "She caught me off guard."

"Right. We've established that you have no poker face."

"That's not true."

"Does this mean I get to amend the rules?"

Her eyes widened. "No," she shouted, drawing the attention of several customers standing nearby. An older man waved her toward him, lifting a potted plant as if to ask her opinion.

"Jenny." Owen gently wrapped his fingers around her wrist.

"Thanks for not ratting me out with Dina, but seriously, why are you here?"

"I was on my way home from the office—"

"On a Saturday?"

He inclined his head. "Anyway, I wanted to see . . ." He was about to say *you*, but that felt like too much to reveal, so he finished with "what the barn looked like in the daylight with customers."

"What do you think?" She stilled, her caramel-colored eyes wary as she met his gaze.

"What you've done here is amazing."

Her lips parted, and he could almost see the wheels spinning in her brain, as if she'd taken his compliment and was dissecting it to figure out where to extract the underlying criticism.

"I've got to get back to work," she said after a moment.

He let her go and she moved toward the customer, her features relaxing again as she spoke to the man.

Owen turned to go only to find Cooper standing behind him.

"Dina told me you were here," the boy said. "She's putting her son down for a nap."

"It's nice of you to help with them," Owen answered. "You're a good kid, Coop."

127

Cooper shrugged but Owen could see the corners of his mouth turning up.

"The barn is crowded today," Cooper said. "Mom asked me to refill the stock as people buy it. We've got another flat of tomatoes and peppers out in the greenhouse."

"Want some company?" Owen asked. He'd planned to go back home and work more on a report he was supposed to review for his CFO. But the beautiful day and the rich scent of earth filling the air made him want to do something that would take his mind off everything going on with work.

Cooper flashed a full-on grin. "Yeah, you can help." He led Owen out of the barn and around the side toward the small greenhouse on the edge of the property. "Are you trying to suck up to my mom?"

"Not exactly." Owen nudged the kid. "Maybe I'm trying to suck up to you. Let's go haul some plants."

The smile Cooper gave him made Owen's crappy morning fade to a distant memory.

CHAPTER ELEVEN

"You hit the man-jackpot with that one."

Jenny turned from setting the table to where Dina stood in front of the sink, staring out the window with a goofy smile on her face.

Don't walk over there. You don't care about the man in your backyard. It's a game. It's an act.

But even as she mentally repeated every excuse she could think up, she felt her feet moving her closer.

Dina turned off the water and made room for Jenny in front of the sink. Her breath caught as Owen ran by the patio carrying Dylan on his back. The boy laughed wildly while Cooper chased them, holding tight to Emma's hand as he did. Jenny loved the flagstone patio with its old-fashioned planter boxes and view of the mountains far in the distance. She'd added a table and chairs with an oversize sun umbrella and spent as much time as she could out there in the evenings.

"I thought they were playing soccer," Jenny muttered. "That looks like chase."

"It looks like fun," Dina said, her voice wistful. "Do you know the last time John played with our kids?" She rolled her eyes. "Never. My dad spent hours with us in the backyard. Kids need that." She glanced at Jenny. "Did you have a fun dad?"

"I didn't have a dad." Jenny grabbed the sponge from the back of the sink and wiped at an invisible spot on the counter. "Cooper doesn't either, and he's turning out fine."

"Now he has Owen. He's great with the kids."

"Yeah," Jenny said. "Imagine that." Her skin got the same hot, prickly sensation she'd had the night of the party where she'd set it up to look like she was cheating on him.

Owen Dalton was a man she could easily fall for, and she'd learned a painful lesson from the two men she'd been foolish enough to love—first her father and then Trent. If she made herself vulnerable and gave her heart to someone, she was certain to have it broken. Jenny had spent her whole life aching for the dad she never knew and a good portion of it bitter after being deserted by the callous teenager who'd walked away from her and her unborn son.

She would not make that mistake again. No matter how perfect Owen seemed, she couldn't trust him. Or herself. Mostly herself.

The problem was her. She couldn't be certain about her father, but Trent had gone on to marry and have a wife and kids. He simply hadn't wanted her or their unborn child enough.

The boy who was the center of her world.

As she watched, Owen dropped to his knees in the grass at the edge of the patio. For a few seconds Emma rode him like a horse, then he pointed to a nearby bush. All of the kids gathered around him to peer at whatever was in the branches.

Like it was the most natural thing in the world, Owen sat back on the lawn, putting an arm around Emma and lifting Dylan to his lap. Cooper turned to the three of them, his expression animated.

A thick ball of emotion clogging her throat, Jenny walked to the oven and peered in. "I think your casserole is done. I'll pour milk for the kids."

"Oh. My. God." Dina's voice sounded dazed.

"What happened?" Jenny hurried back to the window and felt all the blood leave her head and rush south to the girly parts of her body, which were doing frenzied flips and cartwheels like some sort of overcaffeinated gymnastics team.

Cooper, Emma, and Dylan were taking turns drinking out of the hose. Owen, who had obviously just been sprayed by the kids, wiped off his face with the hem of his gray T-shirt.

The shirt was hiked up around his waist and . . .

"Holy crap, he has abs," Jenny murmured.

Not just any abs. A six-pack, all rigid planes and rippling muscles with the sexiest damn happy trail she'd ever seen leading down into the waistband of his dark jeans.

He hadn't been ripped like that before, had he? They'd taken things slow, but surely she would have noticed that kind of body. A little whimper escaped her lips. Five days in a house with that man. How would she survive?

Out of the corner of her eye, she noticed Dina staring at her and turned. "He's all mine," she said quickly, hoping to cover the fact that—

"Why does it sound like you didn't know he had those abs?" Dina asked.

Jenny scoffed. "I knew. Of course I knew. But he's been working out more lately, and it seems like his body changes every time I see him."

Dina stared, her brows scrunched together like she definitely wasn't picking up what Jenny was laying down.

"It's hard to find time for . . . you know . . . getting down to business with Cooper around." She nodded when Dina's features relaxed the tiniest bit. "I have to set a good example, and we're not married yet."

"You should go on a real date night," Dina suggested, giving Jenny a tight hug. For someone who was a total mean girl, Dina certainly liked to break the barriers of Jenny's personal space. Jenny tolerated her friend Chloe's affectionate nature, but there was room for only one hugger in her life. "You've done so much for me; I'd be happy to watch Cooper."

"He's twelve," Jenny answered, pulling away. "He doesn't really need a babysitter."

"Then you have no excuse." Dina's tone was firm. "Don't get into a rut with Owen. That's what got John and me in trouble."

"John's wandering penis got the two of you in trouble," Jenny said.

Dina made a face as she grabbed two pot holders from the counter. "That, too. I'm going to pull out the casserole. Would you call everyone in for dinner?"

As soon as Jenny stepped onto the patio, Owen's dark gaze found hers. A heat that was becoming quickly familiar spread through her as he flashed a boyish grin.

"I think dinner's ready," he said to the three kids. Cooper scooped up Dylan and took Emma's hand, leading the way toward the house.

Owen turned off the spigot at the back of the house, then joined Jenny on the patio. "I don't have to stay."

"Are you kidding?" With the pad of her thumb, she wiped a drop of water off his cheek. "You worked your ass off the better part of the day *and* you've proven you could have a second career as a nanny. It will break Dina's heart if you leave right now."

Ever so slightly he leaned into her touch. "Dina's heart isn't my concern."

His body crowded hers, but she didn't step back. This close, she could see the golden flecks around the edges of his brown eyes and feel the heat of his body. She wanted to reach out her hand, snake it up under the hem of his shirt, and flatten her palm against his hard belly. To press her nose into his neck and lose herself in the scent of him.

"I don't know," she said with a small laugh, trying to distract both of them. "After we break off our arrangement, she might be in line to become the real Mrs. Dalton."

One side of his mouth curved. "You think there's a line?"

"I have no doubt."

"There's no line." He leaned in so close she could feel his breath on her skin. "And I'm going to kiss you now."

Her eyes darted to the house, but Dina and the kids were nowhere in sight. She should have protested. It was definitely a violation of one of the rules.

But right now she needed Owen's mouth on hers in the same way she needed to breathe. She licked her bottom lip with the tip of her tongue and heard him growl low in his throat. The next moment, he cupped her face in his palms and his mouth met hers, sending sensation swirling through her. Their bodies remained a few inches apart and he didn't make a move to pull her closer. But the way he kissed her made her know he wanted more.

She wanted more. She wanted everything.

That thought had her breaking the contact, and she tried to force her heartbeat back to a normal rate.

"We should go in for dinner," she said, clearing her throat so that it wouldn't be so raspy.

"Dinner," he agreed, and took her hand as they walked toward the house.

She was going to have to add no hand holding to the list of rules. For now, she simply enjoyed his touch.

They'd reestablish the rules tomorrow, when her brain was working again.

Almost two weeks later, Jenny sat in a coffee shop in the Highlands neighborhood northwest of downtown, her knee jiggling erratically under the table. It would be helpful to blame her nerves on too much caffeine, but she'd taken to drinking decaf. Her turbulent emotions didn't need any more of a jolt. She and Owen were leaving for West Virginia in three days and she was terrified at how quickly she'd come to depend on him in her life.

They'd established a routine since the Saturday he'd come to the garden center that she craved at the same time it terrified her.

Owen came to her house almost every night after work. He helped with the nursery, either moving plant stock and doing whatever odd jobs she asked him to handle, or he'd entertain Dina's kids and Cooper in the backyard. A few of the evenings, he'd brought carryout, and once had grilled steaks Dina purchased at the local market.

Jenny had picked up her mother a couple of times from the nursing home to join them for dinner. Mona seemed to blossom among the unexpected mix of people suddenly filling Jenny's world. Her mother loved watching Emma and Dylan play in the backyard, and Owen was so sweet and charming that Mona became immediately smitten.

But Jenny's life was far from perfect. She was constantly running on all cylinders to balance the projects she managed for the landscaping company with her work on the nursery. Dina vacillated between steadfast commitment to her decision to leave her husband and late nights crying on Jenny's shoulder about how much she missed him.

In the midst of the surges and ebbs of almost daily chaos, Owen remained at her side. Jenny found it far too easy to forget that nothing about their relationship was real when her feelings for Owen felt all too genuine.

"You can't hurt him again," Kendall said gently.

Jenny jerked back, the words landing like a blow to her heart. Coffee sloshed over the rim of the cup she was holding, making her skin burn slightly where the steaming liquid hit.

"I thought we were friends," she muttered as she took the napkin Kendall handed her.

"We are. I'm telling you that not just for Owen's sake, but for yours. You were just as devastated by what you did as he was. Don't let it get to the point where you irrevocably sabotage whatever is between you two."

Jenny wadded the napkin in her clenched fist and looked around the crowded coffee shop, needing a moment to collect herself before she responded to Kendall.

"Did Chloe and Sam nominate you for this little intervention?" she asked finally.

Kendall shook her head. "Ty saw Owen yesterday and heard that you're going to the wedding with him. He wanted to talk to you directly, but I asked him to let me speak with you first."

Pain sliced across Jenny's chest. "You and Ty are my two best friends in the world. What does that say for my character when neither of you trusts me?"

"What does it say when you haven't told any of us about your little wedding date arrangement?"

"I knew you'd try to talk me out of it."

"If you need money for the business, we can help," Kendall offered.

Embarrassment dulled Jenny's pain. "I'm tired of Ty bailing me out of life," she said, not bothering to hide the bitterness in her tone. "He must be sick of it as well."

"He loves you, sweetie," Kendall said. "We both do. You know that."

"Then I need you to trust that I know what I'm doing."

Kendall didn't answer, only studied Jenny over the rim of her coffee mug as she took a sip. Kendall was a master at reading people, and knowing that she sucked at hiding her emotions made Jenny's anxiety ratchet up another notch.

"Don't use those investigative reporter mind tricks on me," she said, taking a hefty swig of coffee and wishing it was a double shot of espresso. She'd need the extra energy to maneuver through the conversation without accidentally revealing how much Owen truly meant to her.

Kendall had gotten her big journalistic break two years ago when she'd been the lead reporter on a story that had exposed the corrupt land dealings of one of the biggest real estate developers in the state. It just so happened that the man who ran the company was also Ty's father.

Kendall and Ty had met while she was working on the story, but the ramifications of it had almost torn them apart. Their love had triumphed in the end, and they were happily married and expecting their first child. "There's no scoop here. Owen did me a favor and now I'm doing one for him."

"And you don't have feelings for him?" Kendall placed a hand on her belly, an unconscious gesture that Jenny remembered from when she was pregnant with Cooper.

"We're friends." It wasn't a total lie. Jenny didn't bother to mention that she'd never before had a friend who also made her want to rip off her clothes and climb him like a spider monkey.

Kendall drew in a slow breath, then nodded. "If you're sure. With everything Owen is dealing with at work, I know he's not in the best frame of mind to—"

"What stuff?" The coffee Jenny had just drunk turned to thick tar in her stomach. She pushed the mug to the side as she leaned forward, elbows on the table.

"The baby's kicking." Kendall's gaze softened, and she pressed one hand to the low part of her abdomen as she took a bite of muffin. "I swear she loves carbs. If I eat a donut, she goes crazy."

"Cooper liked watermelon," Jenny said, happy for her friend's obvious joy. "But let's focus here, Mrs. Pregnancy Brain. What stuff is Owen dealing with at work?"

"The difficulties he's having with getting the Labyrinth Web military technology off the ground."

"Dalton Enterprises doesn't work with the military," Jenny argued. "Their focus has always been individuals and communities—connecting people through their personal devices."

"That's the point," Kendall answered. "No one can figure out why Owen is so determined to make the Labyrinth Web work. I know he comes from a family where military service is important, so maybe that has something to do with it. According to Ty, upper management and the board of directors are losing patience. Stockholders will too if he can't make progress before the next quarterly earnings announcement."

She popped another bite of muffin into her mouth. "Ty said information trickles over to the foundation slowly, so it could be worse now."

Jenny felt her shoulders stiffen. "Why hasn't Owen mentioned anything to me?"

Kendall's gaze sharpened as if she'd finally realized how much not knowing this huge thing in Owen's life meant to Jenny. Her voice turned placating. "The only reason Ty found out is through people at the office. I guess he tried to talk to Owen about it but got nowhere." She reached forward and patted Jenny's hand. "I didn't mention it to make you worry. It's just that I do think you need to be kind of careful with Owen right now. He's not in the best place."

"I will." Jenny mentally kicked herself for not guessing something was wrong. Owen was privy to almost every detail of her life, and she now realized how little she understood about what made him tick. It was difficult to know whether the fault of that lay with him or her. Maybe a combination. Maybe she was the type of woman who didn't inspire trust or faith in a man.

It was a good reminder that what she had with Owen was . . . nothing.

He was a nice guy and her life was a shit show, so he'd stepped in to help. He didn't want or need anything from her, at least beyond the sexual chemistry that was becoming harder to ignore.

"Enough about Owen and me. Tell me about all the baby plans," she said, pasting on a bright smile.

"Jenny." Kendall's voice was so tender it made Jenny's head pound.

"Seriously, Ken." She swallowed when her voice cracked. "I can't get emotional because I screwed things up with the perfect guy and now there's nothing between us. I own what I did, sucky as it was. But between my mom's care and working my ass off to make the garden center a reality, Cooper is getting caught in the crossfire. The one thing I've always done is put him first, and that's not going to change. I need some stability right now. Too many things have changed in the past six months."

She wrapped her fingers around the coffee mug, pressing them tight against the porcelain so Kendall wouldn't notice they were trembling. "I'm not going to hurt Owen. Once we're past the wedding, things will go back to how they were before. We'll be friendly when we need to and ignore each other the rest of the time."

"Are you sure?"

Jenny nodded. "Now talk to me about your pregnancy and when you're going to get hormonal acne and blow up like a balloon. You know we can't be true friends unless that happens."

"My boobs are huge," Kendall said with a laugh. "Does that count?"

"Don't make me punch—" Jenny sucked in a breath. Of course she'd been about to say "punch you in the throat." That was her signature phrase. Owen had even mentioned it. She didn't want to think about all the other things he knew about her because it was too scary to imagine that he could read her true feelings so easily.

That was a trip to disasterland for both of them.

"It doesn't count," she amended. "At least tell me you have cankles? Even Kim Kardashian got cankles."

She smiled and nodded as Kendall talked about the pregnancy, her plans for maternity leave, and life in general. Even if Jenny had just been called on the carpet with regards to her intentions toward Owen, she was still grateful to have people in her life that understood and loved her unconditionally.

She'd listened to Dina on the phone with a variety of friends over the past week and each time, Jenny had to fight the urge to grab the phone and tell every one of those two-faced witches to go to hell. By the way Dina had responded to the pauses on her end of the line, Jenny could tell they'd been trying to convince her to return to John.

The separation was taking a toll on Dina. Jenny had quickly come to care for her unlikely new friend and hated to hear the muffled crying Dina couldn't quite hide late at night. Jenny would never allow herself to be so emotionally vulnerable to anyone. It was better to end up alone than to risk the kind of heartbreak that could come from letting a man see the soft and vulnerable places she hid deep inside.

CHAPTER TWELVE

Owen paced back and forth in the small commuter terminal that serviced the municipal airport on the south side of Denver. His plane had been waiting on the tarmac since their scheduled departure time over thirty minutes earlier. A member of his ground crew signaled to get his attention, but he continued to ignore the man, embarrassment flooding him.

Jenny was a no-show.

The plan had been for her to drop Cooper at the camp fifty miles northwest of Denver, not far from Estes Park, then head straight to the airport.

He'd received a voice mail from her an hour ago, but it had cut out so much that he couldn't understand more than a few garbled words. Now she wasn't answering, and he worried that her doubts had gotten the best of her and she was flaking on their agreement.

It shouldn't have been a total surprise. The more time he'd spent with Jenny, the edgier she'd become until she could barely look at him without immediately shying away.

He should have given her some space, but a part of him liked pushing her buttons. He liked knowing he had some effect on her given that he was in a constant state of frustration since she had been back in his life.

Because she wasn't really back. They had a temporary arrangement. As much as he wanted it that way, it also annoyed the hell out of him. He wasn't going to put himself on the line for anyone, especially not the woman who'd responded to his declaration of love by groping another guy in a coatroom where Owen was sure to find them.

Despite what he knew to be prudent, his defenses had begun to fall away the more time he spent with Jenny. And there he was, once again on the verge of being humiliated.

No more.

He could make up some excuse to his family. Maybe it was time he manned up and dealt with why his father's approval still meant so damn much to him anyway. He signaled to the ground personnel that he was ready to go just as Jenny burst through the terminal doors.

"I'm sorry," she called, dragging the biggest suitcase he'd ever seen behind her. "We're here." Cooper followed, eyes downcast. A backpack was slung over his shoulders, and he carried another smaller duffel bag that matched Jenny's luggage. "You got the message I left before my phone ran out of battery, right?"

A wave of idiotic relief that his father would call pansy-assed rushed through him. "It kept cutting out. What happened to camp?"

"I changed my mind," Cooper muttered. "Sleepaway camp is stupid. Too many bugs and . . ." His voice cracked. "It's stupid."

"And yet," Jenny said, her voice tight, "somehow we didn't figure that out until I paid the entire nonrefundable registration fee." She aimed the words at Owen, but they all knew she was speaking to Cooper.

"I don't have to go with you to the wedding," Cooper said, his lips barely moving. "You can take Grandma out of the nursing home to stay with me."

Jenny snorted. "So she can burn down the house? I don't think so."

"Dina will be there," Cooper continued. "She'll be happy to have me around."

"I always want you around," Jenny said, sounding miserable. "But—"

Owen stepped forward. He could not stand to see this woman looking like she was on the verge of tears. "Have you ever been on a private jet?" he asked Cooper.

The boy's eyes widened as he shook his head. "We went to Disney World when I was little, but that was the only time I've even been on a regular plane."

"Then you're going to love the Gulfstream."

Cooper started to smile, then darted a glance at Jenny. "Mom?"

"This is Owen's trip," she said quietly. "If he's fine with it, then I'm happy to have you along."

"Awesome." Cooper pumped his fist. "Can I go out now?"

Owen nodded. "James will take you. He's part of my ground crew. Your mom and I will be out in a minute."

James stepped forward and took the duffel bag from Cooper. "Ma'am," he said, turning to Jenny, "may I take your luggage?"

Her grip tightened on the handle of the suitcase. For a few seconds Owen wondered if she was going to bolt out the door. Then she rolled it forward. "Thank you."

"You know we'll only be there for five days," he said, watching James and Cooper walk out into the bright Colorado sunshine. "It looks like you packed enough for a monthlong stay."

Her eyes narrowed. "I wasn't sure what to bring. I want to make a good impression."

His head jerked a little to think she would care what his family thought of her.

"I assumed that was part of the deal," she added quickly, a blush rising to her cheeks. "You're basically paying me a whole lot of money to be your arm candy for the week. That is why I'm going, right?"

He almost laughed at the idea of Jenny thinking of herself as arm candy when to him she was more like the only thing that might get him through the next few days in one piece.

Meant for You

"You're going," he answered, schooling his features into a blank mask, "because you owe me and my family thinks I have a fiancée thanks to the wonders of social media."

Something flashed in her eyes that he couldn't decipher, which was unusual, because normally everything Jenny felt was clear on her delicate features.

It was only there for a moment, and he wanted to freeze time and take the emotion from her, hold it in his hands and study it like a child might do with a seashell, turning it over and over to memorize the texture and patterns until he could make sense of what it meant.

He shouldn't allow himself to want more from Jenny than she was willing to give. She'd made it clear that this was business for her. In spite of how her body might respond to him, she would never give away her heart. Owen had spent half his life trying to wrench love from a man who had none to give him. If it were possible to draw water from a stone, Owen would have found a way.

But stones stayed dry, and he'd learned that lesson too many times to let himself be fooled into believing he could change Jenny.

"What about Cooper?"

He looked out to the tarmac, running a hand through his hair. "He's on the plane already."

"I know the plan wasn't for him to come with us. I'm sorry. Something happened when we got to camp. He saw these boys he knew from school—kids I thought were his friends. Suddenly he refused to stay." Her gaze met his and there was that sliver of vulnerability again that about did him in.

"Did he say why?"

She shook her head. "It was strange and so unlike him. But I couldn't leave him there and get on a plane not knowing he was okay. He doesn't—"

"It's fine." Unable to stop himself, he wrapped his arms around her. She rested her forehead against his chest with a sigh. "It's fine, Jenny," he repeated. Taking the weight of her troubles onto his own shoulders and easing her pain felt like an accomplishment worthy of a standing ovation. "Cooper is a great kid. My family will love him."

"You shouldn't be holding me," she muttered, but pressed so close he could feel her lips moving against his shirtfront. "There's no one watching us."

"The rule covers kissing. This is a hug. You didn't say anything about hugs."

She gave a small laugh. "Obviously, I wasn't planning on Cooper actually witnessing this charade."

Owen cringed. *Charade* was such an ugly word in terms of what was between Jenny and him. "We'll be careful."

"I won't be able to maul you in front of your brother."

It was his turn to laugh. "Was that your plan?"

"As usual, I didn't have a plan." She pulled back. "But we'll come up with one on the plane, okay? The three of us."

"The three of us," he agreed.

Owen wished he could have changed the jet's flight plan en route to take them anywhere but back to his hometown. The three hours spent in the air with Jenny and Cooper felt like they might be the best part of the trip.

Cooper didn't seem bothered at all by the show they were about to put on. He'd been the one to make up most of the details of Owen and Jenny's courtship, even fabricating the exact way Owen had asked her to marry him, in case anyone was curious.

Cooper had spun a story in which Owen had taken Jenny to dinner at her favorite Mexican restaurant. But as they arrived, she discovered that he'd rented the entire place and hired a twelve-piece mariachi band.

He'd gotten down on one knee and proposed over a plate of chicken enchiladas, which Cooper assured Owen was Jenny's favorite dish.

Jenny had smiled and confirmed the truth of that. But when the boy had started down the road of a fireworks display going off while he and Jenny shared a dish of fried ice cream, Owen had laughed and told him to stick with the enchiladas. The kid had a future career as a romance novelist.

He and Cooper spent the rest of the flight trying to outplay each other in a variety of games on their phones while Jenny napped across the aisle. She looked so peaceful sleeping, and Owen knew she needed the rest from months of firing on all cylinders. He wished he could do something more to help—pay for the expansion of the garden center or cover her mother's bills. What was the use of having so damn much money if he couldn't spend it on the people he cared about?

But Jenny was just as stubborn as his father, and also as likely to spurn any assistance he offered. If it wasn't for Cooper's intervention, he doubted she would have even agreed to keeping the ring. In fact, he wouldn't put it past her to try to return it to him after this week. The woman had more pride than sense.

She woke as they landed, stretching slowly, then pulling back her red curls into a loose ponytail. His body reacted to the languid movements. Her guard was down for a few moments, and it made her sexy as hell. More than anything, he wanted to see her wake in his bed some morning, soft and sleepy after a night spent in his arms.

One more dead-end fantasy on his part.

As the jet came to a stop on the landing strip outside Hastings, Cooper turned to his mother. "You have to put on the ring."

She swallowed and shot a glance to Owen. "Right." She reached behind her neck to undo the chain. "Damn it."

"Mom," Cooper groaned. "Swear word."

"I'll owe a dollar to the jar," she mumbled. "But I can't get the clasp to work. Cooper, will you—"

The boy had already grabbed his bag and headed for the exit at the front of the Gulfstream.

"I'll get it," Owen told her.

Jenny looked like she wanted to argue, but turned in the cramped aisle and lifted her hair off her neck.

The intoxicating scent of citrus and lavender drifted up to him and her skin was pale above the collar of her shirt where the necklace sat. The need to lower his mouth to her neck and breathe her in was almost overwhelming. He only unhooked the clasp and allowed it to drop into her hands.

The ring slid off the chain and she slipped it onto her left hand. "Are you ready?" she asked.

He nodded but answered, "Hell, no," earning a smile from her.

"I've got your back, Owen," she told him, and the words were spoken so solemnly they felt like a vow.

"Then I'm as ready as I'll ever be," he answered and followed her out of the plane.

His sister was waiting inside the terminal. Gabby had always been the life of the party in their family, animated and full of so much energy it was hard to contain her. Owen braced for her to launch herself at him, which was her customary greeting since he'd left home.

It didn't matter where he saw Gabby, whether in the mountains of Vermont where she made her home during the off-season or at ski events around the world. Each time she greeted him like they'd been apart for years. He tried not to let more than a few months pass without traveling to see her. Since her return to West Virginia after the accident on the slopes that had effectively ended her professional career, they'd only connected via the phone or FaceTime.

Now she took measured steps toward him and he forced his gaze to remain on her face instead of straying to the slight limp in her left leg. She still wore her blond hair long and straight, falling almost to the middle of her back. Her pale blue eyes and delicate features were at odds with the strength she harnessed while racing down the steepest mountains in the world. She'd built a successful career on her talent as a professional skier, but the way she looked hadn't hurt. She'd just been coming into her own as far as sponsorships and endorsement deals when she got hurt.

He wasn't sure Jenny or Cooper would notice her gait, but Owen knew the injury had changed more than just Gabby's physical abilities. Her identity was wrapped up in how she performed and she could no longer do the one thing that had always given her so much joy.

"Hey there, hot stuff," he said, moving forward to meet her halfway. He hugged her to him but she pulled away far too soon.

"More like lukewarm stuff these days," she said with a laugh that sounded more bitter than amused. "I'm glad you're finally here. You can stop me from killing our annoying, bossy, smug jackass of a brother."

"Do you mean the one who's getting married?" Cooper asked, coming to stand next to Owen.

Gabby's blue eyes widened. "A kid, too? Nice touch, Owen."

Jenny was at his side the next moment. "My son isn't here to be part of our arrangement."

Owen hid his smile as Cooper scoffed. "Of course I'm part of it. It was my idea." He pointed at Gabby. "Wait until you hear what I came up with for how Owen asked Mom to marry him. It's awesome."

"Cooper, this is not a game," Jenny said, her voice tight.

Gabby threw her an assessing look. "It kind of *is* a game."

Owen felt Jenny bristle, and quickly cleared his throat. "Gabby, let me officially introduce you to my fiancée for the week, Jenny Castelli, and her son, Cooper." The last thing he needed going into the wedding was Jenny and his sister at odds. "Cooper had a last-minute change of summer camp plans, so he's with us."

"Nice to meet you, Coop." Gabby held out a hand.

"It's Cooper," Jenny said under her breath.

Cooper smiled at Gabby, who had a way with kids. She'd earned the money for her first pair of racing skis by babysitting neighborhood kids for the whole of one summer. "I like 'Coop.'"

"If you're the brains behind this fiendish operation," Gabby said, leaning a little closer to the boy, "what's in it for you?"

"A vacation to Hawaii," he answered without hesitation. "And we're going to borrow Owen's jet for the trip."

Gabby burst into the familiar cackling laugh Owen hadn't heard for too long. She turned to Jenny. "You've got a great kid."

Jenny nodded, still looking like she might break out with a throat punch comment at any moment.

But Gabby was a master at smoothing rough waters. She'd had enough experience at it while growing up. She gave Jenny a wide grin. "Honestly, I don't care how it started or why you're here now. I'm just glad my brother has someone in his corner this week."

"Gabby." Owen used his best big-brother tone. "Jack and Kristin can't be that bad."

She snorted. "They're worse."

"I can handle them," Jenny said firmly, and something in her tone made Owen study her for a few seconds.

She met his gaze, her brown eyes rich with determination. He let out a slow breath. The tension that had been building inside him since they'd boarded the plane began to dissipate. Maybe he didn't have a future with Jenny, but he believed her when she said she had his back.

He couldn't remember the last time he'd allowed himself to depend on someone. When he wasn't the one offering assistance. An odd sort of tingling radiated through his chest at the knowledge he wasn't alone, even for a short time.

Gabby looked between the two of them and then gave a short nod. "Great to meet you, Sis," Gabby said to Jenny. "Can't wait to spend the week with you."

Jenny flashed a calculating smile. "I think we're going to have some fun together."

The two women walked toward the terminal entrance, heads bent together so intently it looked like they were either plotting his ultimate destruction or coming up with a solution to world hunger.

"This is going to be awesome," Cooper said as he and Owen followed behind.

Owen wondered if *awesome* was another way of saying *unmitigated disaster* in preteen speak, but kept his mouth shut. There was no turning back now.

CHAPTER THIRTEEN

Hastings, West Virginia, was much as Jenny expected—quaint in some parts and rundown in others. Owen's parents lived in a modest, two-story brick home on a tree-lined street just outside Hastings's small downtown area.

Jenny kept her gaze trained out the passenger window of Gabby's Jeep as her pretend soon-to-be sister-in-law pulled into the driveway. Gabby had insisted that Jenny and Cooper drive with her while Owen followed behind in the rental car. She and Cooper had done most of the talking, which was helpful since Jenny's nerves were sucking away most of her brain cells.

A blast of hot, humid air washed over her as she climbed out of the car. She hadn't noticed the oppressive heat at the airport with her nerves humming, but now—

"It feels like we're in an oven," Cooper said, wiping his forehead with the back of his arm.

"This is the difference between a dry climate and a humid climate," Jenny told him. "Think of it as a science experiment."

"Like how hot can a person get before his insides start to boil?"

Jenny ruffled his overlong hair. "You're a kid. You can adapt to anything."

"This isn't even the worst of it," Owen said as he walked over to join them. "You should try living through August."

"At least Mom and Dad have central air now," Gabby added. "Dad refused when we were growing up. He said the fresh air was—"

Gabby stopped and shot a look toward Owen that Jenny couldn't read. "Why the meaningful glances about fresh air?"

Owen shrugged. "I told you I had allergies as a kid. It meant I couldn't keep my windows open."

"His room was a furnace," Gabby confirmed. "I don't know how you ever slept."

"Couldn't they have installed a room air-conditioning unit for you?" Jenny asked.

Owen shared another look with his sister, then turned to Jenny. "It was a long time ago. I turned out fine and now they have AC. Discussion over."

It was far from over, but the muscle clenching in his jaw stopped her from saying anything more. She grabbed his hand, and they walked up the cobblestone path toward the front door, Gabby leading the way with Cooper.

Needing to ground herself and him, Jenny interlaced her fingers with Owen's. She rolled her eyes when he shot her an incredulous look.

"It looks better this way," she said, although that wasn't the reason she'd taken his hand. She also wanted to remind him he wasn't alone, because right now he looked about as happy as if he was meeting a drug lord whose stash he'd just flushed down the toilet.

He quirked a brow but didn't answer as they entered the house. The living room was neat and cozy. The candle burning on the coffee table gave off the sweet smell of vanilla, and framed photos hung on the walls. As a girl, Jenny had been envious of kids with houses like this one. They looked so normal, as if every one was filled with happy families living the American dream.

She'd quickly learned not to judge a person's family dynamics by the hominess of their environment and understood the Daltons were no exception.

A woman who was a doppelgänger for Gabby, only thirty years older, walked out of the kitchen. Her gaze traveled past her daughter and over Cooper, flicking briefly to Jenny before settling on Owen. The flood of love in those blue eyes almost leveled Jenny with its ferocity.

"You're back." Tears welled in her eyes.

"Hey, Mom." Owen seemed slightly confused and more than a little embarrassed by the intensity of his mother's greeting.

She rushed forward but stopped midstride when a door slammed from the back of the house.

"Karen, I'm ready for the steaks." A brawny man, who looked like he could have single-handedly moved a mountain in his heyday, strode into the room and stopped short when he saw Owen. The man's light hair was graying around the temples and his belly had gone soft, but there was no mistaking that he was the ruler of his domain.

His features went tense in the same way Owen's had when they started up the walk to the house, and Jenny knew without a doubt she was looking at Hank Dalton.

Owen's mother hugged him, but her movements had become stiff and halted. "It's nice to see you," she said, the love in her eyes warring with a look of regret Jenny couldn't understand. "I hope you had an easy flight."

"He has a private jet," Hank said, his voice booming. "Of course it was easy. I bet he still can't appreciate the honor that goes into a day of physical labor." He stopped and shook his head slightly, as if he wasn't sure why that outburst had poured forth. It was like riding Owen was a habit so ingrained in his father's makeup that Hank had no control over his own words.

Owen sucked in a breath and tried to pull his hand away from Jenny's but she held fast. No way in hell was she letting go of him now.

"Hank," Karen said through clenched teeth. "He just got here."

"You do realize he built Dalton Enterprises from the kernel of an idea to one of the most respected technology companies in the world?" Hank's gaze zeroed in on Jenny's left hand and she tipped up her chin. The engagement ring seemed to grow warm under Hank's stare.

Jenny let her protective instincts take over. It might only be a temporary bit of make-believe, but at that moment Owen belonged to her, as absolutely as anyone she loved. "That takes more hard work than you can imagine. It's a company that bears your family's name. Your son's name. His reputation."

"It's okay," Owen said quietly.

"And besides running a major corporation and philanthropic foundation," Jenny continued, taking a step toward Owen's father, "he's helping me to expand the garden center I own." She dropped her voice to an overdramatic stage whisper. "Which involves physical labor."

"Dad, this is Jenny." Owen tugged her back to his side. "My fiancée."

There were no words for all the ways Jenny wanted to take down Hank Dalton after only having the briefest of interactions with him.

But she gave him a dazzling smile and stuck out her hand. "It's lovely to meet you," she said, her tone sickeningly sweet. "Owen told me so much about you."

To her surprise, Hank threw back his head and laughed, the rich sound echoing in the awkward silence of the room. She looked around to make sure she hadn't missed anything. Owen's mom and Gabby looked as stunned as she felt. Cooper made a funny face, and Owen . . . well, she didn't dare look at Owen.

Hank took a step forward and enveloped her hand with both of his. "You've got the personality to go with that hair," he said, his grin wide. He turned to Cooper. "Is this your boy?"

"I'm Cooper Castelli, sir," Cooper said, making eye contact just as she'd taught him. But his voice was unsure, his nervousness obvious. She wondered how Hank Dalton would react and steeled herself to go on the defensive once more.

Even if Owen hadn't told her about his father's military career, it was clear from the high-and-tight cut and the Semper Fi emblem on the front of his T-shirt that his time in the marines remained a big part of Hank's identity.

He gave Cooper an approving nod. "Nice to meet you, son. Let me know if you want to get a haircut while you're visiting."

It was clear Hank was teasing, but Cooper's eyes widened. "Um . . . maybe, sir."

"You've got manners and backbone," Hank told him, and Cooper's shoulder straightened a little under the unexpected praise. "That's a great combination." Jenny tried not to be affected by another subtle display of how her son clearly valued male approval. "Must be because your mom raised you right."

Cooper nodded. "She's the best, sir."

"Don't ever forget that, son," Hank said and winked at Jenny.

She felt herself return his grin. How was this gruffly sweet bear of a man the same person who minutes earlier had been so blatantly dissing Owen?

Abruptly Owen dropped her hand, as if with a giggle she'd changed sides from his to his father's.

Before she could find a way to reassure him of her loyalty, Karen moved closer and took her hands. "It's lovely to have you here." She smiled at Cooper. "Both of you. We didn't realize Owen had gotten serious with a woman until we saw your picture on Facebook. I would have thought he'd tell us first but . . ."

Jenny could almost hear Owen grinding his teeth. "I explained that I didn't know those photos were going to be posted. I would have called first if—"

"We understand you're busy," his mom interrupted. "We're happy to have you here now. Are you sure you won't stay with us? There's plenty of room."

"I've rented a place not far from here."

Karen pressed her lips together but nodded. "Jack will be glad to catch up with you. They should be here any minute. He and Kristin have been so busy, but now that he's—"

"I'm going to put the steaks on the grill," Hank interrupted. "Gabby and Cooper can set the table."

It was clear Hank was used to giving orders and after Jenny nodded, Cooper followed Gabby and Owen's father into the kitchen.

"He really is glad to have you here," Karen said quietly, laying a hand on Owen's forearm.

"Mom, don't."

Before Karen could reply, the front door opened and another big, blond hulk of a man came into the room. With the exception of Owen, the members of the family looked so similar to each other they could have been the poster family for a strong, sturdy Scandinavian gene pool.

Maybe that had something to do with why Owen never fit into his family. As a girl, Jenny had spent hours gazing into the mirror trying to figure out which features she'd inherited from the father she never knew. What was it like for Owen to be like a changeling child among his siblings? Something niggled at the back of her mind and she sucked in a breath at the sudden realization surging through her brain.

Owen went rigid next to her, obviously misinterpreting her reaction. She took a closer look at his brother. Jack Dalton was handsome, his thick hair a little longer than a military cut and his features chiseled. He was as broad as a bodybuilder, with muscles corded through his arms and bulging under the black T-shirt stretched tight across his chest.

"There's the whiz kid," he said as his gaze landed on Owen. His voice was so deep and rumbling it almost sounded forced.

"Hey, Jack." Owen smiled but didn't move forward. "Congratulations."

Jenny's stomach took a nosedive as Jack held open the screen door for the tall, leggy raven-haired beauty following him into the house. She'd imagined Owen's former fiancée as a mild-mannered wallflower, but Kristin was a knockout.

The pale yellow sundress she wore stopped just above her knees and hugged curves that made Jenny think the woman either had a body a supermodel would envy or she'd invested heavily in shapewear. Unfortunately, she doubted it was the latter.

"Owen," Kristin said with so much affection Jenny hated her on principle. "I'm thrilled you're here." Unlike Gabby, Kristin had no problem launching herself at Owen and hugging him tightly. "We have a ton of things to catch up on," Kristin told him, her voice a breathy trill.

"You look great, K," Owen answered, and Jenny swallowed down the growl that formed in the back of her throat. He had a nickname for his ex-fiancée.

"I'm Jenny," she said, snaking her hand around Owen's waist and pressing herself to his side. "Owen's fiancée."

Kristin's hazel eyes dimmed slightly but her smile remained in place. "You two sure kept a low profile. It's difficult to believe Owen got engaged without any of us even knowing."

"He did. To me." She reached up on tiptoe to plant a smacking kiss on Owen's cheek. "We're mad about each other. Isn't that right, pookie?"

She couldn't read the look he gave her, but his mouth quirked at the sides as if he was amused. He hooked an arm around her neck and pressed a kiss on the top of her head. Even though she knew it was for show, she felt it straight to her toes. Just a simple touch of his lips and he could wreck her.

Jack moved forward and took her hand. "Welcome to the family," he said, pumping her arm. "You're not my brother's normal type."

Jenny couldn't stop her gaze from darting to Kristin, and a few moments of awkward silence descended on the group.

"Jenny is perfect for me," Owen told his brother as Jack continued to study her.

The burly man nodded. "Kristin's got a lot crammed into this week, but let's plan a night to go out for drinks. We'll hit the Red Hornet. We're having the rehearsal dinner there, too."

Kristin's smile grew bright again. "They named a drink after Jack," she said. "The JKrita. It's their featured special this week. Isn't that the coolest?"

"It's great, K," Owen answered.

Every time he called her "K," Jenny's temper flared. "You know in Denver—" she began.

"Signature drinks are a big trend," Owen interrupted. She'd been about to tell them that the hospital on the south end of the city had just named their new surgery wing for Dalton Enterprises after Owen's foundation made a large donation to the facility's capital campaign. Why wasn't he shouting his accomplishments from the rooftops to these people?

Kristin nodded. "People might think Hastings is just a tiny dot on the map, but we're up on the latest styles."

"Let's go see what's going on out back," Owen suggested. "I want you guys to meet Jenny's son, Cooper."

"I thought it was just the two of you this week," Kristin said with a frown that Jenny would have described as petulant.

"There was a mix-up with the camp he was supposed to attend," Jenny told her. "If it's a problem adding another person to the guest list for the reception, I'm sure he'll be fine at the rental house for a few hours."

"No worries," Jack answered for his fiancée. "We've got plenty of room."

Kristin didn't look convinced, so Jenny added, "You can sit Cooper and me wherever. I'm sure Owen will be at the head table with the bridal party."

Next to her, Owen cleared his throat, and Jack dropped his gaze to the floor.

"What?" she asked.

Kristin's smile brightened in a way that made Jenny's hackles rise. "We're having a small bridal party and there was only room for Jack's high school friends and a few guys from his squad. Being a marine bonds them, you know, like family."

"Except Owen *is* family," Jenny said.

"It's fine, Jenny." Owen gave her shoulder a little squeeze.

"Is Gabby a bridesmaid?"

"Well, yes," Kristin admitted. "But—"

"Owen understands." Jack's unwavering tone was an exact replica of his father's.

"I understand," Owen agreed, but his voice sounded hollow.

"Let's have some dinner," Jack said, chucking Owen on the arm a little too forcefully for Jenny's taste.

As he and Kristin moved toward the kitchen, Jenny tried to pull Owen aside.

"It's fine," he repeated, not meeting her eyes.

"Your family—" she began, but he shook his head.

"I don't want to talk about them now, Jen. Yes, they have issues. But you and I have no room to talk. Our relationship is a sham. The whole week is for show. Can we just get through this evening and head to the rental house?"

She fought the urge to flinch as his words cut through her. She wanted to argue, but that wasn't her place.

Their engagement was fake. His feelings for her were pretend. Given those two things, she had no right to intervene in his family's dysfunction.

"Fine," she agreed, and feeling more alone than she had in years, followed him toward the back of the house.

Money might not be able to buy happiness, but it could arrange a stocked refrigerator in a rented house with no problem.

Owen was eternally grateful as he pulled out a beer and dug in one of the drawers to find an opener. It had been nearly ten before they'd gotten to the rental. Jenny had immediately gone upstairs to unpack and get Cooper settled.

He hadn't thought dinner at his parents' would last so late, but Jack had suggested a game of badminton after dessert. Although his mother had never participated in family game nights, everyone else had mile-long competitive streaks.

For Owen, that meant growing up had been the equivalent of being picked last in gym class each time they started a backyard game of whiffle ball or badminton or even H-O-R-S-E at the basketball hoop. His father and Jack always did a round of rock, paper, scissors to decide who got Gabby on their team and who was stuck with Owen.

He'd become so desensitized to the continual insult that he hadn't even realized how fucked up it was until Jack made the suggestion again tonight. With an outraged gasp, Jenny had immediately shut Jack down, claiming both Owen and Cooper for her team. His father had decided to sit out, so that left Gabby, Jack, and Kristin as a team.

Cooper wasn't much more athletic than Owen had been as a kid, but Jenny shouted encouragement for every shot her son took. Owen had never found her more beautiful.

Even his father had cheered the boy from the sidelines, which Owen found difficult to believe given how hard Hank had ridden him as a kid.

Maybe it was the long-overdue indignation that spurred Owen on, or the fact that he'd grown into his body and athleticism as a man. He no longer felt like the weak link in every sport. Although it was a simple lawn game, Owen took it as seriously as if they were playing for an Olympic medal.

Jack was no different, and the match became a heated contest complete with trash talking, a few elbows through the net, and general unsportsmanlike conduct on both sides. Gabby and Kristin took the whole thing in stride, used to the competitive nature of everything the Daltons did.

Owen had expected Jenny to get into the fray. He had felt her anger at the dynamics of his family attempting to bubble up to the surface most of the night. But while she'd first been amused, in the end she'd seemed more than a little annoyed. She'd missed an easy lob over the net that cost them the final point and allowed his brother to triumph. Owen had a sneaking suspicion she'd whiffed on purpose.

To Owen's surprise, his father had cut short Jack's typical gloating victory dance, chastising both Owen and Jack for setting a bad example for Cooper. Jack had seemed shocked to find himself on the receiving end of Hank's blustery temper. As was her way, Owen's mother tried to smooth over the rough waters, quickly bringing out old photo albums to show Jenny and Cooper.

Of course, that hadn't done much to rectify the situation since Owen showed up so infrequently in the images.

"I always thought I wanted a big family." Jenny's voice cut into the quiet of the darkened kitchen. "Yours makes me grateful I didn't have one."

He took a long drink of beer, then reached back into the fridge and handed one to her. "I'm pretty sure we take dysfunction to new heights."

"Or lows," she murmured.

"How's Cooper?" The boy had been silent most of the drive to the rental house and had immediately gone up to his bedroom. "I bet he regrets bailing on summer camp after tonight."

She shook her head. "He's just tired. Although it's hard to watch someone get treated the way your family treats you, Owen. It's so blatant."

He didn't want to acknowledge the truth of her words and did his best to ignore the pain that squeezed his heart. He'd become accustomed to the dull ache of tacit rejection that always accompanied his visits home, but having witnesses made it like feel like a knife blade.

"It was a mistake for you to come here," he said quietly.

She studied him as she drank her beer. "Because I cut into your quality time with your future sister-in-law?"

He laughed. "I don't want time with Kristin. But I'm also not sure I want witnesses to my fucked-up relationship with my dad and brother. When I'm here by myself, it just feels normal."

She moved closer and he backed up against the counter. His emotions were strung too tight to let Jenny into his space. "It's *not* normal," she said quietly.

"It's my normal," he countered. "It's what I know. When you challenge them, I notice it in a different way."

"Isn't that why I'm here?" She eased another inch toward him, placing her beer on the counter. "To make some waves."

"I thought so." He shook his head. "But now it's screwing with me as much as it is my family."

"You haven't been back in a while," she answered. "Maybe what's different isn't me. It's you. You're not the same person you were as a kid."

He set his beer next to hers and scrubbed a hand over his face. "Why is that so damn hard to remember when I'm in that house?"

Her hand brushed his arm and the touch felt particularly electric. He should walk away right now. He was in no shape to handle Jenny or hold himself back from anything she might offer.

She was toe to toe with him now, so close that her citrusy scent enveloped him. But her touch remained feather light, one finger tracing small figure eights along his arm. The only sounds were their breathing and the hum of the refrigerator.

"Do you want to remember?" she asked after a moment, her voice pitched low. "Or do you want to forget?"

"Forget," he said, and before he could talk himself out of it, he wrapped an arm around her waist and pulled her close. The fact that she didn't hesitate only made him want her more. He couldn't hide the raw desire he felt. He claimed her mouth, deepened the kiss, and left no question about what he wanted.

She met his need with her own, and it wasn't long before nothing mattered except this woman and the way she made him feel. She pulled at his shirt, and he tugged it over his head as she did the same with hers. Lifting her, he turned to seat her on the edge of the counter. Then he bent and licked her nipple through the delicate lace of her pale pink bra.

She let out a little whimper and arched toward him, and he cupped her other breast in his palm.

"Remind me why we didn't do this before," he said as he pulled her jeans down over her hips and peeled them from her legs.

"You wanted to think I was a good girl," she told him, her voice a throaty rasp.

His fingers stilled, and she whimpered in protest. "I'm not going to talk if it makes you stop."

"You," he told her, claiming her mouth again, "are good for me."

"We both know that isn't true, but I'm not going to argue. For the love of God, tell me you have a condom."

He pulled his wallet from the back pocket of his jeans and took out a packet. "Are you sure, Jenny?"

She met his gaze, her eyes so dark he couldn't see where the iris ended and the pupil began. "Now, Owen. I can't wait any longer."

He ruthlessly shut down the part of his brain screaming a warning that this was too much. He was a guy, for Christ's sake. He could handle no-strings sex with a woman. He welcomed no-strings sex.

He shrugged out of his jeans and boxers, then rolled on the condom. As he moved closer, Jenny grazed her nails over his shoulders and back. It was enough to almost send him over the edge, and strings or not, he refused to go there alone. He drove into her and set the rhythm hard and fast, spurred on by every moan and whimper that escaped Jenny's beautiful mouth.

When he lifted his hand to gently squeeze her taut nipple, he felt her shatter in his arms. It was the most powerful thing he'd ever experienced and sent him reeling into his own oblivion.

He held her as their breathing returned to normal, but when he started to nuzzle her neck, she pushed him away.

"We had rules." She hopped off the counter and tried not to make eye contact with him, suddenly far too self-conscious.

He moved to the trash can to take care of the condom, put on his jeans, then picked up both of their shirts from the floor and held out hers.

She grabbed at it, but he didn't let go. "Jenny, look at me."

When she did, her brown eyes were fierce but he could see the hint of vulnerability she worked so hard to keep buried. The fact that it was there soothed him as much as her touch, and he made his voice gentle as he spoke.

"You and I were friends before anything else, and we can be again."

She let out a disbelieving laugh.

"We both know there is no future for us." The words felt like sandpaper across his throat, but he forced himself to keep going. "This is you doing a favor for me."

"That wasn't pity sex. I wanted you, Owen." Her eyes blazed. "I want you."

"I wasn't talking about what just happened," he told her, letting her have the shirt and shrugging into his. "But my ego appreciates you clarifying that. I meant this week. When it's over, we're going to end our engagement." Now he barked out a harsh laugh. "At the rate my family is showing their crazy, you'll have the perfect excuse for not wanting to tie yourself to me."

"I wouldn't do that."

"But you're going to," he countered. "Because this is all pretend."

She stilled for a moment as she buttoned her shirt. "All of it?"

No. A piercing denial ripped through his body. Even now, he wanted to prove exactly how real this was for him. Minutes after pulling out of her, he was already hard again.

"You know it's how it has to be," he said as an answer. His heart beat a thunderous rhythm in his chest, as if that traitorous organ was conspiring with the rest of him to once again turn his world upside down for this woman. He marveled at his lack of self-preservation instincts.

She stared at him for a moment, then gave a sharp nod. "So the sex means nothing?"

"It means we're physically compatible." He used the tone he employed when speaking to his board of directors. It was distant, precise, and the exact opposite of the riot exploding inside him.

But Jenny seemed to take it in stride, which meant he was doing the right thing. He wasn't going down this road with her only to end up with his heart in a messy pile on the floor. Despite what his body wanted, his brain was in charge and it was going to keep him safe.

"At the end of the day," he said dully, "I'm paying you to be my fiancée, which means—"

"That this was a one-off," she said, her voice as matter-of-fact as his. "The rules still stand."

"Fine."

"Fine," she repeated.

There was nothing keeping her there, but she didn't move. Was it as difficult for her to break the connection between them as it was for him?

After almost a minute of silence, he said, "Go to bed, Jenny. We're fine."

She opened her mouth as if to argue, then shut it again and hurried past him.

The kitchen was suddenly too quiet, much like his life when Jenny wasn't a part of it. He opened the refrigerator, the light making him squint, took another beer from the top shelf, then headed for the family room. He couldn't stand to walk upstairs into the master bedroom knowing Jenny would be sleeping across the hall.

He'd spent most of the first two years after he founded Dalton Enterprises sleeping on an old sofa in the corner of his makeshift office outside the lab space he'd leased. The overstuffed couch in the rental house looked just as comfortable. It was just what Owen needed to remind himself that no matter how far he'd come, he would always be the man struggling to find his place in the world.

CHAPTER FOURTEEN

"Did someone turn up the sun a few notches?"

Jenny threw a glance at Owen, who was shading his eyes from the morning light even while wearing a baseball cap pulled low and with polarized sunglasses covering his eyes.

He'd been in the shower when she'd gotten up this morning, but based on the empty beer bottles on the coffee table and the way the couch cushions had been arranged, he'd had a late night after she'd gone to bed. Not that she'd slept. It felt like she'd tossed and turned for hours, reliving the memory of his hands on her. She was still working to convince herself both that it had been a bad idea to give in to her desire for Owen and that she wouldn't do it again.

"It's called a hangover." She spoke quietly enough that Cooper, who was walking behind them toward the car, couldn't hear. "You need greasy food and a milkshake."

"Great," Owen muttered, stopping at the edge of the sidewalk. "Let's get breakfast on the way to the airport. We can be wheels up in an hour and on our way back to Colorado." He took off his hat and wiped a hand across his brow. "It's not even nine and already I'm roasting. The last thing I want to do is play golf with my brother and his friends."

"Would you rather be going to a bridal shower for your future sister-in-law?" Jenny lowered her sunglasses on her nose and gave Owen a look over the top of them. "According to Gabby, we have to play party games."

"Which is why we should—"

"Stop, Owen." She put a hand on his arm. She wanted to do more. After last night, she wanted to wrap her arms around his neck and pull him down for a kiss. She wanted to recapture the way she'd felt at that moment, as if all of the crap in both of their lives didn't matter. As if nothing mattered but pressing her body to his.

But last night had been great sex. Nothing more. He'd actually said those words. While they'd about killed her, she understood. Just like she understood he needed to see out this week with his family. She might not be able to be the woman Owen wanted or needed, but she could give him this. "We're not leaving. You're staying for the wedding and we both know it."

A muscle twitched in his jaw but he nodded. "Thank you for being here with me."

She forced out a laugh. "You're paying me."

"Right." He shifted so that she had to drop her hand. "Cooper, are you ready for a morning of driving the golf cart?"

"How fast can it go?" her son asked as he climbed into the backseat.

"We'll have to test that out," Owen answered.

"Not too fast," Jenny cautioned automatically, earning a groan from Cooper and a small smile from Owen.

"I'll take care of him," Owen told her as he started the car.

Emotion rose thick like molasses in Jenny's throat. She rolled down the window and stuck her hand out as they drove through the neighborhood toward the Daltons' house. The morning air was already heavy, and she could almost feel the moisture against her outstretched fingers. The climate of West Virginia was so different from what she was used to in arid Colorado, and it only made her more aware of how narrow her life had been.

They hadn't had the money for vacations when she was a girl, and then she'd been focused on making a life for her son. There had been no time for the vacations and life-expanding trips other women she knew had taken in their early twenties. Her mother had splurged for a trip to Disney when she retired. That was the only time before this week that Jenny had been on a plane.

She wanted more for Cooper. She had no doubt Owen would take care of him, and it embarrassed her how much that meant to her. It's what Cooper deserved, a man in his life to teach him to golf and throw a ball and cast a line and all the other little things boys with great dads took for granted. Cooper deserved a man who would do the things a father should.

She hated to admit that she wanted a man in her life. Not just any man—Owen. Last night had been amazing, but also a mistake. A friendly romp between the sheets was one thing, but sex with Owen was more. It had meant something to her that she couldn't even put into words, but she knew risking her heart could destroy both of them if she wasn't careful.

Her need was like the sultry air of summer in the rolling hills that surrounded Owen's hometown. Sometimes it was difficult to take a breath and not have her desire for him threaten to choke her.

But it was nothing to him. She was nothing. She'd lost her chance and she wouldn't ask for another one because she'd just end up hurting him again. Owen deserved better than that—better than her.

He was quiet as he drove, and she wondered if he regretted what they'd done. Hell, she'd been the one to set up the rules. Yet at the first opportunity, she'd tossed them aside.

She had to be stronger. She was there to help Owen and she couldn't do that if she spent all her time mooning after him like a teenage girl with her first crush.

They pulled in front of his parents' house a few minutes later, and Cooper hopped out to open the back cargo area. Hank was waiting on the front porch, a set of golf clubs at his side. He slung the clubs over his shoulder and started toward the SUV.

"I seriously need some greasy food right now," Owen muttered, lifting the sunglasses to the top of his head. "Or a drink."

"It's a few hours of hitting around a ball. You'll be fine." She pointed a finger at him. "Just don't go after your brother with a golf club."

He smiled at her ridiculous warning. "I'll try to restrain myself."

She unfastened her seat belt and leaned over the console, using one finger to turn his face toward hers. His jaw was rough with stubble and the feel of it sent another wave of desire pulsing through her. She kissed him on the mouth, gentle and slow, and only moved her head back when she felt some of the tension ease out of him.

"What about the rules?" he murmured against her lips.

"Your father is watching," she whispered, not knowing or particularly caring if that was true. "It's all part of the show."

She kissed him again and felt his smile against her lips because they both knew she was lying.

"It's definitely better than a milkshake," he told her, his dark eyes gentle on hers. "Thank you."

She started to remind him that he shouldn't thank her. For all intents and purposes, taking care of Owen was her job this week, and he was compensating her far more than she deserved.

Instead, she pretended that he was simply grateful for her taking care of him the way a woman took care of the man she loved.

The man she loved.

The thought, unbidden and unwelcome, made her jerk away as if she'd touched her mouth to a hot flame instead of Owen's firm lips.

Opening the door handle, she lurched out of the car. Thick hands wrapped around her arms. "Whoa there, missy. Where's the fire?" Hank gave her a knowing smile as if he could read the incendiary thoughts inside her head.

She glanced over her shoulder and saw Owen flip his sunglasses down over his eyes before turning to look at her. She might not be able to read his expression, but the frustration radiating from him was clear.

Why did it bother her that the kiss felt real to both of them? Her real feelings mixed with their pretend engagement farce to make her emotions a complete jumble.

Hank gave her arms a small squeeze and guided her to the sidewalk in front of the house with surprising gentleness. "You girls have fun today."

"'Bye, Mom," Cooper said as he climbed back into the SUV.

"Put on sunscreen," she called lamely, earning another smile from Hank.

"We'll take care of him," he said, sounding just like Owen, who kept his eyes straight ahead.

She stood on the edge of the Daltons' yard and watched the car pull away, Cooper waving from the backseat. He seemed to be taking everything that happened this week in stride, likely keeping his eye on the prize of that Hawaii vacation he wanted.

After a few moments, she turned for the house. Karen was waiting at the front door by the time she got there. "Come on in. Kristin called with a last-minute request for cream-filled cupcakes that they only have at the bakery in Jasper, which is the next town over. Gabby went to pick them up, so we have a few minutes to visit before she gets back."

Jenny blew out a breath even as her stomach clenched. She had her own reasons for wanting to speak privately with Owen's mom, but she hadn't been prepared to have the conversation this morning.

"I'd like that," she said, pasting a smile on her face and following Karen into the kitchen.

"Have a seat," the older woman told her. "I made a fresh pot of coffee and baked a batch of my special tea cookies." She tsked softly.

"I'd offered to bring them to the shower, but Kristin had her heart set on the store-bought cupcakes."

Jenny slid into the same chair she'd sat in for dinner last night, thinking that her mother would have liked Karen Dalton. "Kristin seems to have very particular ideas about every aspect of this wedding."

"Oh, yes," Karen agreed with a laugh. "I think she's been planning her wedding day since she was a girl." She pulled two mugs from the cabinet and filled them with coffee. "I guess that's the way of most young girls."

"I don't think I ever planned an imaginary wedding," Jenny admitted, adding a spoonful of sugar from the dish on the table to her coffee. "Although I did have a whole stable full of fantasy horses."

Karen laughed again as she sat across from her. "You sound like my Gabby. Have you and Owen set a date for your wedding?" She shook her head. "I wish he'd told us about you sooner. He was always so closed off from the rest of us."

Maybe because you allowed him to be ostracized, Jenny wanted to answer, but took a sip of coffee and said nothing. She had a deeper grievance to air on Owen's behalf, but for once wasn't sure how to broach the subject.

"It's good he's found you." Jenny could hear love, regret, and guilt clashing in Karen's voice. "He deserves—"

"Why haven't you told him?" Jenny asked, unable to hear that she was what Owen deserved.

Not at this moment when she was about to force his mother to reveal a secret that could destroy their entire family.

"Tell him what?" Karen's fingers tightened around her coffee mug.

"About his father."

Karen's tinkle of laughter was so sharp it could have cut glass. "My husband has always been tough on Owen, but—"

"I'm not talking about Hank," Jenny said calmly, "and we both know it." Based on Karen's reaction and the fact that she didn't immediately deny the veiled accusation, Jenny knew she'd been right in her hunch that Hank Dalton wasn't Owen's biological father. It didn't give her any comfort to have an explanation for the role Owen had unknowingly been forced to play in his family.

"No one," Karen said, her eyes filling with tears, "has ever guessed. I don't understand how you realized it so quickly. Does Owen suspect—" She broke off, a little sob escaping her lips. "Have you told him?"

Jenny shook her head. She wasn't even sure if it was her place to confront his mother, but Owen's relationship with Hank Dalton had shaped so much of his identity. And all of it had been based on a lie. "He only knows that the man he thinks of as his father finds him lacking in almost every respect. From what I can tell, he's spent his whole life trying to prove himself to your husband, but he was never going to measure up because he isn't truly Hank's son."

Karen set her mug roughly on the table, coffee sloshing over the side. "Hank loves Owen," she said through clenched teeth. "He's strict and demanding, but he loves him and he's raised him without ever hinting that theirs wasn't a true father-son bond."

"A bond?" Jenny snorted. "Is that what you call Owen being made to feel like a second-class citizen in his own family?" Her mother-bear instincts kicked in hard. She couldn't imagine allowing anyone to treat Cooper the way Owen had been treated by the man he called Dad. "How could you have stood by all those years and let it happen?"

Karen's head snapped back as if Jenny had actually struck her. She swiped at her cheeks with her fingers. "I protected Owen the best way I could," she said, her eyes suddenly fierce and clear. "Do you know what he would have gone through growing up with no father?"

"I do," Jenny shot back. "I don't remember my father, and my son counts only me and my mother as his family." She leaned forward and bit down on her lip to keep her emotions in check. "We struggled when I was growing up and a lot of times it sucked. But my mother loved me. I never had to question that."

"Owen doesn't question my love." Karen spoke the words like she was willing them to be true. "Things are different in a small town like Hastings. I was eighteen and rebelling against my strict parents. The man who is Owen's—" She shook her head. "No. I will not say he is Owen's father. Hank has always been a father to all of our children. The man who got me pregnant was trouble. He was arrested during the time we were together, and I broke up with him. I found out I was pregnant on the day he went to prison."

She pushed back from the table suddenly, moved to the sink for a dish towel. Lifting her coffee mug with still-trembling fingers, she wiped at the coffee that had spilled on the table.

"I'm sorry," Jenny told her. Trent had been an idiot and she'd hated him for breaking her heart. Yet she couldn't imagine how Karen must have felt carrying the child of a man who was on his way to jail.

"Hank was literally the boy next door," Karen said quietly. "He'd enlisted the day we graduated high school and was getting ready to leave for boot camp. He found me on the back porch step of my parents' house, crying my eyes out. I told him the whole story and he asked me to marry him on the spot."

Jenny swallowed. "Wow."

"We went to the courthouse the next day. Hank told everyone he'd been in love with me for years and the fact that he was leaving finally gave him the nerve to tell me. He convinced everyone . . ." She laughed. "Even me—that it was a whirlwind courtship. My parents were so relieved to have me away from my bad boy that they didn't ask questions. They gave us five hundred dollars to go to Myrtle Beach on our honeymoon. We spent a long weekend there before Hank left for Parris Island, and Owen was born a few weeks late, so it all seemed to work out."

She dropped into the chair again, wringing the dish towel between her hands. "I *know* Hank loves Owen. He was so gentle when Owen was a newborn. Every night Hank would carry him back and forth along the hallway in our tiny house on base until he fell asleep. He read stories and sang lullabies and—"

"When did that stop?" Jenny couldn't help but ask. "It did stop, Karen. You have to see that. Was it when Jack was born?"

Karen squeezed the towel harder. "Maybe. But it became more noticeable as Owen got older. Other than his coloring, Owen looks like my side of the family. My brothers both have dark hair and eyes. No one questioned the fact that he didn't resemble Hank." She raised a brow. "Not until you, anyway. Jack and Gabby favor their father, both physically and in temperament. I think Hank was worried that Owen was going to take after his biological father if we weren't tough with him."

"Owen is one of the most honorable people I know," Jenny said fiercely.

"He always was. But I followed Hank's lead and I may never be able to make amends for the way it affected my relationship with Owen. I was afraid if I challenged Hank, then he'd tell Owen the truth and . . ." She squeezed shut her eyes. "I couldn't risk that."

"This family has shaped Owen," Jenny said. "Everything he's done has been an attempt to prove his worth to his father. You have to tell him the truth. It's not too late."

"He'll hate me." Karen suddenly looked far older than she was. "He'll hate Hank. What if he goes looking for his biological father?"

"Is that man still in Hastings?"

Karen shook her head. "No, and I don't want anything to do with him." She studied Jenny for a long moment. "How did you know so quickly?"

Jenny wasn't sure how to explain it—instinct, a suspicious nature, or some indefinable connection to Owen that made her recognize what no one else had seen. "There was a look you gave Owen when we came into the house that vanished the moment Hank walked into the room. So much love replaced with an equal amount of guilt."

She sipped her coffee. "From what I've pieced together from Owen, his father and Jack were the two who had trouble with him. Gabby was his ally, and you . . ." She paused, then finished. "You let it happen."

Karen began to cry again, silent tears that almost broke Jenny's heart. "This is not a conversation I ever expected to have, but now I'm even more thankful he has you," she said, her voice cracking. "I know things weren't easy for him, but I did what I thought was right. Hank did, too. He loves Owen, even if he never learned how to properly show it. Owen deserves a woman who can give him the kind of love we weren't able to."

Jenny shook her head. She couldn't be the person Karen described and Owen needed. She was nowhere near that person. "I have to tell—"

"Mom, I'm home." Gabby's voice came from the front of the house and a moment later Jenny heard a door slam shut.

Karen grabbed her hand. "You can't say anything. Please. I'm begging you."

"Don't ask that of me."

"It's for Owen." Karen stood and wiped her cheeks, turning her back to the kitchen doorway. "This will break him, Jenny."

"Hey, ladies," Gabby called as she walked into the kitchen.

Jenny watched Karen take a breath, paste a smile on her face, then turn to her daughter. It was a classic mom coping mechanism. Karen would hold it together in front of her child no matter what.

"Did you get the cupcakes, sweetie?"

"Yup. I'm going to please Queen Kristin today." Gabby moved to the table and looked between her mother and Jenny. "Is everything all right?"

"Yes," Karen answered, wrapping an arm around Gabby's shoulder. "We were just talking about . . ."

Jenny wanted to ignore the silent plea in the woman's eyes but couldn't deny that Owen's mother had done what she thought was right. Even if it was so very wrong.

"My mom," Jenny finished. "She has Alzheimer's, which has progressed quickly over the past year. She lives in a nursing home now." She paused, allowing the emotion she felt toward the situation with the Daltons to seep into her voice. "It's been difficult."

"I'm sorry," Gabby said.

"We're managing," Jenny said, "and Owen is a big help." She clapped a hand to her mouth as Gabby shot her an incredulous look. It probably seemed like Jenny was laying it on too thick, but the truth was, having Owen in her life these past few weeks had made everything seem easier. Better. Right.

"We should probably get to the shower," she said quickly, taking her empty mug to the sink so she didn't have to look either Karen or Gabby in the eye. "I don't know Kristin well, but I'm guessing she won't appreciate anyone being late."

Gabby chuckled. "She won't appreciate anyone, period."

"Gabrielle," her mother scolded, "be nice."

"Doing my best, Mom."

Karen gave Jenny's arm a squeeze as they walked to Gabby's Jeep. "Please."

"I won't say anything until after the wedding," Jenny told the woman, compelled to make the promise because of how the news would rock Owen. "But he needs to know."

Karen gave a tight nod. "We'll find a good time to talk to him."

Jenny wasn't sure how she would keep this secret from Owen or if it was the right thing to do. She tried to tell herself that she'd done her part by confronting Karen. She and Owen would go their separate ways after this week, and it would no longer be her problem. That thought only made her chest ache harder.

CHAPTER FIFTEEN

Owen knew Jenny had made the comment about not going after his brother with a golf club as a joke, but he was sorely tempted by the time they returned to his parents' house.

"Is Mom back yet?" Cooper asked as he carried Hank's clubs toward the garage. Somewhere during the round of golf, the boy and Owen's father had become great friends. Hank had patiently shown Cooper how to set up a shot, explained when different clubs were used, and taught him the art of putting. "I want to show her my swing."

Jack had made a couple of asshole remarks about Cooper's lack of hand-eye coordination. They were subtle, mostly centered around how Owen would be the perfect role model for the boy since they had *so* much in common. Cooper seemed to take the comments as compliments, making Owen's affection for him grow exponentially.

To Owen's surprise, Hank had been the one to shut down Jack's veiled attack. Jack had seemed shocked, clearly unused to any kind of reprimand from their father. He'd gone into good ol' boy mode, with a few overly enthusiastic back slaps and guffaws to play off the whole thing. But Owen had seen the way his brother's grip tightened on the shaft of the golf club, and he'd missed an easy two-foot putt on the sixteenth green.

Gabby and Jenny were in the kitchen listening to Kristin have what appeared to be a full-blown meltdown, sobbing about the color of the bridesmaid dresses. "They're supposed to be a beautiful shade of apricot," she said by way of explanation, "and instead the color is bright orange." She let out a little whimper and added, "Like Jenny's hair."

Jenny rolled her eyes when Owen met her gaze across the kitchen, even as she awkwardly patted Kristin on the shoulder.

Seeing the two women seated next to each other, opposites in almost every way, Owen wondered what had ever attracted him to Kristin. Had she always been shallow and narcissistic, or was that the role she'd taken on to make herself the perfect complement for his sanctimonious brother?

"Babe," Jack drawled as he took a can of beer out of their parents' fridge, "pull it together. Who gives a shit what color the bridesmaids are wearing?"

Kristin slammed her palms to the table. "I do," she cried. "It matters to me, Jack, so it should be important to you, too. This wedding is going to be the talk of Hastings for years, and I want it to be perfect. Orange isn't perfect." Her watery gaze shot to Jenny. "No offense."

Jenny raised an eyebrow in response.

Jack popped the top on his beer and took a long swig. "We run this town," he assured his bride-to-be. "People won't even notice the bridesmaids once you walk down the aisle. Trust me, the wedding is going to be killer."

Killer. That was one way to describe the joining of two people for the rest of their lives.

"How are *your* wedding plans, Jenny?" Gabby asked sweetly, and Owen inwardly cringed. Both Jack and Kristin looked at his sister as if she'd just thrown a giant pile of dog poop onto the middle of the tile floor.

Jenny shot a fierce glare across the table, which made Owen want to grin. Maybe it was the red hair, but Jenny was damn cute when she was pissed—at least when the anger was directed at someone besides him.

"This week isn't about Owen and me," Jenny answered. "I wouldn't want to steal any spotlight away from Kristin."

"But I'm sure," Gabby continued, refusing to be deterred, "with Owen's millions . . ." She tapped a finger on her chin. "Or is it billions now? Where exactly are you on the Forbes, Owen?"

"He's number fifteen," Cooper offered, walking into the room followed by Hank.

Owen was embarrassed to feel color rising to his cheeks as his dad and brother stared at him. They knew he was wealthy, but it was an unwritten rule in the Dalton house that no one discussed the extent of his financial success.

"Good to know," Gabby murmured. "Anyway, I'm sure with all that money, your wedding is going to be a spectacle."

"True love isn't about money." Jenny's voice was low and sure. "When you marry the right person, it doesn't matter if it happens in a cathedral or . . ." She darted a glance at Owen's father. "At the county courthouse."

Her words seemed to placate Kristin, who moments earlier had looked ready to launch across the kitchen and claw out Gabby's eyes. Now she turned sweetly to Jack. "I love you, schmoop."

"I love you right back, honeybun."

Suppressing a gag, Owen crossed the kitchen and wrapped a hand around the back of Jenny's neck, massaging gently.

She glanced up at him and said through her teeth, "If you call me pookie right now I'm going to elbow you in the nuts."

He bent and kissed the top of her head, letting the scent of her soothe all the things that had been put on edge this morning.

"She's a keeper," Hank called from across the room. "Plus you get an awesome kid as a bonus."

He felt rather than saw Jenny's flinch. Cooper was beaming from Hank's side and Owen worried that the boy had forgotten this was all pretend. Cooper would earn a beach vacation, but nothing more.

Regret twisted Owen's gut. Had it been stupid to begin this farce in the first place? Or was he simply off-kilter from watching his father bond with Cooper, who was similar to Owen in so many ways? All Owen ever wanted from his father were some crumbs of kindness, and there he was handing Cooper the whole cake. Was he seriously jealous of a fatherless twelve-year-old boy? Christ, he needed to get a handle on himself. Cooper was a great kid, and Owen was glad his dad recognized that fact.

"I'm a lucky man," he answered. "But we should get back to the house. I have a couple of hours of work to do."

"You're still going to make the bridal party dinner at the Red Hornet tonight?" Kristin asked. "Everyone will be there."

"I'm not sure my presence is necessary," Owen answered, "given that I'm not part of the bridal party."

He saw something like satisfaction flash in Jack's gaze. What the hell was that about? It wasn't enough that his brother had been the golden child of their family. Was he purposely trying to humiliate Owen even when the wedding made Jack the undisputed center of attention?

Kristin's glossy pink lips turned down at the edges. "But I want you there. Everyone has to see there are no hard feelings even though . . ." She shifted, her eyes dropping to the floor. Even Jack had the good sense to look away.

"Even though you dumped me for my brother," Owen finished for her.

Jenny jumped up from the chair and pressed against his side. "Of course we'll be there," she said with the conviction of a soldier going into battle. "Kristin, I'm going to buy you the biggest JKrita they can make as a thank-you."

"Thank me for what?"

"For letting Owen go so that I could find him." She reached up on tiptoe and gently grazed her lips over his jaw. "I'm not sure what I would have done if he'd been taken when we met." She turned to grin at Kristin. "It probably would have involved me clawing your eyes out."

"Good one, Mom," Cooper shouted, then flushed when all eyes turned to him. "I mean, I'm super lucky to have Owen, too."

"Sure," Kristin said, but her smug smile dimmed as she looked between Jenny and Owen. "I only drink skinny-ritas. Just so you know."

"Duly noted," Jenny answered. "We can stay for one round. I don't want Cooper to be on his own for too long."

"He can spend the night here with Karen and me," Hank said. "We've got no plans, and the Reds are playing."

Owen cleared his throat. "Cooper doesn't like—"

"That sounds awesome," Cooper said. "We'll work on my throw during commercials. Right, Hank?"

"You bet, buddy. If your mom says it's okay."

"Sure," Jenny said, her voice sounding thick. "Are you sure you don't mind, Hank?"

"Things are too quiet around here," Owen's father said with a broad grin. "It'll be good to have a boy in the house again."

"Can I show you my golf swing before we leave?" Cooper asked Jenny.

"You'll be impressed," Hank told her. "He's a natural."

Jack let out a little snort, prompting Hank and Jenny to shoot him the same warning glare.

"Let's check it out," Jenny said, and walked forward to place a hand on her son's shoulder. They disappeared through the door to the garage, Cooper talking animatedly about the principles of golf that Hank had explained.

Before following them, Owen caught Hank's gaze on him, filled with what looked to be a silent apology. As if his father was trying to mend fences with Owen through his kindness to Cooper.

Some of the bitterness he'd always held on to, as a toddler might cradle a favorite stuffed animal, started to disappear, and Owen cursed himself as ten times the pansy-assed fool. Hank's obvious affection for the boy had nothing to do with his constant disappointment in Owen.

"Later, bro," Jack said as Owen walked by, throwing a punch that seemed a little too enthusiastic.

Owen sidestepped the blow, the way he wished he'd been able to do as a boy.

"See you tonight," he said without stopping.

Although Cooper appeared to be taking everything that was happening this week in stride, Jenny was still concerned about him getting too attached to the Daltons.

How could she blame him when she felt far too connected to Owen? She broached the subject before they left for Hank and Karen's, both of them lying on her bed and talking the way they used to when he was younger.

"It's like when Aidan and I are playing Magik of Myth. We get so into it that the game starts to feel real, like we're really heroes. When the bad guys are closing in, my heartbeat starts to race and my palms get all sticky."

Well, that pretty much described Jenny every time Owen looked at her. It seemed a lot simpler to believe she was in some alternate video-game universe.

"Then you call me for dinner. We turn it off and it's over." Her wise-beyond-his-years son sighed. "That's how this will be unless . . ." He lifted his bare feet into the air and wiggled his toes. "Unless you and Owen decide to stay together. Like maybe he'll fall in love with you."

Like maybe there was a snowball's chance in hell of that happening.

"Owen helped me the night of the reunion," she told Cooper, proud that her voice didn't waver despite her tumbling emotions. "Now I'm returning the favor. He doesn't love me."

Cooper dropped his feet back to the mattress and they both bounced slightly. "Do you love him?"

"This is going to end," she said instead of answering the question. How else could she respond to a question her mind refused to consider, even when her heart already knew the answer? "It's make-believe, buddy."

His voice went soft. "All of it?"

"Not the part where Hank and Karen really care about you. You're an easy kid to like."

"Don't tell Karen," he said casually, "but her cookies aren't as good as Grandma's."

Emotion welled in Jenny's throat at that unsolicited bit of loyalty toward her mother. How she wished Mona was mentally capable of seeing Jenny through this conundrum of her feelings for Owen and the secret she now carried regarding his parents. Her mom was always thoughtful and levelheaded. Jenny figured she'd inherited her temper and impulsiveness from her father.

What did Owen inherit from his biological father? Didn't he have a right to know where he came from?

It was all too much to consider, and she tipped her head close to Cooper's. "No one makes cookies like your grandma."

"Yours come in second," her son answered, and his steadfast faithfulness made her heart ache.

As strange as the circumstances were, these past few days away from the stress and relentless scrambling to keep her life on track had turned out to be a gift. When was the last time she'd had a few minutes to just visit with her son? He was no longer a little kid, and it was even more important to keep their connection strong over the next several years.

What if she could give him everything she'd never had?

A life without worrying about money and where he fit in the world. A family that was whole.

The thought was almost too much for her heart to carry, and with a last kiss on his forehead, she climbed off the bed with the excuse of needing to shower and get ready for the evening.

An hour later, she and Owen pulled up in front of the Red Hornet bar and grill, located around the corner from Hastings's charming main street. Turn-of-the-century architecture and historic buildings were home to a variety of mom-and-pop shops that looked like they'd been handed down within the same families for generations. There were also a few artsy boutiques and a number of trendy-looking restaurants on either side of the tree-lined street.

The building looked like something out of an old-school movie about life in a stereotypical small town. At any moment she expected to see a young Kevin Bacon roaring through the streets in a beat-up pickup, the people milling on the sidewalks on this summer night breaking into song and dance.

"My family likes you and Cooper better than they like me," Owen said as he opened Jenny's car door, bringing her back to the present moment.

Although purple and pink streaks were just starting to color the sky above them, the temperature still hovered in the low nineties. Jenny had a new appreciation for the cooling night air in Colorado. Even when summer was at its hottest, there was some relief each evening.

"That's not true," she said with firm conviction, even though she understood why he might feel that way. Hank and Karen were thrilled to keep Cooper overnight. When they'd dropped him off twenty minutes ago, Karen had been in the kitchen prepping homemade cinnamon rolls for tomorrow's breakfast, while Hank tinkered in the garage.

"Your parents love you," she told him.

He gave her a funny look. "The first night we were here, you were ready to hang all of them up by their toenails for the injustices I endured as a kid. Now you're a fan?"

"Not exactly." She laced her fingers with his because she didn't want him to feel like he was being deserted, especially by the woman he was paying to stay in his corner. "I still think your brother is a jackass."

"But not my dad?" Owen quirked a brow. "I have to admit he's good with Cooper. It's disconcerting to watch. All my life, I blamed how he treated me on the fact that we didn't have similar tastes in things. I wasn't athletic or rugged." He shook his head. "But he's so gentle with Cooper."

"That's true," Jenny admitted. Maybe the truth wouldn't hurt Owen the way his mother thought. There was a chance it would free him, help him understand that everything Hank had done was out of love. Love and fear, which Jenny understood could become convoluted and blurred until it was difficult to know where one stopped and the other started.

Owen laughed without humor. "I guess it's just me."

"No." She stopped just before the bar's mahogany-stained front door. Tugging Owen back to her, she wound her hands around his neck. "You are an amazing man just the way you are."

Disbelief was clear in his eyes and she did the only thing she could think of to make it disappear. She pulled him down to her and kissed him. An open-mouthed invitation that he immediately accepted, angling his head to deepen the connection.

All the desire she'd tried to convince herself had been sated by their one frenetic coupling roared to the surface, like a riptide pulling her under and over the waves. She couldn't breathe, couldn't think other than to hold on to Owen like a lifeline. He was her anchor in the tumultuous sea of her own need.

When the door banged open, they broke apart. A man walked past, giving them a sidelong glance. "Glad to see you back in town, Dalton," he said when he realized who it was he'd just caught in a crazy-passionate PDA on the sidewalk.

"Nice to be here," Owen said, curling his arm around Jenny's waist when she would have stepped away.

"The new computer lab is working out great," the man told them. "I'd love to have you visit the kids when school is in session."

Owen inclined his head. "I'll check my schedule in the fall."

"Great." The man threw a questioning look at Jenny but didn't ask for an introduction. Owen didn't offer one. Jenny wasn't sure why that small oversight grated on her nerves. If the guy was a friend of Owen's, someone to visit on his next trip to Hastings, it made sense that Owen wouldn't want to involve her. She wouldn't be part of his life at that point.

Yet she could no longer fool herself into believing she didn't want to be.

"Who was that?" she asked after the man walked away.

"Tom MacFarlane," Owen answered. "He was a year behind me in school, and now he's the head of the math department at Hastings High School."

"Where you donated the money for a computer lab?"

Owen paused with his hand on the bar's front door. "Among other things," he said quietly. "Tom asked and I was happy to help."

Before she could question him further as to what other things, he opened the door and foot-stomping country music along with a cacophony of voices drowned out anything she would have said.

They were ushered into the back to a private dining room where Kristin and Jack were holding court among their friends. The atmosphere immediately cooled several degrees, which Jenny couldn't understand. Back in Colorado, Owen was a well-loved member of the local community, known for his down-to-earth attitude and easygoing manner.

The reason became clear as the meal progressed. They'd been seated at the end of the table furthest from the bride- and groom-to-be. Owen was deep in conversation with Brandt Tomlison, a sheriff's deputy in Hastings and one of the few people at the table who didn't seem to view Owen as the enemy.

Jenny turned to the deputy's wife, Missy. "Have you lived in Hastings all your life?"

The curvy woman with dark hair pulled into a neat ponytail nodded. "Actually, I was in Owen's grade. We only had classes together through middle school because he was in all the advanced courses during high school." She smiled. "He probably doesn't even remember, but the only reason I passed seventh grade math is because he let me copy his answers on the final exam."

Jenny felt her eyes widen. "Owen cheated?"

Missy took a deep breath. "My mom was diagnosed with breast cancer that year and I was kind of a mess. Owen didn't say much about it—none of the kids did—but he helped me."

Of course, Jenny thought. Owen had cheated to rescue someone in need. Always the white knight.

Missy glanced at her husband and Owen across the table. "It's why I had so much trouble believing the things Jack said about him."

A trickle of apprehension skittered across Jenny's skin. "What things?"

"Nothing horrible," Missy said quickly. "Jack thinks success made Owen's ego inflate."

Jenny actually laughed at that. Owen was the least egotistical man she'd ever met, especially given how much he'd accomplished in life.

Missy smiled. "I know. It seems odd now that we've spent some time with Owen—I think Jack got it wrong."

Jenny thought Jack was an asshole.

"What else did Jack say about Owen?" Jenny asked.

"A few offhand comments about how Owen thought he was better than the rest of us. That's the reason he never came back to visit." She twirled her wine glass between two fingers. "When he first came home, Jack was trying to set up a nonprofit to help injured soldiers, and he'd gone to Owen for funding. Owen said he didn't want anything to do with this town."

"Owen would never make a comment like that."

"Right?" Missy leaned forward, as if sharing a big secret. "Once we found out how much Owen had given the school—he's paid for new computers, a sound system for the theater, and a scoreboard for the football field—it made even less sense. I guess he donated all that money with the stipulation that it be kept anonymous."

"But everyone knows?"

Missy shrugged. "It's a small town. I think Jack was pissed, but then it became personal. He said Owen refused to fund his business because of hard feelings from when they were kids. I mean, Owen wouldn't even agree to be part of the wedding party."

"He wasn't asked to be in the wedding," Jenny said, not bothering to hide her disgust at the way Jack had tried to poison the town against Owen.

"Seriously?" Missy let out a little gasp. "But they're brothers."

"Yes," Jenny agreed, "and Owen is still here supporting his brother despite the purposeful snub." She glanced to the end of the table and met Jack's gaze. By the way his jaw clenched, she figured he must know what she and Missy were discussing. "Do me a favor," she said, "and let people know the truth of the situation." She flashed Jack a saccharine-sweet smile that she hoped he knew was her appropriate-for-public-consumption version of flipping him the bird. "I don't want to cause trouble, but Owen isn't the man he's been made out to be."

"Sure, honey." A small smile curved Missy's lips. "Jack Dalton has always been a little too big for his britches if you ask me."

Jenny's head jerked back. "Too big for your britches" was one of her mom's favorite phrases. In fact, to Mona Castelli, it was the worst criticism she could give someone. It felt strangely prescient to hear the words at this moment.

"I'm going to the restroom for a minute," she said and stood. Owen threw her a questioning look from across the table but she smiled and said, "I'll be right back."

This situation was becoming more complicated by the second. Again, she wished she could call her mother to ask for advice.

Kendall, Sam, and Chloe were too close to Owen to give unbiased feedback, which left only one person to call. She bypassed the bathrooms and let herself out onto the narrow alley behind the bar. The smell of old liquor and rotting food hit her hard in the thick air, so she quickly dialed Dina's number.

Dina picked up on the first ring. "It was a tiny kitchen fire," she said by way of greeting. "I've already repainted the wall behind the stove. Seriously, you need new appliances. John came over and helped with the kids while I—"

Jenny pressed a hand to the rough brick of the building's back wall, reminding herself to stay focused and grounded in this moment. "Dina, stop."

Silence on the other end of the line.

"I didn't call because of the fire." Jenny gave a laugh that she hoped didn't sound as hysterical as it felt. "Or because you let your dirtbag husband into my house."

"John has been really great," Dina argued quietly. "Did Trent get a hold of you?"

Jenny's mind went blank. "Was Trent looking for me?"

There was a pause and then Dina said, "He left a couple of messages. He sounded pretty intent on speaking to you."

"No," Jenny answered numbly. Trent could only want one thing, and the thought of him coming after Cooper sent another wave of panic running through her. But now wasn't the time for a baby-daddy freak-out. She'd deal with Trent when she returned to Colorado. "I'm not calling because of Trent."

"Oh." Dina's voice was hopeful. "Did you call just to talk? Because we're friends?"

"Not exactly," Jenny muttered. "Well, maybe. I called because I'm in over my head here and—"

"Yeah," Dina interrupted. "The trials of dating a bajillionaire. Woe is you."

"Um . . ." Jenny had made a categorical error in calling her uninvited houseguest. She'd forgotten that Dina didn't know about her arrangement with Owen. Hell, she'd forgotten the relationship wasn't real. "Let me call you back."

"You're fine, Jenny," Dina said. "I saw the way Owen looked at you. That man is head over heels. There's nothing that's going to tear the two of you apart."

"I'll call you back," Jenny repeated, and ended the call. She stared at her phone for a few long seconds, trying to decide which of her three best friends to ask for advice.

Then she heard the door to the back of the building creak open.

Jack Dalton stood in the entrance for a moment, silhouetted in the shadowed glow from the hallway. He took a step toward her, letting the door bang shut. Night had fallen in earnest, and the only light in the alley came from a streetlamp in its opening. It was difficult to make out the look in Jack's blue eyes, but from the stiff line of his shoulders, he hadn't followed her out to ask advice on his wedding vows.

CHAPTER SIXTEEN

Jack moved closer and she instinctively took a step back. "Take a wrong turn?"

"I could ask you the same question," she answered. "If you're looking for someone to kiss your ass, you've come to the wrong place."

White teeth flashed in the encroaching darkness. "I guess the stereotype about redheads and their tempers is true in your case."

"Maybe," she said evenly. "Or maybe I got an earful about the lies you've been spreading around town."

He didn't bother to deny it. "So what? Hastings is nothing to my brother. Christ, he's famous all over the world. This is my place."

"This town is important to Owen," she argued. "He loves every member of your family, and you treat him like he's dirt on the bottom of your shoe."

"Let him use his money to throw a big fucking pity party for himself," Jack shot back.

Jenny's temper spiked even harder. She moved toward Jack, unwilling to let his size or anger intimidate her. "Do you realize how big of an asshole that makes you? Owen has spent his whole life trying to fit in to your family and the long shadow you cast. I'm not sure he can even appreciate his success because it doesn't make him you."

"I bet Owen's not the only one who wishes he was more like me," Jack drawled, then easily caught Jenny's hand as she reached up to slap him. "And you've only heard one side of the story. I spent my whole damn life working my ass off to prove I was worth something. It all came so damn easy to Owen."

"What?" she asked. "What came easy? Being left behind on family vacations? Never having your father's approval?"

Jack snorted. "Is that what he told you? Give me a fucking break. Owen didn't go on vacations because he was sick and Mom coddled him. Dad still talks about how brilliant Owen is to anyone who will listen. Since I came back from the marines, he doesn't say crap about me."

Jenny knew from growing up with Ty and his brother and sister that siblings often had different views on how childhood events played out. But the way Owen described his family had seemed so cut-and-dried.

"Your father is proud of your military career," she said, her temper somewhat appeased by Jack's unnerving reaction. "You're just like him."

"Right. Just like him." His face went as hard as a sheer mountain cliff. "You know, Red, things aren't always as they seem."

"Is this a private conversation or can anyone join you in the foul-smelling alley?"

Jenny jumped away from Jack at the sound of Owen's voice, shaking off his brother's grasp and moving quickly toward the door where Owen stood. "I called Dina to check in on things at the house," she told him, but he was looking past her to his brother.

Another time when Owen had looked past her to a man flashed through her mind. A fund-raiser more than two years ago when she'd grabbed the meatstick guy who'd been eyeing her all night and kissed him at exactly the moment she knew Owen would find her.

God, she never again wanted to witness the look she'd seen in Owen's eyes. She couldn't make out their dark depths in the alley, but it killed her to think he believed she would make a move on his brother. Would she ever be able to regain his trust?

All she wanted was Owen, but she had no right to him. No business making demands or promises when she was bound to disappoint them both, purposely or not. This moment was another stellar example of that.

"Are we good, Jack?" The "I don't give a fuck" tone of Owen's voice was at odds with the question.

"Never better, Owen," came the reply from the darkness. Jack hadn't turned around, and stood with his hands on his hips.

Jenny felt Owen begin to surge forward, and threw her arms around his waist. "Take me home." All the emotions swirling through her seeped into her voice. "Please."

He stilled for a moment, then grabbed her hand and hauled her down the hall.

"My purse," she said on a gasp as he moved through the crowded bar toward the front door.

"I'll pull the car around while you get it," he said without looking at her.

"Owen, you know I wasn't—"

"Just get the damn purse, Jenny."

He stalked away from her, maneuvering through clusters of people until she lost sight of him.

She pressed her knuckles to her chest, ruing the pain she'd once caused him. At the same time, it stung to think that he might believe she'd repeat that moment of selfish stupidity or that she hadn't regained his trust.

Glancing over her shoulder to make sure Jack hadn't followed them out of the alley, she entered the private dining room and grabbed her purse from the back of her chair.

"Owen and I need to leave," she said to Missy. At the head of the table, Kristin was deep in conversation with the woman Jenny recognized from the bridal shower as her maid of honor. "Would you make our excuses to the happy couple?"

"Sure, honey," Missy said, gently squeezing Jenny's arm. "You take care of Owen. We're real proud of him around here."

Jenny forced a weak smile, then hurried back into the bar, keeping her eyes trained in front of her. Like most things in life, there was nothing else to do but move forward and hope the moment would pass.

Owen's rented SUV waited at the curb. He was the type of stand-up guy who would never stop being a gentleman, no matter how angry he was. She climbed in and as soon as her seat belt was buckled, he hit the accelerator.

There was so much she wanted to say to him, but all of her words felt inadequate. *She* felt inadequate, and so she let the silence swallow her until she was drowning in it.

Owen didn't speak during the short drive back to the rental house. He parked in the driveway and handed the house key to Jenny as they met at the front of the SUV.

She opened her mouth to speak, but he held up a hand. "I need a minute," he said and stalked around the side of the house, the motion-sensor lights illuminating a path. He kept moving until he stood at the edge of the woods that bordered the far edge of the lawn.

He took several deep breaths of the sultry summer night air, something he hadn't been able to do as a boy for fear an allergy-induced asthma attack would wrap like a fist around his lungs.

He was no longer that helpless kid, but returning to his hometown sent him reeling back decades at every turn. Tonight's highlight was reliving the moment he'd caught his then fiancée cheating on him with his brother.

A low point he'd thought at that time, but surprisingly it hadn't compared to the more recent heartbreaking discovery of Jenny kissing another man at a fund-raising event when she'd been his date. He knew charity functions and the rarefied social circles he sometimes found himself traveling through weren't her cup of tea, but he'd been so damn proud to have her on his arm. He'd fostered the foolish belief that being together was enough to make any situation palatable.

"Nothing happened between your brother and me," she said a moment later, as if he'd conjured her like a citrus-scented ghost out of the darkness. He continued to stare into the dark shadows of the trees. Crickets chirped and the thick, earthy odor of underbrush filled the air.

"I know," he said, giving her a sidelong glance.

In the soft moonlight, her skin looked like alabaster and made the pink of her sweet mouth appear even more delectable. He wanted to pull her to him, rake his fingers through her thick hair, and pretend that nothing mattered but the two of them.

Christ, her beauty slayed him.

She eased closer, nudged him with her elbow. "Then why are you back here sulking?"

He knew she was teasing, trying to ease the tension, but he couldn't snap out of his dark mood.

"Feel free to leave," he said, not caring that he sounded like a complete dick. "If you're finished bonding with Jack, my parents are probably still awake. I'm sure they'd love to see you for some late-night laughs at my expense."

He heard her sharp intake of breath, then she disappeared from the periphery of his vision.

He'd finally done it—used his messed-up family history to push away the one woman he wanted to keep close. Jenny had been different this time around—softer and more open to the connection that still held between them. He'd actually started to believe she agreed that what was between them deserved a second chance.

A moment later the heat of her body pressed against the fabric of his linen shirt. She wrapped her arms around his waist, inching her hands under the hem to splay across his skin, erotic and unexpected. He could feel the rise and fall of her chest and allowed his own breathing to slow until it matched hers.

"There is nowhere I'd rather be than here with you. You and Cooper are the only things that matter to me."

His eyes drifted closed as her words washed over him like the cool shower of a summer rain, washing clean all the broken and bleeding places inside of him.

Her voice dropped even further as she said, "Even if you're acting like a dick."

He felt his mouth curve. This woman was something special.

"Thank you for the reality check," he told her, and turned away from the woods so that he faced her. She tipped up her chin and smiled, but there was a wariness in it.

"Jack and I were arguing," she said.

"I don't want to talk about my brother."

"I need you to know there was nothing more to it," she insisted. "I need you to believe me."

"It's fine, Jenny."

She shook her head. "That's not the same thing."

"I believe you," he said, and was rewarded with a softening of her features.

As he'd wished minutes earlier, the world shrank until it was just the two of them. And he had no other purpose in life than to claim this woman for as long as she would have him. He leaned in and kissed her, the connection turning instantly incendiary. His hands traveled down her body to press her closer.

She gave a little moan and he felt the shiver that rippled through her. He lifted her and she wrapped her legs around his waist. All he could think about was getting her to the house and his bed. It was better that they were coming together while in West Virginia. He wasn't sure if he took her to his bed in Colorado that he'd be able to let her go.

She'd turned on a few lights when she came through the house and he didn't bother with them now. Not when their kisses were making him wild with need.

As soon as he stepped into the bedroom, she hopped down and started to tear at his clothes. He encircled her wrists and lifted them high above her head, turning and backing her against the door.

She whimpered, her eyes darkening. "Owen, I need—"

"You'll get everything you need," he told her, bending to place hot, slow kisses along her throat as his free hand skirted up under the hem of her shirt. "But we're not rushing things this time. We've got all night, Jenny, and I'm going to take advantage of every minute."

His words almost drove Jenny over the edge, and he'd barely touched her. He released her hands as he dragged her shirt up and over her head.

Then his mouth, which had been working wonders on her overly sensitive skin, closed over the tip of one breast. There was something about the heat and pressure coupled with the gentle scrape of lace across her nipple that drove her crazy.

She dug her heels into the carpet and locked her knees, worried she'd melt into an embarrassing heap on the floor before the good stuff even got started.

But with Owen, all of it was amazing. To have the entire night felt exciting and indulgent and she had no idea how to pace herself for so much pleasure. Owen licked and nipped, his attention fully on her body. His hands and mouth were everywhere, as if he was trying to memorize every inch of her.

When he dropped to his knees, she let out another soft groan. Slowly his palms skimmed down her legs and he took her foot out of one and then the other sandal, his thumbs caressing the sensitive arch of each foot. Then he reached up and curled his fingers in the waistband of her panties, pulling them down over her hips.

"Bed," she whispered, her voice hoarse.

"Not yet," he answered, and she heard the smile in his voice. "I'm not finished here."

He took his sweet time with her, as if his only goal in life was to draw every exquisite sensation out of her. Her legs finally gave up the ghost when she spiraled over the edge of pleasure. Owen was there to catch her, which made her melt for an entirely different reason. He scooped her into his arms and, pulling back the covers, settled her gently onto the bed. She felt weightless and boneless, barely able to lift her head from the pillow.

Her senses sharpened again as he did an efficient striptease, tossing his shirt to the side. When he started on the buttons of his jeans, she gasped.

Owen paused. "Problem?"

"Come here," she said, crooking a finger. "And explain to me exactly where in the hell you got all that."

He looked down, the outline of his erection clearly straining against the denim. "Can you clarify 'all that'?" A smile played around the corner of his mouth.

"These . . ." she lifted herself onto one elbow, then reached out, tracing a finger along the muscles cut into each side of his abs, forming a V as they tapered down toward his pelvis. "I don't even know what they're called, but they go with that six-pack you've miraculously developed, like chips go with salsa."

He sucked in a breath as her finger continued to play across his skin. "Not sure if my body falls in the miracle category," he said with a tight laugh. "But I'm going to actually give credit to less chips and salsa and more time in the gym."

"They're my favorite thing." She found herself mesmerized by his body, the rough texture of his skin to her touch.

She popped open one of the buttons on his fly but before she could go further, he pressed her back to the bed with a heated kiss.

"Now that I'm in the favorites category," he said, his voice a sexy rumble, "let's not ruin it by finishing this before we've even gotten started." He shucked out of his jeans and boxers, put on a condom, then climbed onto the bed and covered her with his body.

As his mouth met hers, she instinctively arched toward him, and he drove into her. They both gasped and their breath mingled, sweet and hot as he said her name. It was difficult to know where Owen ended and she began, but for once the intimacy didn't scare Jenny. She craved it. She craved more, and he gave her everything she needed.

Their movements were slow and languid, a discovery of sorts. A dance that seemed choreographed to each sound she made. The pressure inside her began to build and the pace Owen set increased, like he knew what her body needed better than she did.

She gave herself over to the bliss, and minutes later, cried out his name, earning a low growl and a deep kiss. As he found his own release, she wrapped her arms and legs tighter around him, wanting to feel every tremor that shook him. Wanting everything she could give and take from this man.

This time when he curled her into his arms, she didn't resist. She didn't let the fear that fluttered across her stomach take hold and drag her down. She might not have Owen forever, but tonight was hers.

"You are incredible," he murmured into her hair, tucking her closer.

"Says the man who founded one of the most famous technology companies in the world."

"A company is one thing, Jenny." His thumb traced a lazy path over the curve of her hip, lulling her with its rhythm. "But you're raising a son. Plus, you've started your own business."

"Out of a dilapidated barn," she said with a laugh. "And barely that."

"It will become more."

A chill ran up her spine at the thought of how and why. It still made her feel cheap and needy to know she was taking Owen's money. Like she was, indeed, selling herself.

"The ring speeds up the process," he said, once again startling her with his ability to read her mind, "but you would have made it work. It's what you do."

Happiness, sweet and refreshing like strawberry ice cream on a hot summer day, moved through her body. Her life in the past year had been messy and constantly bordering on unrestrained chaos, but Jenny was making it work. Sometimes she had difficulty comparing herself to her friends who seemed to be much better than her at the whole adulting thing. But Owen was at the top of the success pyramid by anyone's standards.

Yet he gave her the compliment so matter-of-factly, and she knew he wasn't simply trying to placate her or blowing post-coital smoke up her butt.

She shifted onto her back, grabbing at the sheet and pulling it up over them both. This moment had quickly shifted to a place where she felt too emotionally exposed. It was dangerous territory, because typically, being vulnerable made her stupid.

She didn't want to be stupid with Owen.

"I need to apologize to you," she said softly, placing her hand on his chest above his heart.

His jaw clenched but his eyes stayed gentle. "You don't—"

She shook her head. "If I could change one moment in my life, it would be those few minutes in the coat closet."

He sifted his fingers through her hair, spreading it over her neck and throat like he was arranging a work of art. "Just so you know, I'll never check another coat at an event as long as I live."

A sound that was a mix between a laugh and a sob rose in her throat. "Me neither," she agreed. "It meant nothing to me, Owen."

"Is that supposed to make me feel better?" There was no anger in his voice but she felt the lash of a whip just the same. "To know that you publicly humiliated me for a guy who meant nothing to you?"

"No." Of course not. Where was she even going with this? Was it another form of self-sabotage? A way to ruin the connection between them by the reminder of what a heartless bitch she'd been? "I just want you to know I'm sorry. The way I felt for you . . . it scared me. When I'm scared, I act stupid. I sabotage the good things in my life. Like us."

He didn't meet her gaze but continued to play with her hair, tickling her skin with the ends of it. "You suck at pillow talk," he told her. "Would you like a do-over?"

She searched his expression for something that would tell her whether he was talking about this conversation or the whole of their relationship.

His eyes gave away nothing.

"Yes," she said, answering either or both questions and deciding to save face and go for the easy out. "You have mad skills in bed."

What man didn't like to have his ego stroked?

Owen only chuckled. "It's not me," he countered, "and it's not you. It's the two of us together."

His gaze slammed into hers and the intensity in his dark eyes made her chest ache. "You get that, right?"

Mesmerized by his attention, all she could do was nod. "Yeah," she admitted. "I do."

He smiled, and propping himself up on an elbow, leaned over to kiss her. As soon as their mouths touched, she was lost again.

It was easier to communicate with their bodies than words, Jenny thought. She had no problem getting that right with Owen. So she rolled him to his back and straddled him. His mouth still fused to hers, he groped blindly for the nightstand drawer.

She pulled it open, took out a condom, and rolled it down Owen's length before lowering herself onto him with a sharp intake of breath. The way she felt joined to this man was the opposite of stupid. It was freedom, bliss, and a thousand starry nights come together in one perfect moment.

Jenny was determined to savor it as long as she could.

CHAPTER SEVENTEEN

"I just need a minute to figure it out."

"Mom, you're going to strangle me."

Cooper yanked at the tie around his neck at the same Jenny tried to straighten the lopsided knot she'd fastened.

It was the morning of the wedding, and she was struggling to get both of them ready through a flurry of nerves that had taken flight inside her chest. While she knew Kristin's claim that *everyone* in town would be attending the wedding was exaggerated, such a public outing on Owen's arm made her both skittish and jumpy.

"What kind of department store doesn't have clip-on ties for kids?" she muttered.

"The one at the mall in Hastings, West Virginia," Owen said from the bedroom doorway. "Can I help?"

"Yes," Cooper shouted and took a quick step away from Jenny. Traitor.

"I almost had it," she said, turning to Owen. Her breath caught as he grinned. Would she ever get used to how he made her feel with just a look—like everything she'd never even realized she wanted from life was in his eyes?

"You look lovely," he told her, and she couldn't hide the blush that rose to her cheeks. She smoothed a hand over the soft fabric of the floral-print dress she'd allowed Sam to choose for her on another pre-Owen shopping trip. The dress had a V-neck and was fitted at the waist before flaring to a hemline just above her knees. It was pretty and feminine and made Jenny feel like she was playing dress up in a way she surprisingly enjoyed.

"We don't normally wear fancy clothes," Cooper announced helpfully.

"Count yourself lucky," Owen told him. "Ties are never comfortable, but there's an art to tying one. I'll teach you."

"I'm not sure we have time for that." Jenny moved from the side of the small bed to make room for Owen next to where Cooper stood in front of the dresser.

"There's time," he said and brushed one finger across her wrist as he moved past. The touch was gossamer light and subtle enough that Cooper didn't notice, but it sent a whirlwind of sparks fluttering over her skin.

"What do I do first?" Cooper asked, holding out the two ends of the shiny fabric.

"Start with shortening the skinny end," Owen answered. "We're going for the classic four-in-hand knot today."

"There are different kinds of knots?" Cooper asked, fascinated.

"Yes, but this is the only one you really need to know." Owen stood behind Cooper, hands resting on the boy's shoulders. "It's the one James Bond uses," he said with a wink at the mirror above the dresser where her son was watching him.

"Cool," Cooper murmured. "I wouldn't have learned this at sleep-away camp. I'd probably be making stupid crafts and stuff."

Owen's gaze darted to Jenny over Cooper's head. She gave a small nod, then moved to the doorway and grabbed the knob tightly in her fist. She'd tried to broach the subject of camp with Cooper several times since they'd arrived in West Virginia, but he'd managed to avoid giving her an adequate explanation.

"I thought you were excited about camp," Owen said casually.

Jenny backed into the hallway as Cooper glanced toward the door. "I didn't know Brad and Emmett were going to be there," he answered. "They're trouble."

"What kind of trouble?"

Cooper shrugged. "Emmett's older brother is in high school and smokes a lot of pot. I overheard Emmett talking to Brad about how he had a joint in his bag. Maybe it was just talk, but I didn't want to deal with that."

Jenny sighed. And she'd thought potty-training had been tough. Guiding Cooper through his teenage years was going to be a million times more difficult. She'd heard that kids were experimenting with drugs in junior high, but the idea of her son being exposed to it made her crazy.

She watched as Owen crouched down to eye level with Cooper. "You made a smart choice, buddy. I'm glad you told me. You're going to need to talk to your mom, too."

"She'll freak out."

Owen laughed and Jenny felt one corner of her mouth lift at how well Cooper understood her. "Maybe," Owen agreed, "but tell her anyway. She loves you."

"I'll tell her." He pulled at each side of the tie. "So what do I do next?"

Owen patiently instructed her son on wrapping the wide end around the narrow and looping it through.

It took several tries before Cooper ended up with anything that looked like a decent knot, but Owen quietly encouraged him and gave hints on how to hold the knot as he pulled and tightened.

The moment was a small one, but the significance of it crashed through Jenny like an emotional wrecking ball. This was what she wanted for Cooper, someone to teach him how to be a man, from big things like character to something as basic and essential as tying a tie.

He could have that with Owen. She could have the love she'd secretly craved if only she was brave enough to open her heart to this man.

She pasted a bright smile on her face when Cooper stepped around Owen to show her his handiwork. "I'm like James Bond, Mom. It wasn't even that hard."

"Not when you've got an expert on hand to teach you," she agreed. "Did you thank Owen for the lesson?"

"Thanks," Cooper said, still gazing down at the result of his new-found skill.

"Any time," Owen said, reaching out to make a small adjustment to the knot.

He lifted his gaze to Jenny's and her heart hammered in her chest. "Any time," he repeated, and the way he spoke the words felt like a promise. It was a promise she very much wanted to return.

Owen sat with Jenny and Cooper in a center pew of the church he grew up attending and watched his brother recite vows to the woman Owen had once planned to marry.

He felt nothing.

Not quite nothing. There was a vague sense of relief floating through him, like his insides were an antigravity chamber with random feelings and thoughts bouncing off the edges. Jenny had told his parents that it was a blessing Owen and Kristin hadn't worked out because it had allowed Jenny time to find him.

The opposite was true.

He'd discovered her, as if she were a secret garden at the end of an overgrown path, just waiting for him to come along. He still remembered their first meeting. She'd been new to the design end of the landscaping business, unsure and defensive about her lack of education and experience.

But the plans she'd drawn had been perfect for his company's headquarters, exactly what he'd envisioned to complete the space. The longer they'd spoken the more she'd relaxed and opened up to him. He'd watched, fascinated as her defenses had slowly dropped, a thousand veils drifting to the ground. There had never been anyone like Jenny in his life.

Then she'd broken him, and he'd assumed he'd unwittingly played the role of Icarus in their story, ascending too close to her bright sun and paying the ultimate price.

Now he understood the truth was more complicated than he'd realized. Jenny had also been burned by love, and she still nursed the scars, faded as they might be.

But she was wearing his ring. He tried not to consider Cooper's plan to sell it. In the halcyon glow of the past two days, it was easy to forget that what was between them was only pretend.

After the scene with Jack in the alley, Owen had decided that he'd done more than his fair share of fawning over the happy couple. His first idea had been to leave town before the wedding, but Jenny convinced him that would do more harm than good.

She did agree, however, that forgoing the rest of the pre-wedding festivities was in everyone's best interest. They'd picked up Cooper and headed to the reservoir tucked at the far end of the state park about fifteen miles outside town.

They'd bought a picnic lunch from a gourmet deli and driven out to spend the day the way Owen had always wanted to as a kid. They swam and skipped rocks, jumped off cliffs and got eaten alive by mosquitos.

He'd picked up a couple of fishing poles from the local sporting goods store and taught Cooper how to cast a line. Owen had spent a lot of money learning to fly-fish with a private guide when he'd first moved to Colorado. It gave him a ridiculous amount of pleasure to spend an afternoon fishing with Cooper. Several times he'd caught Jenny staring at him, a wistful look on her face, and knew he wasn't the only one longing for something more.

The trick was going to be convincing her to admit it.

Owen realized the ceremony was over when everyone around him stood. His brother and Kristin walked past arm in arm. For a moment Owen forgot all the bullshit that was between them and simply wished Jack the best with life.

He glanced down when Jenny took his arm.

"Are you crying?" he asked as she swiped at her cheeks with her other hand.

She sniffed. "Your brother is awful, but weddings always get to me."

An older woman who Owen recognized as a friend of his mother winked at him on her way out of the pew. "You're next."

He felt Jenny recoil and a corresponding quiver pricked his heart.

"Mom, let's go." Cooper gave them both a little shove. "We've got bubbles to blow for Jack and Kristin when they come out of church."

Owen placed a hand on her waist, and she shifted away slightly. Shit. One offhand comment from a stranger and it felt like the connection between them had been irreparably severed.

Their bond was tenuous, in part because there was so much he couldn't find a way to say to her. A million emotions he didn't trust himself to share.

"Okay, buddy," she said as they moved toward the front of the church with the rest of the wedding guests. As Owen looked around, he was overwhelmed by the past and memories of his childhood. Even though it made him look like the jackass Jack had believed him to be, he couldn't bring himself to meet the curious gazes of old neighbors and his brother's childhood friends.

He tried to protect Jenny from being jostled as they walked. As they came to the door, he saw his parents and his sister standing to one side of the wide stone steps leading up to the chapel. His mother blew him a kiss.

It was something she'd done since he was a boy and he automatically raised a hand and pretended to catch it in his fist. Once he did, he raised his knuckles to his mouth. His mom's eyes were gentle, and she gave him a small smile.

Jenny linked their fingers and they stood behind Cooper as he waited with his bubbles. After a few minutes, Jack and Kristin walked out of the church, hands held and raised over their heads. The guests cheered and bubbles floated through the air, glistening with the promise of two lives joined together. The newlyweds made their way down the stairs and into the waiting car.

Once they had driven away from the church, Cooper went over to greet Owen's mom and dad. As the rest of the guests left the church steps, Jenny turned to Owen. "Are you ready?"

"To head to the reception?"

She placed a hand on his cheek. "To go home."

A dozen thoughts ran through his mind but the one word that spilled out of him was, "Yes." He picked her up and swung her around. "Hell, yes."

Jenny laughed, swiftly kissing the crook of his neck. "I didn't realize you'd been waiting for permission."

"I'm just happy it was your idea," he told her. "When my mom protests, I'm blaming you."

"That's what I'm here for," she answered. "Scapegoat."

He set her down and lifted her knuckles to his lips. "You are the best part of this week."

Her eyes were gentle. "That goes both ways."

He sent a quick text to his assistant to contact the flight crew he had on standby, then led her over to where his parents stood. Instead of incriminating Jenny, he took the easy excuse and blamed his work.

Gabby punched him lightly on the arm, but he could tell by the smile she gave Jenny that his sister was happy with the way things had turned out.

Neither of his parents looked pleased, but they didn't argue. His mother wrapped her arms tight around his neck. "It was so nice to have you home," she told him. "Don't be a stranger."

It was a teasing comment, but it hit Owen like a fist to the gut. In many ways, he still felt like a stranger in his own family. But the week had shown him that he was no longer that sad little boy who didn't belong. He'd made a life in Colorado and had finally come to terms with his past. He could own where he came from, but it didn't need to dictate who he knew himself to be.

Hank ruffled Cooper's hair and promised to continue their baseball lessons during their next visit. He turned to Owen and gave him an awkward—but sweet—hug. "You're doing good, son," he said softly. Owen held his father's gaze, trying to decipher what prompted him to finally offer that small bit of praise. After a moment, he simply nodded. But something that had long been wound tight in Owen's chest loosened.

Jenny also hugged both of his parents. He watched as his mom whispered something in Jenny's ear that elicited a palpable reaction from his tiny redhead. She tried to play it off but he could tell from the way her skin paled so much that her freckles stood out in sharp relief and the way she refused to meet his gaze that she was upset.

Jenny was silent as they packed up their suitcases at the rental house, and remained out of sorts on the way to the airport. Her hands were clasped tightly in her lap and she was biting down so hard on her bottom lip Owen thought she might actually draw blood.

"What did my mom say to you?"

She shrugged in response, then looked to the backseat. Owen flicked a glance in the rearview mirror. Cooper had headphones on and his eyes trained to whatever game he was playing on his phone.

"Something about our wedding plans," Jenny said, her mouth pulled down at the corners. He reached for her hand but she crossed her arms over her chest. "I hate deceiving them. It was a lot easier to create a pretend relationship before I knew your family. Before I understood . . . how things are. Now I just feel dirty, you know?"

He knew. He wanted to say he had no regrets in what they'd done, but it wasn't true.

His biggest regret remained that Jenny still seemed convinced it needed to end.

"Where have you been? I thought you'd deserted me."

Mona's gentle reprimand made Jenny's heart hurt. She hugged her mother, letting the familiar smell of Olay lotion soothe her ravaged nerves.

"Cooper and I went to a wedding with Owen," she answered, sitting on the bed next to her mother. "Remember, I told you I'd be gone when I came to visit last weekend?"

Mona's eyes narrowed as if she was searching for the memory along the tangled pathways inside her brain.

"I asked Ty to check in on you this week," Jenny said.

At that, Mona perked up. "He and Kendall both came. They're going to make wonderful parents."

"Yes," Jenny agreed. "It's exciting. But it isn't fair that Kendall isn't puking or getting fat. All she has are bigger boobs and a gorgeous pregnancy glow."

Mona nodded. "The glow gave it away. I could tell with you, too," she said quietly, although it was just the two of them in her room. Some of the residents were watching the Rockies game in the community lounge. With Cooper's newfound love of baseball, he'd joined them.

Jenny smiled and tucked a lock of silver hair behind her mom's ear. "I wasn't glowing. I was scared to death and trying to hide my morning sickness from you *and* studying for midterms."

"You were beautiful," her mother replied, mimicking Jenny's touch. Mona's fingers were cool, the skin smooth like tissue paper as it grazed Jenny's ear. "I knew you would be an amazing mother, sweetheart."

"I could never live up to you." Jenny's voice cracked on the last word. Mona had always been a shining beacon, never wavering in her beliefs. She'd been dealt some tough blows, but always took the high road and stayed true to her steadfast moral compass.

Jenny's inner life was like a tiny steel ball in a pinball machine, constantly battered from one side to the other. Tumbling and turning so she never got time to truly get her bearings. Every time life slowed down enough for her to feel like she was making headway, something else would launch her spinning again.

Sometimes she hit a target and scored, like with Cooper. But sometimes she slammed into a bumper and spun down the drain, as she had when she'd betrayed Owen. When she was younger, the constant scrambling had felt like part of who she was. Now she wanted something different . . . something more.

She wanted peace.

She felt that peace when she was working in her nursery, which strengthened her resolve to make her business a success. But she'd also had it in Owen's arms, and she was terrified of losing that.

"What's this?" Mona asked. Her voice soothed like being wrapped in a favorite blanket. "My girl isn't usually one for tears."

Jenny sniffed. "What if I mess everything up again? I don't even know how to figure out if the things I'm doing in my life are right or wrong. I don't know where to go from here."

Mona pulled her close. "What does your heart tell you?"

"My heart is the last thing I should listen to," Jenny said with a laugh. "It never fails to steer me wrong." Her heart had allowed her to believe that Trent would do the right thing and marry her, be a father to their baby. It had warned her not to get too close to Owen. Her heart had convinced her that she could make the garden center a success on her own, that she'd paid enough dues to finally earn her place in the world.

She definitely didn't trust her heart.

"I should have listened to my heart when your father asked me to go with him," Mona murmured with a sigh.

Jenny lifted her head from her mother's shoulder. "He took off on tour with his band," she said. "He left you behind."

Mona's smile was wistful. "Yes, but he'd asked me to go with him. You were just a baby, and Joseph had promised to settle down. To quit touring and get a regular job that would support our family." She placed her hands in her lap and rubbed her thumb across the empty ring finger of her left hand. "I gave him an ultimatum—it was either the band or us. I should have known better. Your father was never one to be tied down."

"But that means he didn't desert us," Jenny murmured, everything she'd known as truth in life suddenly shifting as the foundation of her world split apart.

"He loved you," Mona said. "I always told you your father loved you."

"I didn't believe you. If he loved me so much, why didn't he ever come to visit? How could he just vanish from our lives?"

Mona bit her lip. "Because I told him if he left that he was never welcome back. I was angry and heartbroken, and then he was gone. By the time you were old enough to ask after your daddy, I'd lost track of him. The truth was, I didn't want him back in our lives stirring up old feelings and making you want things that weren't right."

"You never mentioned that part." Jenny couldn't help the accusation in her tone and saw her mother wince. Emotions vied for position in Jenny's heart—shock, anger, frustration. She felt everything and nothing at once but worked to remain calm so her mom could speak without becoming too agitated to continue.

"I told you he loved you," Mona insisted. "That explained everything you needed to know." She stood and paced to the edge of the room. "You've got to get ready for the dance recital on your own this afternoon. Mrs. Bishop needs me to set the table for her garden party, but I left your ballet slippers and leotard at the end of your bed. I'll be back down to the carriage house to drive you. We'll get you there on time, baby girl."

"Mom, it's okay." Jenny stood, walked to her mother, and enveloped her in a tight hug. When Mona got agitated, her short-term memories faded and she slipped into the past as her reality. Part of the reason Jenny paid so much for the tranquil assisted living community was to keep her mother calm and rooted in the present. "I don't even care about the stupid recital."

The words were an exact copy of what Jenny had said to her mother as a ten-year-old, when they'd been late to the recital because Libby Bishop had kept Mona late. Jenny's mother would never say a word against Libby or the fabricated demands she placed on her. To Mona, the Bishops meant security and an entry into a level of society that never would have been available to Jenny otherwise.

Mona hadn't realized that Jenny never wanted that life. Now she knew it could have been different. The curiosity she'd tamped down for decades sprang to life inside her. Maybe the outcome would have been the same if Mona had left with Joseph, but Jenny would have known the father who hadn't simply tossed her aside like so much waste and baggage.

The father who had, in fact, loved her.

Which made her . . . lovable.

It had been stupid to believe otherwise, but that was the way her mind had processed being rejected by a parent. Even now, it was difficult to think otherwise. Her mother should have explained the whole truth about Jenny's father years ago, but there was no point in arguing that now. Mona was not capable of having that conversation.

"How is Owen?" Mona asked suddenly, and Jenny wondered if her brain actually broadcast thoughts onto her forehead. What other explanation could there be for how easy she was to read?

"He's fine."

He was perfect and handsome and set her heart racing every time she thought of him. Their good-bye at the airport had been tense, mostly because of how on edge she'd been by the time they touched down. The flight from West Virginia had been excruciating. Jenny had listened to Owen and Cooper discussing baseball stats, and she'd wanted nothing more than to make Owen part of her world forever.

But the week was a sham, and it had to come to an end. The lessons Jenny had learned about trust and vulnerability and how the combination of those two only led to pain were too deeply etched into her soul. She could not risk her heart. She would not.

Owen had left things up to her, as if giving her the control was some sort of test. He'd said that she should think about what came next and let him know. If it was indeed a test, she wondered if he expected her to pass or fail.

"You should bring him to see me," her mother said. "I liked him. He's not the kind of man to go chasing his dreams on the stage of every roadside bar this side of the Mississippi." She shook her head. "All I ever wanted was to take care of you, sweetie."

Jenny could hear the faint undertone of disquiet in her mother's voice and gently steered her toward the door. "Let's go find Cooper."

"Oh, yes," Mona agreed. "That boy is getting taller every time I see him."

It was beyond frustrating how the disease's progression continued to erode her mother's brain, but Jenny smiled around the lump that clogged her throat. "Every time," she agreed and they headed down the hall.

CHAPTER EIGHTEEN

Jenny was working in the barn later that night when she heard the crunch of tires on the gravel drive. She'd dropped off Cooper at a sleepover birthday party after leaving her mother's and had spent the rest of the evening repotting vegetables and flowers. She'd hoped surrounding herself with the comforting scent of dirt and mulch would pull her mood out of the toilet.

Gardening had always been her salvation, but now everything she was doing seemed tainted by the knowledge of how her garden center's future would be built on the money she was taking from Owen.

The money that would come from selling her engagement ring. Owen had put the choice of whether their relationship would continue in her hands, and it broke her heart. Jenny had always hated that saying about the silk purse and a sow's ear, but the phrase had played through her mind on endless repeat since that afternoon. She knew which end of the idiom described her.

A tear dripped off the end of her nose, and she swiped at her cheek with the back of a sleeve. She refused to cry over a situation she'd created for herself.

The door to the barn creaked open.

"That was the shortest reunion dinner on record," she called over her shoulder.

Dina had taken her kids out to eat with their father. Apparently John Sullivan had a complete change of heart—and Jenny hoped conscience—once he'd spent a few weeks without his wife and kids. According to Dina, he'd been visiting them at Jenny's farmhouse every night and pitching in to help with cooking and housework. Something he hadn't ever done in their years of dating and marriage.

Jenny still didn't trust the guy, but she was coming to understand the truth of a situation wasn't always as clear-cut as she might like.

"I didn't realize we'd begun the reunion portion of the evening," came a deep voice.

She whirled around, her hand knocking the pot she was planting off the wooden workbench. It fell to the hard ground and smashed into a dozen pieces, dirt flying everywhere.

"Sorry," Trent said from the doorway, looking anything but apologetic. "I didn't mean to startle you."

She bent to clean up the mess, willing her hands to stop shaking. "Do you always go prowling around other people's property at night?"

He stepped farther into the space and the light caught on the flash of his teeth. "I wouldn't have needed to come prowling if you'd returned my calls."

"I just got back into town," she said, although that was only part of the truth. She'd listened to the voice mails as soon as she got home once Dina told her how insistent Trent's calls had become.

"Right. Dina said you went back to Dalton's hometown to meet his parents. How cozy."

Jenny cursed Dina a little under her breath. Her houseguest hadn't thought to mention the fact that she'd actually spoken to Trent when she'd told Jenny about the messages. The memory of how tenacious Trent could be when he wanted something seeped under Jenny's skin like the first frost, chilling her all the way to her bones.

Meant for You

He hadn't liked to be told no as a teenager, which had led to his ardent pursuit of Jenny. At the time, she'd been flattered by his tenacity. Now it made him seem like a spoiled brat.

"What do you want, Trent?"

"Your little lecture at the reunion got to me, Jennifer. I'm here for my son."

Every mama-bear instinct Jenny had went into overdrive. She straightened and stalked toward Trent. "No way," she said through her teeth. "That isn't how this shit works, buddy." She jabbed a finger into his chest, satisfaction bursting at the smear of dirt she left on his bright white shirt. "You don't get to prance in here and pretend like you haven't been a deadbeat dad for the past twelve years."

"Of course I do," he returned, brushing at his shirtfront. "It's what you wanted." He leaned in closer. "Or were you just busting my balls? I went home and told my other kids they'd soon be meeting their older brother. You wouldn't want me to break their little hearts?"

Panic cut off her breath. "I don't—"

"What about Cooper?" he continued. "The boy needs a father."

"He has Owen," she said, even though it was no longer true. She'd walked away from Owen today, and a sad, sorrowful part of her knew it was for the last time.

As much as she hated to admit it, Trent was right. Everything Jenny had learned about Owen's family and the truth her mother had revealed about Jenny's father coalesced in her mind and her heart. How would it have changed her life or who she believed herself to be if she'd known her father hadn't abandoned her? What would be different for Owen if he understood the circumstances of his birth and the choices his parents had made to protect him?

No matter what she wanted and in spite of the doubts that still circled through her, she had to do what was best for Cooper. If Trent wanted the chance to be a father to him, how could she stand in his way? "Okay," she said with more calm than she felt. Her heart was racing inside her chest. Every cell in her body urged her to fight or run. To keep Cooper all to herself. But she kept talking. "We have to do this the right way. You have another family, but Cooper is my only priority. I want to start slow."

Shock flashed in his eyes. As if he couldn't believe she'd acquiesced so quickly. His gaze shifted away but not before she'd seen something that looked like guilt replace the shock.

"What?" she demanded.

"I . . . uh . . ." He stepped away from her. "I didn't expect you to agree."

"Then why are you here? Does your wife know you're here?"

He kicked at an invisible rock on the barn floor and refused to look at her. But she'd seen enough guilt etched into this man's features to recognize it a mile away. He wasn't there for Cooper.

"I'm in town for business," he answered. "She doesn't—"

"What the hell is going on, Trent?" Jenny had trouble controlling her tone.

"I thought you'd fight me harder." He laughed without humor. "Based on our run-in at the reunion and the fact that you haven't returned my calls, I figured there'd be no way to convince you."

Yet she'd blindly trusted that he was finally doing the right thing. After spurning her when she was pregnant and pretending their son didn't exist for all these years, she'd believed his intentions were good.

"Get the hell out of here," she told him, almost as angry with herself as she was with him.

He shook his head. "You're going to need to give me some incentive to leave."

"Is that what you think? After all this time, I have something to give you? Look around, dumbass." She threw out her arms and turned a circle on the hard dirt floor. "I don't have anything." The only thing of value in her life was Cooper.

"You have access to Owen Dalton."

Meant for You

Jenny dropped her hands to her sides, her whole body going still. "No."

"There are rumors going around the tech world that he's working on something new." His brow arched. "Something big with regards to the Department of Defense."

She thought about the military technology Owen was working to develop. The project had him at odds with his board, his management team, and even his own inner north star. From what she understood, the Labyrinth Web had the potential to change the way troops communicated in combat situations, but it might cost him everything he'd worked for until now.

"I don't know anything."

"You're lying," Trent said, his voice low and deceptively gentle. "I need the information."

"What does it matter?" she demanded. "Why is this so important to you?"

He shrugged. "My company has DOD contracts and relationships already in place. If I can figure out how Dalton Enterprises is positioning this big reveal, we might be able to partner with them on bringing it to market. I had a couple of deals fall through, and my boss . . . let's just say I need a win."

"I'm not going to give it to you," she said through clenched teeth. "I *couldn't* even if I wanted to. I'm not one of Owen's employees. If your company has a business proposition for him, take it through the proper channels."

"I saw the way he looked at you," Trent said. "You can have anything you want from him. I don't have time for the *proper channels*. I need a win, and I need it soon. Find a way to get information on his new technology. Something my company can use."

"Or what?"

"I have rights as a father," he said. "I will make myself a part of Cooper's life and—"

219

"You should want to be a part of his life anyway," she screamed, no longer able to keep her temper at bay. She stalked toward him, stopping only when they were toe to toe. Just barely holding herself back from smacking the hell out of him. "You have an amazing son, Trent." She forced her voice to a lower tone. "He's smart and funny and has the biggest heart of anyone I know. How can you use him like this when you don't even know him?"

"This has nothing to do with Cooper," he shot back. "You tried to trap me into marrying you."

The breath left her lungs in a whoosh, her anger extinguished suddenly like a flame denied oxygen. All that was left was the charred remains of her blackened self-respect. "That's not true. My pregnancy was an accident."

"Sure it was." His lip curled. "It would have been quite a coup for you and your mother to tie yourselves to my family."

"You were the one so intent on having sex with me, Trent. I didn't realize I was just a piece of ass to you. I thought you loved me. I thought you would have done the right thing without being forced." She swallowed against the disgust rising in her throat. "For your baby."

"It would have ruined me." He leaned in, anger flashing in his eyes. "*You* would have ruined me."

"No."

"I don't care if he's a great kid. Cooper was a mistake we both made. I handled it the best way I knew how."

The crack of her hand against his cheek echoed in the silence of the barn. "Don't you ever use the word *mistake* in the same sentence as my son's name. You pretended he didn't exist. That's not handling anything. That's being a coward."

He pressed two fingers to his cheek and winced. "I'd been recruited to play football at Notre Dame. A baby would have changed everything."

"I get how becoming a parent changes things," she fired back. "*I* was the one raising him."

He shrugged. "If you would have listened to me and gotten an ab—"

"Get out!"

"You have until end of business tomorrow."

She wanted to hit him again. She would have liked to claw out his eyes, rip him limb from limb until he disappeared into pieces so small they couldn't hold sway over her.

"I will never let you see Cooper," she said. "Not when I know you just want to use him."

"You know how to make sure that happens." He turned and walked out of the barn, the heavy door slamming shut behind him.

Jenny sank to her knees on the dusty ground. She wrapped her arms around her waist and leaned forward, unable to catch her breath. How was she going to untangle this mess without hurting either Cooper or Owen? It would destroy her son to learn that his father was only interested in using him as a pawn in some kind of scheme to salvage his own career. She could never let that happen.

But she couldn't tell Owen about Trent's demand. He was already bailing her out of her current financial crisis with the ring still tucked into the top drawer of her dresser. She couldn't ask him for more when she couldn't give him anything in return. Not when her goal had been to finally make it on her own.

Attending the reunion had been one more stupid decision added to her long list of mistakes. What had she thought she would prove to anyone? Her big plan to confront Trent had blown up in her face, and now it had given him an entry back into her life.

She'd told herself she would do anything to build the life Cooper deserved. What price would she pay in the end?

"You love her."

"So what?" Owen called over his shoulder, then concentrated on pulling air in and out of his lungs as he pedaled his mountain bike up the dirt path deep in the foothills west of Denver.

"So stop being such an asshat"—Ty panted as he moved just ahead of Owen at a place where the single-track trail widened—"and tell her."

Owen dug in hard and forced his legs to pump double time. He inched past Ty, but the last hundred yards of the trail got even steeper. He let his anger at Ty's words propel him forward. He reached the place where the trail leveled off and an outcropping of rocks provided the perfect spot to view the Denver skyline in the distance.

He unclipped his riding shoes and climbed off the bike, bending forward with his hands on his knees and gulping in air.

A few minutes later, Ty joined him. He was breathing just as hard as Owen and leaned against a tree as he struggled to take normal breaths.

The trailhead was over seven thousand feet in elevation and, according to the GPS on Owen's bike, they'd climbed over a thousand feet during the five-mile ride. Altitude could be a real bitch.

"You realize I'm your boss," he said when he finally caught his breath. "And you just called me an asshat."

Ty took off his helmet and dropped it next to the bike, then sprayed his water bottle over his head. "I called my friend an asshat," he clarified. "Right now I'm talking to the guy who is messing with a woman who's been like a little sister to me since she was in diapers. You're not my boss right now."

While Owen didn't appreciate being called out, he liked the fact that Ty could separate their working relationship from their friendship. Since Dalton Enterprises had become a runaway success, and particularly since he'd taken the company public, Owen had a difficult time figuring out who were his true friends and who wanted something from him.

It felt like everyone wanted something.

"She doesn't want to be with me," he told Ty. "Jenny made it clear that our arrangement was short-term. There was practically a trail of scorched earth behind her with how fast she took off after we got back from the wedding." To save face he added, "I'm not looking for a commitment, so it's really a moot point."

"You keep telling yourself that," Ty countered, "but I know you don't believe it."

"I have to," Owen muttered, then he took a long drink from his water bottle, letting the cool liquid wash away the fire that had nothing to do with the way his lungs burned.

"Why?"

How to answer that? Because he wasn't sure he'd survive another broken heart care of Jenny Castelli? Because she was already so deep under his skin, he could feel her pulsing through his blood with every beat of his heart?

"I'm not looking to be on the receiving end of the kick in the teeth when she has another emotional freak-out." He tipped the water bottle toward Ty. "You understand our little redheaded friend has some definite issues with love?"

Ty leveled a look at him. "But she's worth it. You know she's worth it."

Owen looked out to the edge of the overlook to the city he called home. He'd always loved Denver, but the happiness he felt with Jenny blew out of the water anything he'd known before her. As different as they were, she fit him like the piece of a puzzle he hadn't realized he'd been missing. Work had always been his life—his refuge.

Jenny gave a feeling of sanctuary and purpose that was more than he could have ever imagined.

Yeah, she was worth all the trouble she caused.

Because he loved her.

"Take it from me," Ty continued, "if you can work out the messy details, it makes the reward on the other end all the sweeter. The women that make you work for it are the game changers."

"I think I can take credit for your happy marriage," he told Ty, "since I dated your wife while you were falling for her."

"Nothing like a little competition," Ty said, inclining his head, "to motivate a guy to up his game."

Owen gave a short laugh. "I was never competition and we both know it."

"When two people are meant to be," Ty said as if Owen had played into his hand, "there's no denying it."

"Now you're an expert on romance?" Owen clutched a hand to his heart. "God help us all. So tell me, oh wise sage of matters of the heart, do you have any great tips from all your experience with women?"

Ty gave him the biggest shit-eating grin Owen had ever seen. "Don't be an asshat."

Owen returned to his office after stopping at the company's health club for a shower and change of clothes. He hadn't expected to get the chance to try out Ty's advice so soon, but his secretary waylaid him as he got off the elevator.

"Jenny Castelli is in your office," she told him, her tone almost panicked. "She got here about an hour ago and insisted on waiting. I tried to tell her—"

"It's okay, Diane," he told her, glancing down the open workspace toward his corner office. A heavy thrumming pounded through his body that he realized was coming from inside his chest. Jenny had come to his office. He'd given her the choice, and she'd chosen him.

Anticipation made his skin tingle, like Jenny was an itch he'd finally been able to reach. He was ready to take a chance again, to convince her to take the risk with him. They could make it work. He was certain she felt more for him than she'd been willing to admit. And if she wasn't ready to admit her feelings, his love for her would have to be enough.

The way they'd left things at the airport had been awful. She'd barely been able to make eye contact as she said good-bye. But that was nerves. He understood nerves. She didn't trust herself or her track record.

He had enough faith for both of them.

He walked down the corridor, his heart pumping harder with every step. The door to his office was closed. Unable to stop himself, he burst through, ready to fall on bended knee or whatever it was men did to declare their love to a woman.

He should have known nothing could be so simple with Jenny. As he walked in, he heard the telltale click of a camera phone. Jenny jumped away from his desk, looking as guilty as if she were a toddler with her hand in the cookie jar.

"Do I even want to know?" he asked, all the excitement he'd felt moments earlier draining out of him in an instant.

"It's nothing," she answered, staring at a place just beyond his shoulder. "I was playing Candy Crush while I waited and took a screenshot of my score."

He almost smiled at the ridiculousness of the lie. "You don't play Candy Crush."

Jenny didn't move, but her eyes burned with a mix of guilt and regret that made it difficult for him to keep his gaze on her.

"What are you doing, Jenny? Why are you taking pictures of my paperwork?" He came to the front of the desk, placed his palms on the wood, and leaned forward to see what was on top of the stack she'd photographed.

Then blinked.

His mouth went dry even though what he was looking at didn't make sense. It couldn't make sense.

"This is a report on the Labyrinth Web project." He straightened. "Why are you interested in that?"

"I'm not," she said, regulating her tone.

He straightened, stared at her a long moment. There was something he was missing. There had to be an explanation. Jenny was a landscape designer who owned a gardening store. She had no need for information on emerging military technology. None of her friends would have cared. There was no one . . . except . . .

"Cooper's father."

She tried to hide it, but he saw the small tremor that snaked through her. "What about him?"

"That night at the reunion," Owen said, feeling like a gumshoe detective in a dime-store crime novel. Sorting out the pieces of the puzzle to determine where they fit. Where he fit.

It was almost laughable to think he'd believed he fit with Jenny.

"I have to admit I didn't see this coming. I really must scare the hell out of you."

"You don't—"

"I suppose I should take it as a compliment." He said the words with utter calm, but her face tightened in pain as if he'd thrown a sucker punch.

He didn't feel a thing. Not this time. He wasn't going to let himself believe her reaction meant anything. The walls around his heart rebuilt themselves as if they'd never been lowered in the first place. They'd been crafted with such care and precision as a child to protect himself against the pain of his father's continual rejection. That was nothing compared to the emotional destruction Jenny Castelli left in her wake.

"Owen, you have to understand—"

"I *understand* that you've manipulated me for the last time."

"I didn't—"

"I played right into your hand with my pathetic sob story about earning my father's love with the Labyrinth Web."

"You don't have to earn his love, Owen." She came around the desk and he instinctively took a step back. "I believe your parents love you. They messed up a lot of things, but they were trying to do right by you. To protect you from your real father so that—"

"What the hell are you talking about?" He channeled every one of his raging emotions into his tone.

She shook her head, touching her fingers to the place he'd just touched. "I didn't mean to say that out loud."

"Hank Dalton is my father." He said the words like a pledge.

"He loves you," Jenny repeated, which only enraged him more.

"He's my father."

Her eyes went gentle. "In every way that counts."

"What the *fuck* are you talking about? Tell me what you think you know."

She pressed her lips together, then reached out a hand, which he dodged. "I don't *think* anything," she said quietly. "I spoke to your mother, Owen. She confirmed my suspicions."

"Which were?"

"Hank isn't your biological father. He married your mother when she was pregnant with you. He raised you as his own. He loves you."

"It's a lie." He turned away, unable to face the sympathy in her gaze. It couldn't be possible. Someone would have told him. Surely his mother wouldn't have kept this kind of news from him for his entire life. "It's an excuse for what I just caught you doing."

"No." Jenny wiped at the corner of one eye. "I'm sorry, Owen. I shouldn't have said anything. I didn't mean to—"

"What, Jenny? You didn't mean to turn my fucking life upside down? It was an accident that you went through my private e-mails to collect information to give to your . . ." He laughed again as he turned back to her. "Shall we cut to the chase and call him your baby daddy?"

"Trent came to me last night. He made threats about Cooper and he wanted information by today. I promise I wasn't really going to give it to him, but I need time to figure out what to do. You don't get how messed up it is."

"That could be the understatement of the century," he confirmed.

"I have to protect my son. Trent's trying to use him, Owen. It would kill you to hear him talk about Cooper like his only value is as a pawn in this stupid game."

Owen arched a brow. "Sounds vaguely familiar."

"I'm sorry," she said again.

He was sick of hearing those words from this woman and struggled to process what she was telling him when anger clouded every breath he took.

"You could have come to me. I would have helped you, Jenny. I would have done anything . . ."

Another bright flame of pain flared in her eyes. "I wanted to handle it myself. I need to be able to manage things on my own."

"But you aren't alone." He took a step closer and even now, with the bitter taste of betrayal thick in his throat, he wanted to reach for her. To comfort her. "You *weren't* alone," he amended. "I loved you, Jenny. You must have known that. Hell, I thought you came here for me."

"I did," she said miserably. "That's how it started. But I sat there and thought I don't want to be a burden to you. What we had in West Virginia can't survive. This proves it. You don't trust me, and I will destroy both of us, even if I love y—"

"Don't say it." He dragged a hand through his hair, looked around wildly for something to make sense of this fresh hell he was once again living through her hands. His gaze caught on the small stack of papers sitting on top of the printer.

This time he welcomed the fiery anger that shot through him. It burned away the weak and tender places inside him until rage was the only thing left.

"Get out of here," he told her. "I don't want to see you again."

She closed her eyes and drew in a breath. When she opened them again, her gaze was as empty as his heart felt. She stared at him a moment longer, as if she would argue, then turned for the door.

It slammed behind her and the ensuing silence almost drowned him.

He wished it would swallow him whole. Anything to put him out of his misery.

CHAPTER NINETEEN

"Here's a glass of water and a cool washcloth for your eyes." Chloe held out both items, but Jenny shook her head.

"I'm fine," she mumbled as Chloe sat down next to her on the couch.

"It looks like your face was on the losing end of a battle with a hive of bees," Sam said from where she stood on the edge of the family room, arms crossed over her chest. "I've heard of ugly criers, but you take it—"

"Not helping," Kendall snapped. She leaned forward to pat Jenny's arm at the same time Chloe wrapped her in a tight side hug.

Chloe had some sort of friend-in-crisis spidey sense and had called Jenny minutes after she'd left Owen's office. At the time, Jenny had been parked on the shoulder of the highway about a half mile from Owen's building. She'd tried to keep it together but had finally given in to the heartache swelling through her and pulled over for a good cry.

She'd almost let Chloe's call go to voice mail, but had answered at the last minute and burst into racking sobs as soon as she'd heard her friend's gentle voice. Chloe had talked to her until she was calm enough to drive home. By the time she pulled up her gravel driveway, Kendall and Chloe were already waiting. Sam had arrived minutes later.

"You're going to get through this," Chloe told her.

Kendall nodded. "Owen has forgiven you before for much worse."

"What a horrible thought," Jenny whispered miserably.

Sam stepped forward. "Now who's not helping?"

"I'm trying to stay positive," Kendall said gently. "We all know he cares about you. He'll come around."

"Of course he will," Chloe agreed.

There was a significant pause in the conversation as they waited for Sam to chime in, but for once the willowy blond kept her mouth shut.

"You think I've screwed up beyond measure?" she asked.

Sam shook her head. "There's always hope, Red. I know a lot about self-sabotage. You and I are two of a kind that way. And Trevor and I are proof you can make anything right. But you need to believe it can be different—that you can be different—if you really want another shot with Owen."

"Of course it will be different," Chloe said, pulling Jenny closer. "She loves him. Love trumps everything."

"At the movies," Sam acknowledged with a faint smile. "This isn't a rom com at the matinee. It's life. Jenny and Owen both deserve a happy ending, but that's not always how it works in the real world. Are you ready to risk everything to win him back?"

Jenny's throat was raw from crying, and she swallowed against the burn. "I don't know. I'm not sure I'm strong enough at this point." She extricated herself from Chloe's embrace and stood.

Kendall rose out of her chair at the same time. "Are you going to give up?"

"I'm going upstairs to try and make myself look human again. Cooper comes home from science club in a few hours. He can't see me like this."

She saw both Kendall and Chloe shoot death glares at Sam.

"It's okay," she whispered, hugging each of her friends. "I'm grateful for each of you. It means a lot that you came running when I needed my friends."

"We love you," Chloe said.

"Even when you screw things up royally," Sam added, earning an eye roll from Kendall.

"Get some rest," Kendall told her. "This isn't over, Jenny. I promise."

She nodded and headed for the stairs. As much as she wanted to share Kendall's faith in the future, right now it felt like she'd lost her one chance at happiness.

"Are you sure you're going to be okay? I can stay if you need me."

Dina lowered herself onto the edge of the bed the following afternoon, and Jenny instinctively pulled away. "I'm fine. Alone is what I do best."

Out of the corner of her eye she saw Dina shake her head. "You're not alone, Jen."

It was the same thing Owen had told her. The memory of that agonizing confrontation made Jenny clasp a hand over her mouth as a sob rose in her throat.

"Go away." She pointed to the door. "Go back to your cookie-cutter Stepford-wife life with the husband who is bound to break your heart again."

"Maybe you and John should spend some time together." Dina's mouth curved into a sad half smile. "Birds of a feather and all that."

The gentle rebuke slammed into Jenny like a sledgehammer to the side of the head. "I'm sorry."

How many times was she going to have to repeat those words before she changed her behavior and didn't need to use them?

"I'm horrible right now." Jenny shifted on the bed, placed a hand on Dina's arm. "I didn't mean that about John. I know he loves you. He seems committed to making a new start and earning another chance with his family."

Dina and the kids had moved back to their house after her husband had agreed to marriage counseling. It had been strangely bittersweet to see them go, and she was secretly glad Dina had stopped by to pick up a few last things. The house seemed too quiet.

"But there are no guarantees," Dina said. "I understand that I might be naive and stupid to trust him again."

"Like Owen was stupid to trust me?"

Dina shook her head. "Like you were stupid *not* to trust him."

"I couldn't let him bail me out," she answered. "I'm so sick of owing people."

"That isn't how love works," Dina said with so much patience that Jenny wanted to punch her in the—

Nope. She was done with that expression along with believing she could make smart decisions when her heart was leading the charge.

"It wasn't supposed to be about love with Owen." She'd finally admitted to Dina the whole embarrassing story of her pretend engagement, beginning with that first moment on the sidewalk. "The whole thing was a big fat fake."

"No," Dina said, taking Jenny's hand and squeezing. "Your feelings for him are not pretend, and neither are his for you. He loves you with every fiber of his being."

"Not true," Jenny protested even as her heart perked up at the thought of it. Seriously, sometimes it would be easier to just rip that stupid thing right out of her body. "At least not anymore."

Dina sighed. "Love doesn't just end, even when we want it to. It would be a lot easier if it did."

"Preaching to the choir, sister."

"You're in pain and he's in pain. It doesn't have to be that way."

"I took the e-mails," Jenny said, glancing at her dresser. She'd folded up the sheets of paper and shoved them into her sock drawer, right next to the velvet-lined box that held the engagement ring.

"Don't use them," Dina told her. "Shred them . . . burn them . . . whatever. Put the ring back on your finger and go talk to Owen."

Jenny gave a small laugh. "He won't see me."

"Don't give him a choice."

"I can't do that. What about Trent? How can I let him have access to Cooper?"

"Your fiancé is one of the most powerful men in the country—probably the world. Don't you think he'll be able to figure out a way to get rid of Trent?"

Jenny snatched her hand away from Dina's. "He's not my real fiancé, and this isn't *The Sopranos*. Owen can't pick up the phone and arrange to have Trent whacked."

Dina rolled her eyes. "I wasn't talking about killing him. Although it's not a bad idea and would give me a lot of personal satisfaction."

"Dina."

"There are other ways."

"What other ways? If I could think of one, I would have."

"That's why you need Owen's help."

"It won't work," Jenny insisted, shaking her head. "My original plan was to ask him for help. I sat in his office waiting, looking around at everything he'd built on his own. It embarrassed me. I can't even manage my tiny life, and he runs a multinational company and foundation, and he keeps making things happen. All I make are messes. I wanted to fix one of them on my own."

"But you created more trouble in the process."

Jenny had sat behind Owen's desk for over an hour before snapping that photo. She'd read the Labyrinth Web report and knew it contained exactly the sort of details Trent's company could have leveraged to make itself part of the project. It would have been so easy to have slipped the report into her purse and left before Owen returned. But she hadn't intended to truly betray him. As she'd tried to explain, she needed to buy herself time to figure out how to deal with Trent's threats.

But Owen had no reason to trust her, and she'd lost him for good.

Tears sprang to her eyes. She'd wanted to believe she could actually have a future with Owen, so she had let herself be vulnerable. Allowed herself to fall in love with him.

Then she'd ruined them both.

"You know," Dina said slowly, "Cooper is a pretty smart kid."

"The smartest," Jenny agreed with a loud sniff.

"Seems to me you could tell him the truth and allow him to make his own decision about Trent."

"No way. I won't hurt him like that. Who knows how much Trent's rejection has already scarred him?" Jenny pointed to herself. "Look at me. I'm a train wreck, and most of it stems back to daddy issues."

The thought niggled at the back of her mind that a lot of her issues involved thinking her father had abandoned her before she was even born. But Jenny's mother also hadn't shared the whole truth. Pretty much Jenny was screwed no matter what course she took.

"Do you really think it's better to protect Cooper's deadbeat father, who has never shown one second of authentic interest in that amazing boy, at the price of hurting Owen?" Dina spoke slowly, as if Jenny was a recalcitrant child who needed coaxing. "Owen, who not only loves you but adores your son and has seemed more than willing to step in and become a father for Cooper. How is that a win for any of you?"

Jenny closed her eyes and tipped her head back against the headboard. "I don't know. I'm stupid, Dina. I'm scared." She sucked in a breath as soon as the words were out of her mouth. The realization hit fast and hard, like a bullet tearing through flesh.

She wasn't leading with her heart. Fear was in the driver's seat and it was steering her recklessly through hairpin turns at a hundred miles an hour.

"Oh. My. God." She scrambled to the edge of the bed. "I'm going to be sick."

Dina put a hand on the back of Jenny's head and pressed it down. "Can I get you a bucket?" she asked softly.

"I need to pull my head out of my ass," Jenny replied, gaze on the floor. Her head was throbbing, both from the blood rushing to it and the knowledge of what she'd done. "All this time I thought I was protecting Cooper by keeping myself closed off from people. I thought I had to devote myself to only him because I'd been so angry at my mom for dividing her attention between me and the Bishop kids growing up. I felt compelled to try to be both mother and father to him."

"You're a great mom." Dina rubbed Jenny's back. "I've seen you with Cooper, and that boy knows how much you love him."

"I knew how much my mom loved me. It didn't change the fact that I was seriously messed up in the head."

"The way we treated you at school didn't help."

Jenny lifted her head, pressing her hands to her temples. "Now look at us."

"We're besties," Dina said, and put her arm around Jenny's shoulder. "Do you ever wish you got a do-over in high school? A chance to avoid the mistakes you made?"

"No," Jenny answered immediately. "Because the decisions I made—even if they were colossally dumb—resulted in Cooper. I wouldn't trade that for anything." She paused, then added, "But I'd take a do-over for the last couple of days, even though I have no idea how to make it better."

Dina patted her leg. "You'll figure it out. I have faith in you."

"Why?" Jenny couldn't help but ask.

"Your heart is solid. You helped me realize I was worth more than John was giving me."

"Everything you liked about my life was based on a lie."

Dina raised a brow. "Are your feelings for Owen a lie?"

Jenny shook her head.

Just then a door slammed from downstairs. "Mom," Cooper called, "I'm home."

"I'll be down in a minute," Jenny answered, standing and walking to the mirror that hung above the dresser. She swiped under her eyes and pinched her cheeks to get a little color in them.

"You can do this," Dina said.

Jenny turned. "You know, I never gave much stock to cheerleaders in high school, but now I see the benefit. Thank you."

"Hurrah for you," Dina said, waving imaginary pom-poms. "Let's go fix your mess of a life."

"Amen to that," Jenny murmured.

Three days after Jenny dropped the emotional bomb about his father, Owen walked up the cobblestone path toward the front door of his childhood home, feeling as if he was watching the scene from outside his body.

Sweat rolled down his back and his limbs felt heavy, like he had cement blocks attached to his feet. He would have liked to blame the heat and humidity but knew the blistering weight he carried came from nerves. His tension had gone from a small hum at the back of his neck when he'd boarded his private plane in Denver to a full orchestra hitting an epic crescendo by the time he stepped onto the tarmac in West Virginia.

His mother opened the door, and her eyes widened in surprise before softening. "Owen. What a lovely surprise."

She reached for him but he shrugged off her touch, ignoring the flash of pain in her gaze. "I need to talk to you and . . ." He swallowed down the emotion rising in his throat. "And Dad. Is he here?"

He heard her small intake of breath and knew everything Jenny had told him was true. Not that he'd really doubted her, but he'd hoped she'd gotten the story wrong.

The alternative was that everything he knew about his life was a lie.

"We love you, Owen." His mother's voice was filled with apology. "We never meant—"

Owen held up a hand. "Is he here? I want to talk to both of you."

"We're just finishing lunch," she said, and stepped back to allow him into the house.

He closed the door behind him, but suddenly he felt like even more of a stranger in this place. Blood roared through his head and his heart pounded, but as he followed his mom through the living room, it was like looking at unfamiliar furniture and photos. Who were those happy people, their lives encapsulated in the myriad of frames that sat on every surface?

His father was at the sink when they walked into the kitchen. He turned, glanced from his wife to Owen. "You are my son. You have always been mine."

Owen's mother let out an anguished sob and rushed forward into Hank's waiting embrace. His arm wrapped around her waist as he tucked her against him.

"Sit down, Owen," he said in the commanding tone that used to make Owen quake in his sneakers. "We have a lot to talk about."

"No." Owen shook his head, then placed a hand on the smooth tile countertop. He needed something to ground him as he felt his whole world tilting on its axis.

Hearing the words from Jenny and then seeing the truth in his mother's eyes were nothing compared to the shock of facing the man he'd spent his whole life trying to please.

And knowing all of it had been in vain.

Hank stared at him for several long moments, as if taking his measure, then finally nodded. He placed a gentle kiss on the top of Karen's head.

"Your mother and I had been friends since we were kids," he said slowly. "I'd already been in love with her half my life when she found out she was pregnant."

"By another man," Owen added, forcing down his emotions. He knew it was a coping mechanism—to separate himself from the moment as if he was watching the action from above. There was no other way to get through it.

His mother let out another small cry and shifted to face him, still keeping her head on Hank's shoulder. "A man who didn't love me and never would have taken care of either of us."

"My biological father, nonetheless."

Tears streamed down his mother's face, and she didn't bother to wipe them away.

"You're hurting her," Hank said, his voice whip sharp.

Owen shook his head. "That's not my intention, but I should have known the truth long before this."

"You had parents who took care of you," Hank snapped, tightening his hold on Karen. "A good life. Do you think that bum could have—"

Karen pressed her open palm to her husband's chest. "He has a right to know." She nodded to Owen. "I meant to tell you. I should have told you. But the time was never right. The truth was I didn't want to think about the man who got me pregnant. He was a mistake I made when I was very young and very foolish."

Owen couldn't help flinching at that.

A mistake.

"Not you," Karen said quickly. "Never you, Owen."

He met her gaze but didn't respond. What was there to say?

"I loved you from the moment I found out I was pregnant. You were *mine.*"

"Ours," his father added. "I was honored to be your dad. I still am."

"That isn't how it felt from my end," Owen told him, his voice sounding distant to his own ears. "I never fit in with you and Jack." He laughed softly. "Even Gabby could keep up with your expectations better than me. I disappointed you constantly, and now I understand why."

"I was hard on you," Hank agreed, "but it was because I love you. Maybe I went overboard, but I never wanted to take a chance on you ending up like him."

"Like my father," Owen said, for the first time in his life intentionally trying to hurt someone.

He could see by the way a muscle jumped in Hank's jaw that he'd succeeded. But it didn't make him feel any better. He was more miserable with every passing second. But he couldn't stop himself from asking, "What is his name?"

"Ed Bosch," Karen answered slowly. "I don't know what happened to him after he got out of jail. By that point, your father and I were married and you were almost a toddler."

Owen swallowed. "Jail?"

She took a step toward him but still held tight to Hank's hand. "I'll answer any questions you have. But you need to understand that he was trouble for me, and not the kind of man I wanted as a father for my precious baby. I should have told you as you got older."

She glanced between him and Hank. "I know things weren't always easy for you in this family. But never doubt that everything—even the mistakes—were done out of love." Her voice broke but she took a deep breath and said, "All I wanted was to protect you."

The image of Jenny telling him something very similar about Cooper invaded his mind. Suddenly he understood how desperate she must have felt when Trent Decker came to her. As distant as his relationship with his mother had become, Owen knew she loved him. He looked at his parents, holding tight to each other as they dealt with this ugly secret, and thought about how Jenny had no one to hold on to.

His chest squeezed painfully. "How did Jenny know?"

His mother shrugged, then gave him a watery smile. "I guess being in love gave her some kind of sixth sense when it came to you. No one has ever questioned it before, but she had no doubt about her suspicions."

A sixth sense? More like a perfect understanding of where to poke him so it would really hurt. He couldn't totally blame her. He'd known better than to expose his soft underbelly. Hell, she'd given him the warning herself. But now wasn't the time to discuss his ex-fiancée or the terms of their arrangement with his mother.

"I never understood why I wasn't more like you," he said to his dad. "It felt like I was a disappointment to you every damn day just for being me."

Hank shook his head. "All I wanted was to make sure you weren't like him. That's how it started and then it became a pattern I couldn't seem to break free from . . . even when it hurt you. It was my own fear, because even as a kid you were kind and damn smart, with the biggest heart of anyone. I was always proud of you, Owen. Don't ever doubt that. You were meant to be the man you've become."

"What about me not joining the marines?" Owen gave a harsh laugh. "Do you know how many hours of guilt I've had because I was the only Dalton man in the history of the family not to serve our country?"

Hank moved forward, releasing Karen's hand to place his on Owen's shoulder. "What you've created with Dalton Enterprises doesn't just help the country, Owen. You help the world. There are lots of ways to serve your fellow man, and you've found the one that fits you best."

Owen looked up at the ceiling, as if it held all the answers to the questions swirling around his mind. "You never said any of that." He was unable to keep the bitterness from his tone.

"I'm sorry," his father said, tightening his hold on Owen's shoulder.

"Gabby was the baby and Jack was the golden boy." Owen shrugged away from the touch, still needing space. "I was the oddball science geek."

"You were brilliant," Karen said.

"Which is why," Hank added, "I gave Jack so much praise. It's not easy being the younger brother of someone so clearly destined for success."

Once again, Owen felt like he'd walked into an alternate universe. "Jack was the football star and the war hero with the military career cut short by the security breach on his last mission with MARSOC."

"Wait," his father interrupted. "What are you talking about?"

"I don't know the details," Owen answered. "It's crap a highly elite, specially trained member of the corps can't discuss with a civilian like me."

"Oh, sweetie." His mother's voice was painfully gentle. "Did Jack tell you that?"

"Yeah." Owen ran a hand through his hair. "He seemed to take a lot of pride in whatever it was he'd contributed to the mission."

"Owen," Hank said slowly, "your brother will always be a marine, but he skated through his enlistment. He was only a grunt."

"And he was never part of MARSOC," his mother added almost apologetically.

The shock from this truth was almost as devastating as what Owen had learned about his birth. Why the hell would Jack go to the trouble of creating such an intricate web of lies?

"I've got to get out of here," he muttered, more to himself than his parents.

"Don't go," his mom pleaded. "Not when you're upset like this."

"Let me call Jack and get him over here," his father offered. "We need to clear the air." Hank reached for him, and Owen felt the weight of his father's hand as if it were made of lead.

"I can't talk to Jack right now. I need . . ."

There were so many conflicting emotions churning through him right now, and he needed time before he could truly process what these new revelations meant for his life.

"I need to go." He placed a hand over his father's. "Give me some time."

His father looked like he wanted to argue, but he nodded. "Call us when you're ready. We'll be waiting."

"I love you," his mother said quietly.

"You too, Mom," he answered, then turned on his heel. One more minute in this house and he was going to lose the very thin grasp he had on his emotions.

He stalked through the house and slammed out the front door, heading toward the rental car. His instinct had been that this little family visit might go south, but he'd had no idea how bad it would get.

"Owen, wait."

He was almost to the black sedan when Gabby's voice rang out behind him. She was at his back a moment later and wrapped her arms around his waist. "I'm sorry. I had no idea. You're my brother. That's all I know."

"It will be okay, twerp," he told her, using the nickname he'd given her as a young girl. "We're all adults now."

"Then why are you running?"

He encircled her wrists with his fingers and pulled away her arms, turning to face her. "I need some time."

"But you're not going away for good?"

Looking past her to the front porch where his parents stood watching, he shook his head. "We're family. You're stuck with me."

She hugged him again. "I love you," she whispered against his chest. "Even more now that I have an explanation for why you're so much smarter than the rest of us."

"You too, Gabs." He smiled despite all the turmoil, which he knew was her intention.

She released him, and after a last wave to his mom and dad—a peace offering of sorts—he got into the car. He needed time to process what he'd learned, but they'd get through it. That's what families did.

The question was if he could sort out the puzzle that was his current life, where nothing seemed to fit the way it should. It had sent him reeling to find Jenny snapping a photo of the Labyrinth Web documents in his office. But what if she'd been trying to tell him the truth and hadn't planned to actually give them to Cooper's father?

It wasn't just their past that made him react so harshly to what he thought she'd done. In the deep, secret place inside him, it had been difficult to believe she could actually want him the way he wanted her. Owen had spent a lifetime feeling like he'd taken the scraps of his father's love. Now he realized his wasn't the only outlook on the dynamics within his family.

Jenny cut a wide swath of self-destruction with her reckless decisions, but she made him *feel* more than anyone had since he could remember. She was frustrating as hell, but could also be gentle and protective of the people she loved. She'd certainly done that for him in West Virginia.

As he drove toward the tiny airport outside Hastings, he realized that as disturbing as the truth about discovering the true origins of his family was, there was also a sense of peace in knowing where he belonged. If only he hadn't pushed Jenny away in the process.

CHAPTER TWENTY

A week after Trent had come to her barn, Jenny sat at a table in the center of Union Station, the railway depot in downtown Denver. The historic terminal building and rail yards had been renovated to house a mixed-use development, with seating for several restaurants. She'd texted Trent to meet her at this public venue, refusing to invite him to her home.

Cooper was at the house with Kendall, Sam, and Sam's niece, Grace, although he'd campaigned hard to come with Jenny when she confronted his father.

Jenny had told her son an abbreviated version of the situation. She'd made it clear that Trent's actions had nothing to do with Cooper and everything to do with Trent being a spineless sack of . . . well, she'd had to make several deposits to the swear jar as she'd talked to Cooper.

Even so, it was a difficult truth to share, especially when Jenny understood the pain of feeling abandoned by a parent. But her friends had rallied around them, and Ty, along with Chloe's husband, Ben Haddox, and Trevor Kincaid, who was now married to Sam, had descended on the house the following morning to invite Cooper on a guys' fishing day with them and Ben's nephew, Austin.

It wasn't the same as having a father, but she knew it meant something that her son had men in his life to love and support him.

Chloe sat a few tables away and gave her a subtle thumbs-up when Jenny glanced over. Jenny wanted to have this conversation with Trent on her own, but appreciated the backup in case it was needed.

She tapped her fingers on the folded sheet of paper in front of her, the one that had the potential to change everything. It still terrified her to think that she might be giving Trent an opening to manipulate Cooper, but she was learning to have faith in the strength of her love for her son. No more secrets or self-sabotaging behavior. She was relying on the truth to set her free.

A mix of tourist families, young couples, and professionals on their lunch hour filled the converted train station. She watched a mother and father snapping photos with their two kids, and for the first time didn't feel a pang of envy at the picture-perfect image. Her life might not be perfect, but it belonged to her and it was good. Happy. There was work to be done, messes to be cleaned up—but she finally believed she could handle whatever came her way.

She'd been waiting for Trent to come through the building's main entrance and jumped slightly when he slammed his open palm onto the table.

"What did you do?" he demanded, his eyes burning as he leaned in close.

Jenny's gaze darted to Chloe, but she shook her head when Chloe started to get up.

"I haven't done anything yet," she said, forcing her tone to remain calm.

"Bullshit," he insisted. "I got fired today, and an hour later the company sent out a press release that they are partnering with Dalton Enterprises to bring the Labyrinth Web to market."

She blinked, blindsided by his words as much as his anger. "I don't know anything about that."

"You cut me out of the deal."

"I didn't." She held up the folded piece of paper. "This is what I have for you."

He snatched the sheet out of her hand, his lips moving as he read, then pressing into a thin line. "What is this?"

She pushed back from the table and stood. "I think it's fairly self-explanatory." She tapped a finger on the top of the page. "If you're having trouble understanding, the law firm letterhead might give you a hint. I'm filing for sole legal and physical custody, something I should have done years ago. You don't give a damn about my son, and I'm not going to let you use him or me this way."

He crumpled up the paper and tossed it to the table. "If I want to see him, then—"

"Then you'll get your head on straight and do it for the right reasons." She expected panic to flood her at what she was about to say, but felt totally at peace with the decision she and Cooper had made together. "Cooper is a great kid, Trent. He's curious about you, although he has a lot of understandable hurt and anger mixed up with that curiosity." She arched a brow. "But I won't be bullied or blackmailed. Owen isn't a part of this. It's between you and me. If you want a relationship with Cooper, you can start by paying twelve years of back child support, then we'll talk about visitation rights."

If steam could actually drift—cartoon style—out of a person's ears, she would have expected Trent's head to look like a teapot ready to boil. "You know that isn't going to happen."

"Then we're finished here."

"Why screw me over with my job?" he asked through clenched teeth. "You called my bluff. Isn't that enough?"

"I told you it wasn't me."

"It can't be a coincidence that the deal I was working was pulled out from under me."

"Blackmail isn't a deal," she answered.

He grabbed her arm. "Did you have Owen—"

Suddenly Trent let out a grunt and released her, stumbling back several steps, then flopping to the floor in a quivering heap.

"Never," Chloe said to him, holding a small, two-pronged black device, "put your hands on a woman in anger."

He muttered an incoherent curse.

Jenny, along with half the people in the train station, stared wide-eyed at Trent. "Um, Chloe, did you Taser him? Is that even legal?"

Chloe tucked the stun gun back into her purse and took Jenny's arm. "Of course," she answered. "He's not worth getting arrested over."

"Of course," Jenny repeated numbly as her friend led her out of the building, leaving Trent to pull himself off the floor on his own. "I knew you were a quiet sort of badass, but . . ."

"The stun gun was Ben's idea," Chloe told her calmly. "He thinks it's important that I can defend myself."

Jenny understood the sentiment since her friend had escaped an abusive marriage years ago and was now working with victims of domestic violence. Chloe might look sweet as pie, but she was one tough cookie. "Remind me to always bring you along when there's some ass-whooping to be done."

"Sam's a big talker," Chloe agreed. "And Kendall has that hard-nosed journalist stare down to a science. But I can take care of things. Honestly, I didn't expect him to take your decision about filing for custody so badly."

Once they were around the corner, Jenny stopped and sagged against the cool brick of the building. "He told me he got fired today, and his company announced a partnership with Dalton Enterprises." Her knees shook and her heart felt as if it might beat right out of her chest.

She'd stood up to someone she'd always thought held more power than her and lived to tell the tale. "I think Trent's anger had more to do with thinking I'd orchestrated some deal between his company and Owen than the letter from the lawyer."

It had been Chloe's idea to speak to an attorney about what rights Trent actually had with regards to Cooper instead of allowing Trent to call the shots. Because of her work with victims of domestic violence, Chloe had far too much experience with one parent using their kid to manipulate the other. According to the attorney, Jenny could begin the process by filing for sole custody and, based on Trent's response, take the next step of having his parental rights terminated.

"Maybe Owen stepped in," Chloe suggested gently.

Jenny shook her head, then rubbed at the place on her chest where the physical ache of losing Owen felt like it would never ease. She'd been careless and selfish with his heart, and it had cost her more than she could ever repay. "I hurt him so badly. There's no way he wants anything to do with me now, and I don't blame him."

Chloe put an arm around her shoulder. "You're making things better. That counts for a lot, Jen."

Jenny took a deep breath, the first one she'd taken in far too long without feeling like there was a weight sitting on her chest. "Let's go home. I've got a lot of work to do before the garden center opens again this weekend, and I want to give my kid a hug."

"Am I throwing a party?" she asked as Chloe parked her car next to the hulking black Range Rover in front of Jenny's house.

Chloe unbuckled her seat belt. "All your friends are here. We wanted you to be surrounded by people who love you."

Jenny slowly climbed out of the car, swallowing her tears. She was claiming her life, and it made her happy. Not as happy as she could have been with Owen, but eventually her heart would mend. At least that's what she told herself.

Voices came from the back of the house and she saw Cooper running through the field with several kids chasing him in a frenzied game of tag.

She looked over to the barn, which was still shabby and in need of plenty of work, but it housed her plants and flowers. And tomorrow it would be filled with customers. People who depended on and trusted her. Yes, the problems she solved were as simple as what kind of soil to choose for tomatoes or how much to water hydrangeas. But the nursery belonged to her, and she was good at running it.

"I'm home."

"It's always been here," Chloe said, sounding like some sort of modern good witch.

They walked through the house and into the kitchen. Sam was at the counter cutting tomato slices as Kendall placed hamburger buns on a plate. Both women turned, Kendall dropping the buns and rushing toward Jenny to wrap her in a tight hug.

"Are you okay? Was it horrible? Did you tell him where he could shove his demands?"

Jenny pulled back. "Chloe Tasered him."

"What?" Kendall and Sam asked at once, both clearly as shocked as Jenny had been.

"Let's just say," Jenny told them, "that Trent had a really bad day and decided to take it out on me."

"I wasn't going to let that happen," Chloe added.

"That's my girl," Ben said, coming in from the patio.

"Damn straight," Sam agreed. "Seriously, Red, how did it go?"

Jenny shrugged. "All I care is that it's over and I'm not going to let Trent or anyone make me afraid again. No more fear."

"Mom, you're home." Cooper burst through the back door. "Come to the yard. You need to see what Owen did to my plane. It's so cool." He ran back outside, the screen door slamming behind him.

"Owen?" Jenny's gaze tracked to each of her friends. "Is he here?"

"Go find out," Kendall said gently. Instead Jenny turned for the hallway, needing an escape. She couldn't possibly face Owen and still hold it together. Kendall grabbed her by the shoulders and spun her back around. "What happened to 'no more fear'?"

"This is survival," Jenny muttered.

"Coward," Sam said, pointing the knife at her.

"Are you brandishing a weapon at me?"

"Are you seriously going to run away right now?"

Jenny opened her mouth to argue, then snapped it shut again. She glanced at Ben. "Do you have any manly words of advice to offer?"

"Don't take the stun gun," he said, one side of his mouth curving.

"A chef and a comedian." Jenny rolled her eyes. "How did I get so lucky to have such multitalented friends?"

They all laughed at her lame joke, but in that instant she realized how true it was. She was lucky and blessed, and a lot of that had to do with Owen. Her heart wanted so badly to believe he was there to forgive her, but the chances of that were so slim as to be virtually impossible.

Even so, she needed to talk to him. Needed to apologize. She only hoped she could do it without making a fool of herself and begging him to give her another chance.

Only one way to find out. Drawing in a fortifying breath, she walked out to the back patio.

Her heart gave a little leap at the sight of Owen, standing with Ty next to the grill. They were talking intently, the way men did about cooking meat, and a swift stab of longing went through her.

This was what she wanted. *He* was what she wanted.

He wore a gray T-shirt, loose cargo shorts, and flip-flops, looking more like the college student who'd started a company out of his dorm room than the Fortune 500 CEO.

"Mom, look at how high it flies," Cooper called from the far side of the backyard. He stood with Sam's niece, Grace, and Ben's niece and nephew, Abby and Austin. She felt Owen's gaze lift to her but kept her eyes straight ahead, moving forward until she was at the edge of the lawn. The helicopter dipped and swooped, much like her heart was doing at the moment. It looked more like a tiny fighter jet than a cheap toy she'd picked up when they first moved to the ramshackle property.

After a few minutes, the plane went down on the far side of the barn. The kids headed that way and she had no excuse not to turn and face Owen.

She found him standing a few feet behind her. "Seriously, is it legal for a toy to fly like that?" she asked, nerves making her voice sound breathy.

He shrugged. "I wouldn't mention it to the aviation commission," he answered, "but what they don't know won't hurt them. Cooper is happy and that's what counts."

She smiled but the ache in her heart only grew. Glancing over Owen's shoulder, she saw that the patio was empty.

"Don't think for a minute that they aren't watching from the kitchen window," he told her.

"I'm sorry," she said quietly. "I should have never tried to protect Cooper by hurting you."

He inclined his head. "I went to visit my mom and . . ." He paused, then said, "My parents."

"Hank is your father, Owen. He's been there since the start." She took a step forward until they were toe to toe. "I should never have—"

"I'm glad you did." He took a visible breath, his dark eyes unreadable but his face relaxed in the soft light of early evening. "It explains a lot, although I still have plenty of questions."

"Your mom—"

"How did you know?" he asked suddenly.

She blinked.

"I told you I never fit in with my family, but how was it so obvious that I wasn't even Hank's son?"

"It had nothing to do with Hank," she answered. "There was a look your mother gave you when we first arrived. It was a mix of love and guilt and longing. Like there were regrets she'd lived with for a long time. I recognized them because . . . well, why doesn't matter. But coupled with what you'd told me, it made sense."

"Nothing about it makes sense."

"I think if I'd had that option, I would have taken it." She gave a small laugh. "If Ty hadn't been like a brother to me and he'd offered marriage, I would have said yes to give my baby a real family. To protect him."

"The way you did when you took that picture."

"That was wrong," she said, shaking her head, "even if I never planned to give any information to Trent. I know it doesn't excuse what I did, but—"

"The package you sent arrived yesterday. Why give back the ring? You earned the ring."

She shook her head. "I couldn't sell it. It's . . ." She broke off, took a step back.

"It's what, Jenny?"

"That ring belongs to the woman you marry. It represents something and—"

He used one finger to tip up her chin. "It belongs to you."

"I talked to the bank," she said quickly, "I can get another loan and—"

Owen leaned in and kissed her, a soft brush of his lips. But the connection ricocheted through her, making her heart squeeze painfully. This was what she wanted, but how could she let herself believe it was real?

"The ring is yours," he said, "because you are the woman I'm going to marry."

"You can't mean that," she said against his mouth. "After everything I've done."

"You belong to me," he told her. "I'm not going to give up on you, Jenny. On us. You drive me crazy and it's all I want. You and Cooper are what I want."

"And you belong to me," she answered, so much emotion filling her chest she could barely breathe around it.

"That's what your mother whispered to me at the church. It wasn't about our wedding plans. She told me to take care of you because you belong to me now. At the time it scared me because I didn't think I could ever deserve the happiness I felt with you but . . . I love you, Owen." He tipped up her chin, searching her gaze. For once, she didn't hold back. She let everything she felt for him show in her eyes. "I promise I will never give you another reason to doubt me."

"I love you," he said, and kissed her again.

The kiss turned heated and for a few moments, she lost herself in the feel of Owen surrounding her. It was still hard to believe this was happening, but he pulled back when cheers erupted from the house.

Her friends were crowded in the doorway, smiling and catcalling.

"I hate them," she muttered.

"Liar," Owen said, pulling her close. "They are your family."

"You are my family." She snuggled closer to him. "You are my heart, Owen. I'm sorry I had to put us both through so much pain to realize it."

"You're worth the trouble," he said with a laugh, then dropped down to one knee.

Jenny gave a little squeak. "You don't have to—"

"We're getting it right this time." He pulled the familiar velvet box out of his pocket. "Jenny Castelli, will you do me the great honor of becoming my wife?"

"Yes," she answered without hesitation. He slipped the ring onto her finger, then stood and kissed her again.

"About time," Sam called.

"Can we eat now?" Cooper asked as he walked up to them, a broad smile on his face.

"Why don't you look surprised?" Jenny asked her son.

"I asked his permission first," Owen told her.

"Don't worry," Cooper assured her, "Hawaii is still part of the deal."

As Jenny laughed, their friends spilled out of the house, carrying plates of food. "It's an engagement party," Kendall called, and Owen kissed Jenny again.

"Are you sure?" She needed to hear it one more time.

"I'm positive," he told her. "This is all I want. *You* are all I want. I love you, Jenny."

She took a breath, finally allowing happiness to wash through her. It filled her, bright and golden, erasing all of her fears and doubts. She was living the life she'd always dreamed of and Owen was essential to that. Essential to her.

"Forever." He laced their fingers together.

"Forever," she agreed.

EPILOGUE

"This is the best honeymoon ever." Cooper dropped to his knees in the sand next to Jenny's lounge chair.

"I'm glad you think so," she said with a smile. "How are the surfing lessons?"

"I'm pretty good." Cooper grinned. "But it's hard to concentrate when I'm too busy taking pictures to prove this all really happened."

"I know the feeling." So much had changed for Jenny and Cooper in the past month. She and Owen had been married in a small ceremony in her backyard the week after he'd proposed for real. Neither of them had wanted to wait to join their lives together. Cooper had been over the moon, and Owen's parents and Gabby plus Jack and Kristin had flown out for the occasion.

There was a noticeable easing of the tension between Owen and Hank that made Jenny wish Owen would have learned the truth about his family earlier.

But Jenny was coming to understand that things happened in their own time and every moment—good or bad—was a chance to learn and grow.

To that end, Jenny'd had a somewhat awkward but ultimately sweet phone conversation with her biological father, Joseph Fienas, who she'd tracked down with the help of one of the jazz singers he'd once toured with. Joseph lived in Kansas City and had responded to her initial e-mail within minutes, asking to speak to her. Jenny hadn't mentioned anything to her mother, but she and Owen were flying to Missouri when they got back from Hawaii so she could meet her father in person.

She'd done a lot of learning and maturing in the past few weeks. The attorney she'd hired had filed the petition for sole custody, and although the court date wasn't until next month, Trent's attorney had already told them that he wouldn't fight her.

Dalton Enterprises' Labyrinth Web was on the fast track, but not with regards to use by the military. As it turned out, the network was even more effective in socially impacted neighborhoods and in the aftermath of natural disasters, when stable and secure communication channels were in high demand. The change in direction had seemed to remotivate Owen, and he spent as much time as his daily schedule would allow working in the lab with his research and development team.

Jenny would have never guessed that she could find talk about mesh networks and secure routers to be a turn-on, but Owen's renewed excitement about his work only made her want him more.

Sometimes it still scared her how much she loved him. She felt unsure and a little fragile as she navigated the unfamiliar terrain of love and marriage. Owen was infinitely patient with her, and she was quickly learning to trust that she wasn't going to screw up the precious love she'd found with him.

Owen had even been the one to suggest making their Hawaii vacation an official family honeymoon.

Cooper shook out his hair, spraying her with ocean water. "I'm going to go out again," he said as he picked up his surfboard.

"Be careful."

"Got it, Mom." Cooper stood and hooked the colorful board under one arm. "Want to come with me, Owen?"

"I'll be out in a minute," Owen answered as he walked up to them. Cooper nodded and ran for the waves. Owen placed a frozen drink with a pink umbrella stuck into it on the table next to Jenny.

"You're the best cabana boy I've ever had," Jenny told her new husband. He wore low-slung board shorts and a faded MIT T-shirt. His hair was longer than normal and tended to curl in the breeze at the beach. He was the hottest techie nerd Jenny had ever seen.

"Just wait until you see the service you get later tonight," he said as he dropped into the chair next to her.

His words made Jenny's skin tingle and butterflies dance across her belly. "If it's anything like the service in the shower this morning, I'm all for it."

"I'm thinking about a bath tonight." Owen took her hand and grazed his lips over her knuckles. "You and me and a tub full of bubbles."

"Now I understand why you rented a four-bedroom house for the three of us," Jenny said with a laugh.

He winked. "It seemed like the best way to have a family vacation *and* a honeymoon."

"Thank you for making this week so perfect for all of us." She shifted on the chair so she could lean over to kiss him.

His mouth was gentle against hers, but he quickly scooped her off her chair and into his lap. She laughed and wrapped her arms around his neck. "I thought you were going surfing."

"One more minute to hold my wife." He grazed the edge of her jaw with his lips.

"I love how those two words sound coming out of your mouth," she said softly. "'My wife.'"

"My heart. My soul. My life."

Her heart tripped over itself. "Owen."

"I mean it, Jenny. I think I fell in love with you the first time you walked into my office. I knew right then there would never be anyone else but you for me."

His words and his love were like a balm to her soul. "I love you so much," she told him. "I never understood it was possible to feel this way. I never trusted myself or my heart until you. You make me so happy."

"That goes both ways, Mrs. Dalton."

"I was meant to be yours, Mr. Dalton." She kissed him again. "Always and forever."

ACKNOWLEDGMENTS

It takes a village to bring a book to the hands of readers and I want to thank the one supporting me, especially:

Everyone at Montlake for the best publishing experience every step of the way. Chris—thank you for the support and the smiley faces. Jessica and the whole Montlake Author Relations team—you guys amaze me with your creativity and dedication. Melody—your expertise is invaluable in making each book so much stronger.

Nalini—I'm so grateful to have you in my corner.

Lana—I wouldn't ever want to be on this journey without you.

Annie—for loving Jenny and Owen from the very beginning.

Jennie—our phone calls are one of my favorite ways to procrastinate.

Mom—you are always the best cheerleader and shoulder to cry on. Thank you.

Matt, Jackson, and Jessie—I love you to the moon and back.

ABOUT THE AUTHOR

 Michelle Major is a bestselling and award-winning author who's written more than a dozen sexy and sweet contemporary romances. She loves second-chances love stories, smart heroines, and strong heroes. A Midwesterner at heart, she's made the Rocky Mountains her home for more than twenty years. Michelle is thrilled to share her books with readers who can connect with her through her website, www.michellemajor.com.